"Funny, adventurous, passionate, and especially poignant, this is a great beginning to a new series . . . Bradley mixes suspense and a sexy love story to perfection." —*Romantic Times BOOKreviews*

"A wonderful start to a very looked-forward-to new series . . . once again showcases Celeste Bradley's talent of creating sensual and intriguing plots filled with memorable and endearing characters . . . A non-stop read." —*Romance Reader at Heart*

"Danger, deceit, and desire battle with witty banter and soaring passion for prominence in this highly engrossing tale . . . Bradley also provides surprises galore, both funny and suspenseful, and skillfully ties them all in neatly with the romance so as to make this story more than averagely memorable." —*Road to Romance*

"A fantastic read . . . Bradley successfully combines mystery, intrigue, romance, and intense sensuality into this captivating book." —*Romance Junkies*

THE CHARMER

"Amusing, entertaining romance." —*Booklist*

"Bradley infuses this adventure with so much sexual tension and humor that you'll be enthralled. You'll laugh from the first page to the last . . . The wonderful characters, witty dialogue, and clever plot will have you wishing you were a Liar too."
—*Romantic Times BOOKreviews*

THE SPY

"Only a clever wordsmith can make this complex, suspenseful tale work so perfectly. Bradley pulls us into the wonderful world of the Liar's Club and gives us a nonstop read brimming with puzzle after puzzle." —*Romantic Times BOOKreviews*

"With its wonderfully witty writing, superbly matched protagonists, and intrigue-steeped plot, the third of Bradley's Liar's Club historicals is every bit as much fun as *The Pretender* and *The Impostor*." —*Booklist*

"A must for readers of the Liar's Club series and a good bet for those who haven't yet started . . . I unhesitatingly recommend."
—*All About Romance*

"Ms. Bradley has an effortless style to her prose."

—*The Romance Reader*

"A Top Pick . . . the best of [the Liar's Club] so far. Bless Celeste Bradley . . . She just seems to get better at it as she goes along."

—*Romance Reader at Heart*

THE IMPOSTOR

"Bradley carefully layers deception upon deception, keeping the intrigue level high and the tone bright . . . Readers will race through this delightful comedy of errors and eagerly anticipate the next installment."

—*Publishers Weekly*

"With delicious characters and a delectable plot, Bradley delivers another enticing read brimming with the mayhem and madness that come with falling in love when you least expect it. The devilishly funny double identities, witty dialogue and clever twists will captivate."

—*Romantic Times BOOKreviews* (Top Pick)

"Don't miss this second book of the Liar's Club series. With humor, passion and mystery, it's absolutely delightful in every way! I can't wait for the next one."

—*Old Book Barn and Gazette*

THE PRETENDER

"Totally entertaining."

—*New York Times* bestselling author Julia Quinn

"An engaging, lusty tale, full of adventure and loaded with charm."

—Gaelen Foley, *USA Today* bestselling author of *Lord of Ice*

"Bradley certainly knows how to combine engaging characters with excitement, sensuality, and a strong plot."

—*Booklist* (starred)

"Bursting with adventure and sizzling passion to satisfy the most daring reader."

—*Romantic Times BOOKreviews*

"A charming heroine and a dashing spy hero make *The Pretender* a riveting read . . . [E]ntertained me thoroughly from beginning to end."

—Sabrina Jeffries, *USA Today* bestselling author of *After the Abduction*

Don't miss the first book in
Celeste Bradley's new series

Desperately Seeking a Duke

Available from St. Martin's Paperbacks

Look for these other books
by Celeste Bradley

THE LIAR'S CLUB

The Pretender
The Impostor
The Spy
The Charmer
The Rogue

THE ROYAL FOUR

To Wed a Scandalous Spy
Surrender to a Wicked Spy
One Night with a Spy
Seducing the Spy

Available from St. Martin's Paperbacks

The Duke Next Door

Celeste Bradley

St. Martin's Paperbacks

THE DUKE NEXT DOOR

Copyright © 2008 by Celeste Bradley.
Excerpt from *Duke Most Wanted* copyright © 2008 by Celeste Bradley.

ISBN-13: 978-0-7394-9498-1

Printed in the United States of America

This book is for the Bradley Girls—many happy adventures lie ahead!

I'd like to acknowledge my husband, who always ends up with the thankless task of making sure we all eat and sleep and survive every deadline. Thank you, sweetie. I would also like to thank Darbi Gill, Robyn Holiday, Cheryl Lewallen, Joanne Markis, Cindy Tharp and Alexis Tharp. You guys are the lifeboat!

Prologue

Once upon a time, a rich, grumpy old man sat down with quill and paper and changed the lives of his female descendants forever. . . .

"I, Sir Hamish Pickering, being of sound mind but ailing body, do make my last will and testament.

"I've climbed as high as a man can, despite having twice the brains, wisdom and fortitude of the layabout aristocracy. Yet, a woman can wed as high as her looks will let her, up to a duchess if she may.

"There, my own daughters have failed me miserably. Morag and Finella, I spent money on you so that you could marry higher but you weren't up to snuff. You expected the world to be handed to you. If any female of this family wants another farthing of my money, she'd best set herself to earn it.

"Therefore, I declare that the entirety of my fortune be kept back from my useless daughters and be held in trust for the granddaughter or great-granddaughter who weds a duke of England or weds a man who then becomes a duke through inheritance, at which time the trust will be released to her and only her.

"If she has any sisters or female cousins who fail, they may each have a lifetime income of fifteen pounds a year. If she has any brothers or male cousins, though the family does tend to run to daughters, more's the pity, they will receive five pounds apiece, for that's all I had in my pocket when I came to London. Any Scotsman worth his haggis can turn five pounds into five hundred in a few years' time.

"A set amount will be given each girl as she makes her debut in Society, for gowns and whatnot.

"Should three generations of Pickering girls fail, I wash me hands of the lot of you. The entire fifteen thousand pounds will go to pay the fines and hardships of those who defy the excise man to export that fine Scots whisky which has been my only solace in this family of dolts. If your poor sainted mother could only see you now.

Signed,
Sir Hamish Pickering
Witnesses,
B.R. Stickley, A.M. Wolfe
Solicitor's firm of Stickley & Wolfe"

So reads the will of Sir Pickering. Now his granddaughters Phoebe, Deirdre and Sophie have come to London to try their hand at winning the prize.

Phoebe, the kind-hearted vicar's daughter with a past, has already lost—and won. By choosing the penniless bastard half-brother of the man who could have been her duke, she walked away from the Pickering fortune with a smile. Rafe, her once rakish, now devoted, husband, has taken her away on their honeymoon—a gift from Rafe's jilted brother, the Marquis of Brookhaven. Their future is bright with love, if not with gold.

Now only the beautiful, Society-bred Deirdre and

the plain, bookish Sophie remain in the game. The Marquis of Brookhaven, soon to be the Duke of Brookmoor, is still up for grabs . . . but not for long, if Miss Deirdre Cantor has anything to say about it.

Chapter One

England, 1815

"The Beast of Brookhaven sets another bride to fleeing! Left him at the altar this very morning!"

Calder Marbrook, Marquis of Brookhaven, froze in his tracks at the newsboy's cant. Since that left him poised in the center of a very busy London street with an ale cart bearing down upon him, it was perhaps not the best moment for him to hear his life story brayed to the public at large.

The driver of the cart cried out a warning, causing Calder's body to react, if not his thoughts. After flinging himself to safety on the other side of the street, he ignored the carter's curses trailing on the breeze and searched the crowd for the voice he'd heard.

"Read all about the Beast! The Voice of Society says 'e can't keep his women from running off!"

The newsboy, who was actually a rather wizened fellow whose voice quavered slightly on the up notes, took Calder's coin and passed him a newssheet without a pause in his oratory. "The Beast of Brookhaven strikes again!"

Then the fellow's gaze flicked upward over Calder's face, then back down to the sketch of a brooding visage on the front page in his hand.

"Oy!" He peered up into Calder's face. "It's you,

ain't it?" The man's momentary excitement faded before Calder's grim gaze. He tugged at his cap hurriedly. "Er . . . good day, milord!"

Calder ignored the man's flight in favor of flipping the folded newssheet open. He began to read as he stood there, a solid, black-clad man-boulder, letting the river of London humanity swirl unnoticed around him.

"The Beast of Brookhaven . . . Can it be denied that all his wealth and rank have never been enough? . . . One must wonder at the mysterious cause of that tragic accident that left him a widower five years ago . . . lovely Lady Brookhaven's untimely demise . . . Has it happened again? . . . Has another young flower of England decided to flee something dark and unnatural, despite the Beast's more obvious attractions?"

The rest was lost, crushed into Calder's tightening fists. Old pain flared, searing fresh scars newly formed. It was incredible how much the insinuations hurt. It was nothing but gossip, thinly flavored with half-facts.

True, this morning he had given to Rafe the woman he'd chosen for his own in a rather unorthodox ceremony in which he himself had reluctantly played the part of the groom. It seemed Society was going to have something to say about how he and his brother had thwarted its expectations with a proxy marriage.

He'd mistakenly believed that with Rafe and Phoebe, the disputed fiancée, safely off on the honeymoon he'd originally arranged for himself, Calder could simply lock himself behind the intimidating grand door of Brook House and hear no more than he chose to hear.

Apparently not.

The paper was thin and the fresh ink still smeared in his hands. It was only cheap fodder for the masses, small news for small minds . . . yet still his chest ached and his breath felt like fire.

Thirty-four years of impeccable existence, of living by the highest standards of honor and decency—save for one mistake, one moment in an otherwise blameless life, and hadn't he done his damnedest to make up for that error?—all wiped away by the blithe hand of this self-proclaimed Voice of Society!

He became aware of the passing throng and the way their eyes slid over him in speculation . . . or was it suspicion? Had they already read this alleged news? Was this morning's wedding already being discussed and dissected by the multitudes? Was his late wife's demise being chewed upon like gristle, the truth spat out again, mangled and twisted and unrecognizable?

All around him, eyes, everyone staring, judging, doubting, sneering . . .

No, it isn't true, he wanted to shout at them. *It wasn't like that. Not then and not now.*

Except, unfortunately, that it was.

He'd changed since then. He'd made the decision never to lose command of himself again, for it had been a breakdown of his well-honed control that had been a precipitating factor in his first wife's, Melinda's, death five years ago.

He remembered that overwhelming sense of betrayal and enraged possessiveness which had gripped him in those dark days, but only as a memory of a memory, like the second act of a play he'd seen long ago.

This morning's loss, on the other hand, still burned like a Chinese rocket in Calder's gut. Years ago Melinda had turned from him, looking for someone more exciting, more romantic. Today, so had Phoebe.

While Society hadn't known the true story about Melinda, it had been bad enough being seen as the stoic and pitiable widower who couldn't keep his bride interested. The world had known nothing of the damage Calder had done to himself and to those he cared most about.

Of course, such a blessing had not lasted before the onslaught of the newest delicious scandal. So soon the tide of public opinion turned. "The Beast of Brookhaven sends yet another bride fleeing into the arms of another man . . ."

The facade of Brook House loomed before him. Had he walked so far while deep in thought? His butler, Fortescue, appeared in the doorway. "Good afternoon, my lord." Then, as he took Calder's hat and gloves, "Miss Cantor wishes to speak to you. She is waiting in the front parlor."

Calder blinked. He'd forgotten—Phoebe's cousins and aunt still resided in Brook House. Originally invited to stay until the wedding only, Lady Tessa and her two other charges no doubt intended to plead their case to remain his guests indefinitely.

Not if he could bloody well help it! Oh, Miss Sophie Blake hardly made a ripple on the surface of Calder's consciousness, for she was a shy, retiring creature.

Phoebe's other cousin, Miss Deirdre Cantor, was highly decorative and passably witty—but she unfortunately came with that screeching harpy of a stepmother attached. Calder longed to permanently rid himself of Lady Tessa with the misty desire of a man in Hell yearning for a cool glass of water.

So Miss Deirdre Cantor wished to speak to him . . .

Picturing the blond, sapphire-eyed beauty, Calder

decided that his wounded pride wouldn't suffer from a bit of female attention—even if it was only to beg his hospitality. Deirdre truly was a sight to look upon, with a delightful figure and a classic grace that reminded Calder of a Greek statue.

At any rate, it was better than standing here with "the Beast of Brookhaven" ringing through his mind!

MISS DEIRDRE CANTOR waited in the marquis's parlor, gazing raptly at the portrait over the mantel. It was of Lord Brookhaven's father—and a good thing, for what sort of man would hang his own portrait to look at day after day!—but there was enough of a resemblance that it might have been a glimpse of the future.

Like his father, Lord Brookhaven was a handsome fellow. Broad of shoulder and dark of hair and eye—the very picture of the brooding lord of the manor in those novels her stepmother didn't know she had read.

If only he would smile once in a while, he would be quite desperately attractive, if one liked the iron-jawed, tanned sort with alarmingly intense eyes.

Which Deirdre did in general, and this man in particular. Most women preferred the sleekly clad languid young men in Society—the sort who even now flocked to Deirdre's side, wanted or not—but Brookhaven had caught her eye years ago.

Over the man in the portrait, she painted Brookhaven the way she'd first seen him, when Tessa had taken her to watch the inquest into Lady Brookhaven's death, public sport that it was. Deirdre would never forget Lord Brookhaven's proud, haughty square-shouldered form and his forsaken eyes and his—

Oh, never mind his flat, hard stomach or his riding-toned buttocks! Get your thoughts together, Dee!—

She'd been instantly captivated. Then, devastated by his wife's death, withdrawn from Society's syrupy pity, he'd disappeared from her sight almost as soon as she'd discovered him.

She'd read every article in every newssheet left lying about by the careless Tessa. She'd gazed with fascination at the brooding profile sketched again and again by artists brave and enduring enough to lie in wait outside Brook House for a chance to spot the suddenly reclusive lord.

She still had every one of those sketches pressed into a book. Of course, she'd been only sixteen then—sixteen to his thirty years, an eternal division. She hadn't let that discourage her, however. Most people looked no further than the face and body she'd been born with, so they didn't realize she possessed a bottomless well of patience and determination.

That was fine with her. Being underestimated was entirely useful in her position, that of Tessa's captive stepdaughter, kept caged and ready in case of future usefulness.

She'd waited to grow up. She'd waited to enter Society until he reappeared. She'd waited for him to decide to wed again. She'd waited through those endless painful weeks when she'd believed Phoebe would go through with the marriage . . .

But Phoebe hadn't. Now, Miss Deirdre Cantor didn't intend to wait one moment longer.

Logic and efficiency were the tacks to take—while looking as demurely undeniable as she possibly could. She reached up to the neckline of her day gown and gave it a quick wriggling yank as she inhaled greatly. It was a move she could do in a blink of an eye and which never failed to elicit a gleam of appreciation in men of all ages.

She smiled grimly at using Tessa's teachings at such a time, but she *needed* Brookhaven to listen to her, and everyone knew that men listened better to an attractive décolletage.

The door opened behind her. *Here I go . . .*

She turned gracefully and subtly inhaled, with a demurely pleased smile on her face. "My lord, I—"

Brookhaven loomed in the doorway, pausing in the shadow even as she stood in the light—which she had planned to best set off her golden hair—and for a startling moment Deirdre felt a stab of real misgiving.

This is not the sort of man to appreciate being toyed with. This man can be dangerous when riled.

Deirdre had a flash of hesitation. Five years ago on the road just outside of London, the late Marchioness of Brookhaven had died horribly, broken like a discarded doll in a terrible carriage accident. At the time, no one had breathed a word of suspicion of the man before her—but perhaps no one had dared.

This man had the power to make the world turn on its axis.

Or in her case, make it stop.

Her mind flashed a memory of this very morning, sitting in the church, watching Brookhaven stand at the altar with Phoebe saying the vows in a voice so low that Deirdre couldn't hear, though she strained to. The pain had been fierce, burning hot behind her eyes and threatening to sap the steel from her spine.

Then, when Lord Marbrook had stumbled in, filthy and starving and hollow-eyed, pleading Phoebe to stop the ceremony—and it had become clear that Brookhaven was *not* marrying Phoebe at all—

Deirdre's breathless, giddy relief at that moment had made one thing perfectly clear. This opportunity was not to be missed.

She had to have this man for her very own.

Chapter Two

God, she was lovely. Calder had somehow managed to put that fact out of his mind once he'd become engaged to Phoebe—who was very pretty herself, of course, though that hadn't been the primary attraction.

Miss Deirdre Cantor, on the other hand, wasn't pretty at all. She was stunning, sensational, an outrageously beautiful concoction of golden hair, sapphire eyes, milky skin and symmetrical features—not to mention a figure that would leave no man wanting.

Beauty is as beauty does. Her own stepmother, Lady Tessa, was a beauty—a ferocious viper, yet still very lovely.

Nonetheless, although he'd never observed Deirdre in anything but the semiformal setting of being his guest, he could not help the feeling that she had depths yet unplumbed.

Oh, damn. What an unfortunate metaphor. Now he was thinking about warm wet depths. More specifically, the intimate depths of the perfectly respectable woman who stood before him.

It had been much, much too long.

She approached him to halt just out of arm's reach,

quite proper and yet still just a bit . . . wary? Bloody hell, had she already read that atrocious newssheet rot?

"Are you afraid of me, Miss Cantor?"

She gazed at him for a long moment. "I am not."

"But you wanted to ask something of me, did you not?"

Her eyes flashed over his face with such intensity that he nearly exclaimed. Then it was gone and she was as serene as ever. She took a breath. "I came to ask for your hand in marriage, my lord."

He leaned back at that, the panels of the door pressing into his shoulder blades. "Ah." She was not the first to wish it, but she was the first to state her request so baldly. How refreshing. However, he had not the fortitude for this today. He rubbed a hand over his face. "Ah, Miss Cantor, marriage is not really a topic I'm fond of at the moment."

"Why, because they're calling you the Beast?"

Here it was still, even within the safety of Brook House. He straightened, smoothing his waistcoat with a tug. "A flattering offer, I'm sure, but perhaps now is not the best time—"

She stepped forward quickly. "Now is precisely the best time, my lord. You cannot allow them to run free with such rot."

He was a bit stunned, really. A woman who could dismiss such deliciously scandalous gossip was not often found, at least not in Society. Either panting to repeat it or desperate to avoid it was more the norm. "How do you know that?"

That wasn't what he'd meant to ask her, but now he found he truly wanted to know.

She folded her arms—really, what a stunning bosom—and gazed at him with one brow raised. "I hardly think that the same man who so kindly arranged to have his fiancée marry another man, simply to make her happy, is the sort of fellow to plot murder or wreak vengeance."

Yet, that is where you are entirely wrong.

On the other hand, it was quite diverting to be held in a heroic light. Oh, he'd been pitied and he'd been respected and he was now experiencing a fresh bout of notoriety, but never in his life had he been considered gallant. Not he, the somber elder brother, with his sometimes jarring directness and his lack of social banter. He was rich and respectable and important, but those qualities apparently did not a hero make.

She continued to gaze at him with absolute certainty. "You are no beast."

Oh, but I am.

Still, it seemed he was looking at the only woman in London who didn't think so. He tilted his head to gaze at her thoughtfully. "You wish to be my marchioness."

"Oh, yes," she agreed easily. "Who wouldn't?"

Melinda, for one. Phoebe for another.

"Can it be denied that all his wealth and rank have never been enough?"

"Miss Cantor, I—"

She gazed into his eyes, not flinching, nor yet beseeching. "I am not Melinda. I am not a spoiled, sheltered child. Neither am I Phoebe, dutiful but unsure. I know precisely who and what I am—and I know I would make you an admirable wife." Her expression became wry. "You could hardly do worse than you already have."

Well, that was true enough. "The gossips would have it the other way around."

Her eyes flashed with something that might have been fury. "Some people have nothing better to do but make up tales."

"How can you be sure?" He was the Beast, was he not? Terror of the Ton, Besmircher of Quivering Brides? Operating on some impulse he couldn't define, he moved toward her, pinning her with the intensity of his gaze. "Do you frighten easily, Miss Cantor?"

She did not drop her gaze or step back. "I wouldn't know."

He moved in close, too close, but by God she was lovely and he had had a very trying day. "How can you not know?" He bent his head until his words were nothing but a breath in her ear. "Everyone has fears."

She turned her head then, meeting his gaze with her own deep blue one. "I don't get frightened," she stated, her voice entirely calm. "I take vengeance."

He was almost startled into laughter. No fainting flower, she. He stayed where he was, challenging her. *See me. Do not underestimate me.*

"You're stalling," she said softly, her breath warm on his face. "I want to know . . . will you marry me? Yes, or no?"

Enough of this game. Enough of the lot of them. He opened his mouth, prepared to send her on her way, packed off with her hellion stepmother, never to darken his door again. All he wanted was to be left alone, always, forever alone in this great, empty, rattling house—

"Yes."

What? Had he said that out loud? The surprise in her eyes told him yes, he had.

Bloody hell! "I—" He couldn't form words with his suddenly dry mouth. He cleared his throat. "I'm sorry, I—"

"You said yes." Triumph flashed in her face. "I heard you."

Damn. "Miss Cantor, I—"

She leaned in close, her lips lifted nearly to his. "You said yes," she whispered. "I fully intend to hold you to it, Lord Brookhaven."

Holding. What a brilliant idea. He swayed closer. An embrace would not be entirely out of order, seeing as they were now engaged—

Oh God. What had he done?

She slipped away in that moment, her face alight with triumph, and practically danced her way to the door. "I'll tell Tessa immediately. I suppose we ought to hold the ceremony as soon as possible if we want to quiet all those gossips!"

The gossips. Oh, hell, what would they make of this? Wedding the cousin of the girl who's left him at the altar?

After this morning's theatrics? It'll hardly make a splash.

She was not suitable.

She is entirely suitable. Her connections are impeccable, her reputation lily white, her beauty undeniable, and by God you'll be the envy of every man in London.

She was too young.

She is young, but not naive—and she was quite correct about Melinda. Astute and intelligent.

He blinked, surprised at the turn of his thoughts. Was he actually considering going through with this?

Why not? It was time he married again. This was a

logical, efficient move, for he had no time to go through yet another wife hunt.

Reassured and comfortably convinced that he'd merely been decisive, not impulsive, he put away the already fading memory of his outbreak of desolation with brisk dispatch.

Yes, she would do perfectly well. Furthermore, there was something about her. In a very secret, never-to-be-admitted way, he liked the way she looked at him, as if he wasn't a Beast at all.

Chapter Three

Two weeks later, on her wedding day, Deirdre longed for her former confidence as she walked down the aisle. She came to a halt before the altar and dipped her curtsy to the powerful figure awaiting her there—her new husband, the Marquis of Brookhaven.

Good-bye, Tessa. Good-bye, painful past.

Hello, Marquis of Brookhaven. Hello, uncertain future.

She was scarcely aware of the vows she spoke or the ones uttered in Brookhaven's deep tones. She was here at last, standing by his side, his bride, his lady.

And soon, his lover . . .

It was all she had dreamed of for these years alone under Tessa's rule. This man was her destiny. This man, though he knew it not, was meant to be hers.

When the moment came to lift the veil, she turned shakily to him, ready to share her feelings at last. When the gossamer curtain rose to leave nothing between them, she broke her formality with an uncertain smile and closed her eyes as he bent to kiss her.

She'd thought it would be wonderful. She'd dreamed it would be astonishing.

She'd had no idea.

His warm mouth touched hers, his lips pressing firmly, even—dared she think it?—possessively. The powerful jolt traveled directly from her sensitive lips to a place deep in her belly, then radiated brilliantly outward like a stone flung into a shimmering pool.

She nearly dropped her bouquet. *Oh, sweet heaven.* All this from a simple, chaste kiss at the altar?

Her wedding night was going to be the death of her!

Their lips parted and her breath left her in a soft involuntary sigh. Reassured at last, she opened her eyes with a small startled laugh, expecting to see an answering gleam in his eyes. After all, it wasn't possible that he'd not felt it, too—

His dark gaze was quite removed, however. In fact, he gazed at her with no more feeling than if she'd been hired to carry his shoes. Chill dismay flooded her, washing away that rush of heat with icy totality. He'd felt nothing, nothing at all.

For the first time, a bit too late to be sure, it occurred to Deirdre that he might never come to care for her. For the first time, she was given a glimpse of a future she'd blindly refused to consider—that she had contracted a cold, bloodless union for herself, with a man best known for having driven away the only other woman who'd ever attempted it.

Suddenly the beautiful ceremony seemed austere, the stylish now shown to be heartless: an event meant to impress, not to celebrate.

Deirdre, Lady Brookhaven, gazed up at her new lord as he walked her back down the aisle on his arm with all due formality. Tall and imposing, proud and rigid, he walked by her side and never glanced down at her once.

If this is everything I ever wanted, then why does it suddenly seem so hollow?

AMONG THE GUESTS, two men sat in the back pew of the bride's side. They were of little account socially— one handsome, somewhat dissipated fellow who hung on the fringes of Society by the merest permission, and one completely unknown, small and bookish.

"Well, she's done it." The handsome one was a bit too loud, or perhaps a bit too drunk, considering that the sun had not yet passed noon, but no one noticed.

The smaller man's face was wreathed in smiles, his spectacles fogging a bit in his gusto. "She'll never need to touch a penny, not with a husband like Brookhaven to provide for her!"

Wolfe seemed very nearly overcome with emotion at the thought of all that lovely Pickering gold sitting safely in their hands for all time. Stickley murmured soothingly and handed over his handkerchief. "Such a wonderful day," he sighed. "A wonderful, *magical* day!"

Wolfe was not so pleased about such an arrangement. The woman could change her mind at any time.

Unfortunately he hadn't heard about the wedding until too late.

"If you hadn't taken yourself on a three-week bender after we successfully kept Miss Phoebe from wedding the marquis, perhaps you would have been in time to offer an opinion," Stickley had stiffly informed him when he'd finally wandered into the office this morning. "I for one am very happy with our result. Lady

Brookhaven has agreed to leave her inheritance in our hands for many years to come. That is, after all, what we intended in the first place, is it not?"

But that wasn't what Wolfe needed. He had debts, big ones, to people who didn't want piecemeal payment, unless that meant pieces of his flesh and bone. This wasn't just about greed and rich living, this was about his life! He would die if he did not pay his debts. He gazed at Stickley with pure hatred. It occurred to him that if he didn't have a partner anymore, he wouldn't have to share the retainer.

Still, the old Stick had his uses. Wolfe certainly didn't want to be the one counting pennies and adding figures. Win the day against the enemy first. There would always be time to deal with his friends after.

AS CALDER WALKED his bride back down the aisle, he scarcely listened to the congratulations coming from all sides. He'd done it. He was once again a married man.

More to the point, he was once again a man with a very beautiful wife.

Perhaps a bit too beautiful. Recall what happened last time?

The hell of it was, she seemed to be getting more lovely by the moment. By God, that smile she'd given him when he'd lifted the veil—as if she *loved* him!

Alas, he knew all too well what a smile from a beautiful woman meant. Very little. She was obviously happy to be wed to a marquis. She'd made no secret of her appreciation of his wealth—or at least she'd made free use of it to produce this admittedly status-appropriate wedding ceremony. It was good that she was content with the arrangement, yet that still did not explain the kiss.

He'd been shocked to his boot heels by the power of that brief contact. Never before had his breath left his body so quickly. His pulse had tripped over itself and his fingers twitched with the compulsion to touch her. Astonishing.

What was there to be so affected by? It was only an instant of soft lips and willing female. After all, he was no callow youth. He'd kissed a few women—perhaps not as many as Rafe had, but more than enough to know that such a reaction was quite uncommon.

Then she had laughed as their lips parted, bringing him back to his senses in a flash. The moment had meant nothing to her, other than perhaps relief that the deed was at last done and that all her careful preparations had succeeded.

He must remember that she was a practical sort. Her proposal had been emotionless and direct. She'd been quite correct that this marriage was to both their advantages. He had a well-bred wife, trained to take her place as duchess someday, who would be mother to his children and mistress to Brookmoor. She had all the wealth and status any woman could want and freedom from her hideous stepmother to boot.

Yes, she would do. The fact that she was stunning enough to make his pulse pound should simply be a delightful side effect.

After that kiss, he now wished he'd waited to launch his little surprise upon her. It would have been quite nice to have more time alone with her. . . .

Deirdre stepped into the daylight to where Brookhaven's driver waited with the grandest carriage in the stables. The intricate Brookhaven crest gleamed gold on the black lacquer door.

Her carriage. Her crest.

From behind her came the voices of some of Tessa's acquaintances.

"What a beautiful wedding," one woman said grudgingly. " 'Tis almost enough to make me wish I were the one to wed the Beast."

The woman next to her tittered. "*Almost.*"

The Beast. Deirdre was sick unto death of hearing it, always in voices just a bit too loud for real secrecy. The man who'd once had Society's pity now apparently had more entertainment value as a villain.

"*My* Beast," she whispered. Her husband bowed as she approached, then straightened head and proud shoulders above the other men.

Her Brookhaven, her very own, to keep forever.

Dear God, she hoped she hadn't made a terrible mistake.

Chapter Four

The ride back to Brook House was only a few short miles, but the time stretched unbearably for Deirdre, locked in uncomfortable silence beside her husband.

Husband.

Yet, he'd not made a move to be so. Oh, why did he not touch her? They were almost back to the house. This would likely be their last private moment for several hours! Not that she wished to be rogered in the carriage like some ladybird, of course.

Oh, heavens, what a thought! What a wonderful, delicious, wicked, scandalous, divine *thought!*

Perhaps he waited for some signal from her, some subtle permission? She shifted slightly closer on the seat and then turned to him with a soft smile, ready to—

Beside her, Brookhaven cleared his throat. "Miss—er, my dear—"

The smile became a slight frown. Was he uncomfortable? Unusual. He might be a bit stiff and even dour, but he usually moved through the world as if he owned it twice over. That confidence was quite attractive.

He shifted again beside her, his brows drawn into a definite scowl. He was truly distressed about something, wasn't he?

Deirdre had no trouble seeing it, although most people would merely think the marquis vaguely irritated. One had to understand how vastly detached his lordship was in order to see that any expression at all was next to screaming aloud, for him.

Since she had years of experience with detaching herself, seeing the difference was quite simple for Deirdre. It had taken all her wit and self-control to live with her vicious stepmother these past thirteen years and not end up the victim of her own loss and uncertainty.

Others might think her steely and unfeeling—though Deirdre cared not a whit for their opinions—or even selfish, but Deirdre had decided long ago that the best revenge on Lady Tessa would be to win a place in Society so high above her stepmother that she could spend the rest of her days making sure that Tessa would be shunned by the lowest squire's wife.

Of course, it was not her primary goal in life, but the fantasy had sustained her through some awful years. Now, enacting Tessa's social demise had attained the level of . . . oh, say, a hobby. A light diversion.

No, what Deirdre cared most about at this moment was discovering everything she could about the man behind his walls—and making sure that that man realized that he could never live without her.

The best part, the part that Deirdre hadn't actually informed Brookhaven of yet, was that once Brookhaven became the Duke of Brookmoor, Deirdre would win a stunning inheritance of nearly thirty thousand pounds from her great-grandfather's trust. With outrageous wealth of her own, no one could control her, not in the slightest way, not by strength or affection or even blackmail, for she'd led a pristine existence.

She was in every way the girl Brookhaven thought her, except that she would soon be as wealthy as a princess. She had been raised from the age of twelve to be a duchess and, although Tessa's methods had been cruel and unusual, Deirdre knew everything necessary to run a great estate and the complicated social lives of such a resplendent couple as she and her husband. She certainly wouldn't want any feelings of "didn't get the right girl" to linger in Brookhaven's mind. The news of the inheritance should erase any such thing right out of his mind.

He cleared his throat again. "My dear, I confess that I have a bit of a surprise for you."

She smiled calmly at him. "I have something surprising for you as well, my lord."

He frowned and opened his mouth again, hopefully to elaborate—but the carriage jostled to a stop before Brook House itself.

Then the carriage door was opened and a liveried footman was there to take her hand and help her down the dainty iron step. "Welcome home, my lady," he said gravely.

The staff stood there waiting in a line from Fortescue on down to the lowest scullery. Fortescue bowed deeply. "My lady." Then he straightened, all proud and distinguished, silver-templed, six foot plus of him. He gazed at her with cool assessment.

Deirdre knew that her first moments as Lady Brookhaven would set the tone for the rest of her life. She drew in a breath to form just the right gracious-but-don't-forget-who's-in-charge greeting.

"*Papa!*"

Since she was gazing at Brookhaven at that very

moment, she didn't so much as register the cry as she did the brief spasm of unholy terror that flickered in his lordship's austere expression. He turned from her to face the creature pattering down the stairs toward him.

Deirdre turned as well, and saw a horrible sight. It was a person—a very little, very dirty, very unkempt sort of person. It hit Brookhaven in a flurry of torn stockings and pointy elbows and tangled hair. Surprisingly, Brookhaven did not pull away, but merely stood stiffly to receive the minor monster's fervent embrace.

"That will do, Lady Margaret," he said finally. "Fortescue, perhaps you might have informed me that her ladyship had arrived a day earlier than expected?"

It turned to look at Deirdre next. Large black-brown eyes glared at her through tangled strands of dark hair. "You!" It approached her. Deirdre stood her ground, staring back. "You're too well-dressed to be a governess," it said. "You look like you think you're getting married." The tone dripped scorn for anyone so stupid.

Brookhaven had a daughter. A *child*.

A child who knew no more about her than she knew about it.

Time bent. Old pain flared anew.

No, Papa! Take her back! I don't want a new mother. I don't want her here.

That wasn't the child's voice but her own, echoing from years gone by. The shock and dismay within her spiked sharply into fury.

"You said nothing," she bit out without looking at her husband. "How could you do this?"

"I did not expect her to arrive until tomorrow." Brookhaven sounded stuffed with forced nonchalance. "I didn't suppose it would be a problem for you."

"Not a problem?" Deirdre backed away from the rumpled little beast and all-too-familiar betrayal in the child's eyes. How could he have done this? He had turned *her* into *Tessa!* She turned on him. "*No.* This—this was not part of our agreement."

Brookhaven gazed at her with nearly the same expression as his daughter. "My dear, this is not an agreement. This is a marriage. You are my wife. You'll do as you're told."

Deirdre stared at him. Who did the big lummox think he'd married? She folded her arms. "I never do as I'm told."

The brat turned to look at her with some surprise. "Neither do I." Then it matched her stance, glaring at Brookhaven. "Fire it straightaway, Papa. I refuse to have anything to do with it." Then the skinny little arms slipped to her sides. "Wife? Papa, did you *marry* the governess?"

Calder took a deep breath, then another, while he fought the impulse to flee screaming into his study and nail the door shut. "Lady Margaret, may I present the new Marchioness of Brookhaven—and your new mother."

He hadn't told either Phoebe or Deirdre about his daughter. The child wasn't precisely a secret. She simply didn't visit very often. The public had seen fit to ignore her existence in the long ago scandal, and Calder supposed he'd simply become used to being close-mouthed about Meggie.

Nor had he wanted to be refused because of her. Meggie had not managed to keep any nurse or governess longer than a few days. Deep down Calder was beginning to fear that his daughter was everything that

Melinda had revealed herself to be in the end—willful, high-tempered and prone to disturbing rages.

Not at all like he himself.

One could not ask a demure and even-tempered young lady like Miss Deirdre Cantor to take on mothering such a hellion. One could, however, trick her into it. As the silence stretched on, he realized that one could also come to regret such a decision.

Meggie stared at him, her eyes wide with betrayal and fury. Miss—er, Deirdre—stood glaring at him with none of the poised charm and agreeableness of before. Calder reminded himself that this was a female raised and nurtured by one of the most poisonous harridans he'd ever had the displeasure to encounter. It would not do to let her detect a moment of weakness.

In fact, a show of strength was definitely in order— which would also have the advantage of putting an end to this excruciating scene. Yes, he ought to have prepared Deirdre. And he ought to have at least hinted at something near the truth to Meggie.

But damn it, something had had to be done and he'd done it! The matter was now put right. The motherless girl had a mother. Brookhaven had a new lady. And he had . . .

He had better act quickly, or the two steaming females before him were going to hit a boiling point. He cleared his throat with authority. "My lady, you will take Lady Margaret in hand and turn her into a proper young lady—" Even as he continued, he had the faintest feeling that he was making a mistake. "You will do as I command, or there will be no parties, no balls, no outings and not a single new gown until you do so!"

The air was being sucked from Deirdre's lungs. He

would speak to her so—in front of the entire staff? Every Brookhaven servant from dignified Fortescue down to the lowest scullery stood behind her, watching each moment of the unfolding drama.

Who, precisely, did he think she was? What picture did he have of her in his mind, that he thought she would swallow such humiliation and bow to his will?

She might have been persuaded to take some responsibility for the child, hiring the proper handlers for her and such, finding the right school, but after this she would no more button that little beast's shoe than she would jump into the filthy Thames!

No. She had not escaped Tessa's tyranny only to find herself in just another cage. She felt her spine turn to steel, bone by bone, hammered to sword edge by the gazes of the very likely scornful Brookhaven staff on her back.

She tugged her gloves off with precise little snaps and gazed at her husband with her chin high. "My lord, if that is how you wish to do battle, you may take your parties and your balls and your outings and your new gowns and you may stuff them in your . . ." She bared her teeth. "Your arsenal."

She turned with great dignity to Fortescue. "I will retire to my chamber at once."

Fortescue's gaze flicked back and forth from her to the Beast of Brookhaven for a moment, then he nodded crisply. "Of course, my lady. This way."

Deirdre knew the way perfectly well, for she'd lived in the house for weeks, but she grasped at any opportunity to begin again with the staff. Dear God, she'd be lucky to get last week's cold bathwater from them now!

Chapter Five

Calder stood in the hall and gazed after his butler and his bride for a long moment. That hadn't gone quite as well as he'd planned.

"You've buggered it now, Papa. She's staying."

Calder closed his eyes, not needing to look down at the tangled head by his side. "There's no need to be crude, Lady Margaret. That is not the sort of language proper young ladies use."

He walked away then, from his bride and his daughter and his staff—and from yet another mangled wedding day.

This was getting to be a habit.

Once in his study, he closed the door with the feeling of shutting out a howling, hair-raising storm. In the blessed silence he paced the length of the room. Details of the new paper factory he was building lay unrolled upon his desk, but he found himself unable to concentrate upon them. Back and forth, from fireplace to window, his gaze unseeing on the fine blue-and-gold carpet.

At last Fortescue rapped twice on the door and entered. Only Fortescue was allowed in the study when Calder was working, and only because the severely poised butler had a certain manner about him that allowed Calder's concentration to remain focused.

Without a word, Fortescue pulled a cloth from his pocket and began polishing the frame of the bucolic country landscape painting above the fireplace. It was a valuable work of art, but that wasn't why Calder had it in his study. Like Fortescue, it did nothing to interfere with his concentration.

Calder ran one hand over his face. "Women."

Fortescue made no comment. He merely continued to polish the frame with tiny precise circular motions.

Calder frowned. "You think I handled that badly, do you?"

Fortescue ignored him. The frame began to shine.

Calder let out a breath. "Well, what was I to do when she defied me so openly? I fear she may be as shallow and unruly as her stepmother. Perhaps the experience of motherhood might do her good."

Polish, polish, polish.

Calder let his hands fall to his sides. "I ought to have spoken to her about it first, I suppose."

Silence but for the friction of cloth on wood.

"And I should have warned Meggie as well. I simply didn't want to . . ." He shrugged. "It just seemed more efficient to tell them both at the same time!"

Fortescue snapped his cloth and then began on the carved scrollwork of the mantel. He said nothing. He didn't have to.

Calder sighed. "But you're right, of course. It was unfair to spring it on them like that, just to save myself the inconvenience of two explanations."

Fortescue tucked the cloth away into a pocket. "If you think so, my lord." He straightened with his hands clasped behind his back. "Will there be anything else, my lord?"

"No, thank you, Fortescue."

The butler left smoothly, his shoes silent on the carpet, the door closing without the tiniest thud.

Calder felt somewhat better. The problem was that the problem wasn't going to go away. He'd married a defiant, willful woman when what he wanted was a compliant, obedient one.

She had looked very fine though, standing there with high color in her cheeks and fury snapping in her sapphire eyes. . . .

The thing of it was, he'd noticed her immediately that long ago night at Rochester's ball—even though he'd subsequently proposed to her cousin the next morning. Miss Deirdre Cantor had outshone every other lady present. It had seemed that everywhere he'd turned, he'd caught glimpses of her shimmering golden hair and her shining blue eyes . . . and her delicious, elegant-but-by-no-means-sparse figure.

When she'd moved into Brook House with her cousins and her thrice-damned stepmother, she'd seemed gracious and demure, but not especially bold. He'd become used to her presence, and after a while he'd found himself less bemused by her perfect features and more interested in the subtle play of emotions behind her poised facade.

Although of course, he'd never thought of her as anything but a future relative.

The plans on Calder's desk refused to make sense to his eyes. He closed them and leaned his head back against his chair. He ought to have considered when he'd married a true beauty—again!—that truly beautiful women had a way of interfering with one's precious concentration.

LADY BROOKHAVEN'S CHAMBER was a spacious, feminine indulgence of lush gold velvet and luxurious cream silk. A bedchamber with the enormous four-poster hung in more gold velvet, a matched sitting room with a grand fireplace, and a dressing room where, apparently, there would be no new gowns to hang.

Deirdre pressed her palms to her cheeks to suppress the furious heat still lingering there. *Stupid, stupid girl!* She'd brought it on herself, of course. How could she have lost her temper at such a crucial moment? She'd put up with Tessa for all those years, she ought to have been able to control herself for a quarter of an hour as the new lady of Brookhaven!

I thought those days were done. At least, I'd hoped. . . .

The familiar oppression of the last ten years pressed down upon Deirdre as if she'd never escaped Tessa. She'd dreamed of having this view, but now she squeezed her eyes closed against it. How could she have been so idiotic? She could have wed one of the many young men, some nearly rich enough, who would have let her run her own life and his as well! She could have married someone like Baskin, whose puppyish devotion would have been irritating but useful, or even some priggish solicitor like Mr. Stickley, who could have kept her quite happily spending his money for the rest of her life.

No new gowns. He thought her so shallow-minded that she'd quail before such a threat? What no one realized was that stylish Miss Deirdre Cantor had never bought costly fashions and worn them just once.

She had been making the same half-dozen gowns do for the entire season with clever trims and distracting accessories and the only reason she had that many was that even Tessa was forced to see the logic behind dangling well-dressed bait.

How had she not foreseen that such a man could be demanding and harsh? His first wife had run away from him—and now Deirdre was beginning to get an inkling of why! Why had she tied herself to another tyrant?

The inheritance, of course—only she didn't really care about that. She never had. It had been Tessa's obsession, once she'd learned of it from Papa. Tessa had imagined that she'd be the natural recipient of Deirdre's eternal gratitude, not to mention the value of such a high connection.

Now, however, that inheritance might mean the difference between continued oppression and real freedom. A man couldn't take what he didn't know about—and Deirdre was strongly considering keeping her future personal wealth a secret forever! She needn't worry ever again that her controlling beast of a husband could affect her freedom in any way.

"It's not right to wish anyone dead," she grumbled to herself, "but if the old Duke of Brookmoor feels the need to breathe his last sometime this week, it would be vastly appreciated."

Several crystal bottles stood lined up neatly on the gold-leafed vanity. Deirdre gently pushed them aside in order to contemplate her own image in the gilt-framed mirror there. How could he have done it? In what mad world was it all right for men to arrange the lives of the women around them without any thought to consent or even a decent, bloody *warning?*

She closed her eyes.

I hate her, Papa! She's cruel and wicked and I hate her!

Her father's weary, vaguely shamed face wavered in her memory. *She's not cruel. She simply wants you to learn to be a real lady, like her. You can do it, Dee. Simply . . . try not to make her angry.*

Had he known by then? Had he finally realized what he'd brought into their peaceful loving home?

What did that matter now? There was no point in carrying on about the past. Her father was long gone, leaving her with Tessa, which she was not sure she could ever quite forgive him for.

She sighed. He'd thought he was doing her good. He'd wanted her to fulfill her destiny to win the Pickering Trust, so he'd done his best to choose a new mother who would be able to teach her what she needed to know. He had been dazzled by Tessa's youth and beauty and somehow hadn't heard a word about her viperish personality—although that was surely why such a well-connected young lady had gone thus far unwed.

Tessa had killed Papa. That fact was carved in cold stone in Deirdre's heart. Her stepmother hadn't taken a knife to Papa or hidden poison in his port, but she might as well have. It was Tessa and her luxurious needs and wants that had drained Papa's wealth like a lovely, black-haired, green-eyed parasite.

Papa had been bemused by Tessa's décolletage or some such thing, for by the time he'd realized the direc-

tion his finances had taken, it was far too late. He'd
aged overnight, a shrunken old man sucked dry by the
evil worm of Lady Tessa's greed.

Then he was gone, his broken heart stopped in mid-
quarrel with his unrepentant bride, his strength too
sapped by ruin and despair to survive it.

Without the presence of her kindhearted husband to
restrain her, Tessa was then able to unleash her full vi-
ciousness on young Deirdre and the staff of Woolton.

Good-bye, Tessa.

Hello, Brookhaven.

Deirdre opened her eyes to slide her gaze across the
room to where another doorway was discreetly set into
the painted paneling. Her ladyship's room came with
his lordship's room right next door.

She stood and swiftly crossed the room, turning the
key in the lock with quick decision. No freedom? Then
no wedding night either. As she stood there, a tap came
on her door. She pulled the large key from the lock and
dropped it into her bodice. "Yes?"

Patricia entered. Deirdre had envied her cousin
Phoebe the pretty maidservant, for Patricia had a talent
for hair and an absolute genius for trimming bonnets.

It turned out she had a kind nature, too, for she only
put the tray down with a quiet smile. "Will you be needing anything else, my lady?"

Oh yes, she'd forgotten. She was the Marchioness of
Brookhaven—rich in all things except command over
her own being.

"No tea just now, Patricia." The smell of food or
drink would only make her stomach roil while she was
this upset. "Perhaps . . . perhaps a hot bath later?" She

ached to wash this day from her . . . and to take off this damned beautiful wedding gown, but right now she had to think.

Patricia merely curtsyed, picked up the tray and left the room, leaving Deirdre with several seconds to spare before the twitching fury began again.

If the worst happened—if Brookhaven continued his tyrannical behavior—if it turned out that she had made the mistake of her life—

She could simply leave.

No.

Actually, yes.

You don't want to leave him. You're angry.

Oh, "angry" didn't even come close.

If you leave him, then how will he ever come to love you back?

Her spine stiffened. She would not stay if she was not loved and she would not beg for that love, not from anyone.

If you stay, you can make him love you.

Better yet, if she stayed, she could make him pay. He had taken it upon himself to declare battle. It was only polite that she return the first volley.

She folded her arms and inhaled deeply. She would stay.

Either way, she won.

Chapter Six

John Herbert Fortescue, manservant extraordinaire, cream of the British butler crop, had been in service at Brook House for ten years. He'd come as an under butler with the previous butler from another great house—though not as great as this one—and when that silver-haired gentleman had retired, Fortescue had stepped into his mentor's place as smoothly as a key fit into the lock it was made for.

In all those years he had never once padded his accounts or skimmed from his budget or pocketed so much as a silver sugar spoon. In fact, in all those years he had never put his own desires before the needs of the household and the master . . .

Except once.

Now he stood in the afternoon shadows of the upstairs hall and watched her walk toward him with her ladyship's tea tray. Patricia, the flame-haired Irish witch who had stirred him so profoundly that he'd been driven to disregard the proper order of things.

The English did not value Irish servants, except perhaps for their near-magical abilities with horses. An Irish girl did not take up service in a great house as anything but a scullery maid. Most worked as factory girls, or in the case of extreme tolerance, as a lowly sort of shop girl.

For Patricia to serve the lady of the house as personal maid was unheard of in this strata of society—a fact that Fortescue had trampled with uncharacteristic lack of respect. None of the staff had dared gainsay his decision, his lordship probably hadn't noticed, and her ladyship had so far made no indication that she thought it was a terrible idea.

If she did—if his lordship demanded that Fortescue put an end to this incredible lapse of custom—if the entire staff of Brook House rose up in mutiny—

Fortescue simply couldn't bring himself to care. Look at her there, with her fiery hair and her emerald eyes and the proud tilt of her head. Patricia O'Malley didn't believe she was inferior to anyone. Quite frankly, neither did he.

He made a noise as she approached. She started slightly, then bobbed a jaunty curtsy with a smile.

"'Twas a fine day for a wedding, wasn't it, Mr. Fortescue?"

He still had his doubts about that, but he only nodded gravely. "Is her ladyship settled in all right?"

A shadow crossed her expression. "She's a bit—" She wrinkled her nose, because no one had yet told her that house servants of their caliber didn't make faces. Fortescue should have, but since he found the expression entirely delightful, he didn't.

"Could be her nerves gettin' the best of her, sir. Me ma used to brew a tea from thistle that worked a wonder on twitchy brides. Should I speak to Cook, d'you think?"

He cleared his throat. "The tea sounds . . . ah . . . delicious, but I believe Cook has a very nice cure for nerves already."

Patricia nodded. "Aye. I doubt thistle be so easy to come by in Mayfair, eh?" She grinned at him briefly, then remembered her station. The easy smile faded and she bobbed another curtsy. "Sorry, sir. Me ma says I'm far too bold."

It was like the sun going behind a cloud. He wished he could tease free another grin, or even a breezy laugh— but he'd been Fortescue for too long to simply be John again. "Well . . . ahem . . . be sure to let her ladyship know that we have already heard from Lady Tessa. It seems that after the ceremony our coachman mistakenly delivered her to the wrong house and then drove away at great speed when she tried to climb back in."

Patricia bit her lip so hard he could see it turn white. He folded his hands formally before him and gazed sternly at her. "It seems there was some mix-up at the Primrose Street house. With no one to watch over them, her staff simply locked up and left—all but for the cook, who has apparently been drinking up everything left in the household accounts."

He thought she'd laugh then for certain, but her eyes went wide.

"Oh, poor Miss Sophie! Can't we save her?"

He tilted his head back and raised a brow. "It is not our business to save anyone, Patricia. His lordship has no obligation to help Miss Blake unless her ladyship requests it." He held up his hand to stop what he knew came next. "It is not our place to nag our employers to do their duty to their family."

She looked frustrated. Then she brightened. "Lady Tessa's maid, Nan, is my friend, sir. Could I ask Cook to make up a basket for a friend in trouble?"

He inhaled thoughtfully. "Why, yes, I believe that it would be entirely appropriate to send Lady Tessa's maidservant a very *large* basket in her time of need. After all, she was, for a brief time, one of our own household."

Patricia didn't bother to repress the sunny smile that blossomed at that. "Yes, sir! I'll tend to it right off, sir!" She bobbed a hurried curtsy, then bustled down the hall, carrying the heavy tray as if it were no more than an empty salver.

Fortescue remained where he was for a long moment. Then, because he was entirely sure he was alone, he rubbed one palm over his chest, right over the spot where it ached the most. He was being quite ridiculous. She hadn't even truly been smiling at *him*.

After a little while, he found he could breathe normally again.

Nearly.

DECIDING TO WAGE Brookhaven's Waterloo was one thing—coming up with a workable plan turned out to be something else entirely. Deirdre had been staring out the window in her bedchamber for quite a while now, seeing little but her own powerless future stretching before her.

Somehow, it was no real surprise when the small voice came from the doorway behind her.

"He doesn't love you, you know."

Since truer words had never been spoken, Deirdre

managed not to turn on the spawn-of-Beast. Instead, she shrugged, never taking her gaze from the scene outside. "Do you want an award for such keen observation?"

"He loves Mama," Lady Margaret continued doggedly. "She was so beautiful that he fell in love with her the first moment he saw her. We all would be living happily ever after if she hadn't been kidnapped and the kidnapper turned the carriage over."

Deirdre rolled her eyes. "That's an interesting version—" Turning, she halted in mid-sarcasm. Little Lady Margaret stood in the precise center of the doorway, neither in nor out, with bony shoulders hunched and grimy little fingers twisted tightly together before her.

Despite the defiance in the little girl's eyes, she knew the truth. Deirdre could see it in every tense inch of her.

It was a familiar sight. She'd seen herself in the mirror often enough as a child. She knew the story as well—how the prince would have loved the princess forever, had she not been tragically taken from him. An ordinary woman became the perfect loving mother, perfect wife, perfect gracious lady, with no distressing actuality to steal the golden glow from the dream.

Yet Lady Margaret's story was an ugly one, tainted with betrayal and secrets that the entire world knew well. How the little monster had held onto her fantasy against that tide of gossip was a testament to her sheer force of will.

"You're dirty." Deirdre waved to the wooden chair that accompanied the dainty escritoire. "You can sit there. Next time, you can sit on the settee . . . if you've bathed."

Lady Margaret considered the offer, apparently

detected no hint of adult condescension within, and moved to the chair with an air of having been on her way there anyway. Wiggling her bottom farther back on the seat, she let her skinny stocking-clad legs dangle, kicking her booted little feet against the spindled rungs.

"You shouldn't be in here, you know. This is my mama's room." She pronounced it the French way: ma*ma*. "I remember her brushing her hair in front of that mirror."

Since Lady Margaret had been all of two years of age when her ladyship died that was unlikely, but Deirdre would be the last person to say so. She had many such scraps of memory of her mother, bits and moments—a smile, a hand taking hers, a scent, a kiss on her brow. Each was as precious as a jewel, taken out and polished again and again in her child's mind.

"Your mother was very beautiful," she said neutrally. "I saw her once, you know."

Hungry eyes locked to hers. "You did?" There was real surprise there, as if until that moment Margaret hadn't actually believed her mother was real.

Or perhaps it was Deirdre herself who wasn't real.

Deirdre moved casually closer, idly arranging the silver brushes on the vanity. "I was just sixteen. It was in Hyde Park. It was a beautiful day and everyone was out. Lady Tessa had allowed me to come to London for a few days and my governess and I could not stay indoors.

"We were strolling in the park alongside the drive and I saw Lady Brookhaven driving in an open carriage with—" With her lover, the man she would flee Brookhaven with only days later. "With a friend. She smiled at me when she drove by. She nodded her head just like a queen. I remember thinking that she was the very loveliest of the ladies of the *ton*. So young and beautiful, with everything a woman could want . . . a fine husband, a great estate—"

"And me."

"—and a lovely new daughter, although mind you, I didn't know about you at the time." Everything a woman could ever long for, and the silly creature had thrown it all away for an *actor*. The fact that she'd left her only child behind, while ultimately fortunate for Margaret, only made Deirdre despise Melinda more. Even Tessa had stopped short of complete abandonment.

Deirdre let her gaze flicker over the little beast's filthy locks for a moment, then turned her attention back to the brushes. "And such hair! Well, I needn't tell *you* that, for you remember it perfectly well. As black as midnight it was, and it shone nearly blue in the bright sunlight that day."

Deirdre sighed in unfeigned admiration. "I remember thinking that if I were ever blessed with hair so beautiful, I should take such grateful care of it."

Lady Margaret sat in silence for a long moment, looking down at her scuffed boots as they thumped the rungs. "Your hair is all right."

Deirdre smiled slightly. "That's very kind of you to say. You'll be rather fortunate in that way yourself . . . someday."

"Um." *Thump. Thump. Thump.* Then the child slid from the chair and walked from the room. At the door, she turned. "I suppose it's all right if you stay in Mama's room . . . since you knew her."

Sympathy rose through Deirdre's anger. Brookhaven

had a great deal to answer for. He'd been nearly as bad as Melinda, leaving his daughter behind at Brookhaven all these years. He really ought to be made to pay for that.

An important step in that process would be to write the solicitors at Stickley & Wolfe about needing her inheritance after all.

But first . . .

"Lady Margaret?"

The grimy child turned back. "What?"

Deirdre smiled. Her manners were hideous. How perfect. "You don't really want me to be your mother, do you?"

Lady Margaret folded her wiry little arms. "You wouldn't want to bloody try it."

Deirdre nodded. "I have no intention of doing so. I do, however, wish to have my balls and my parties and my new gowns."

She seated herself on the pristine cream silk cushions of the settee and patted the one beside her. "Sit with me for a moment, my lady. I have a proposition for you."

Chapter Seven

In Calder's bedchamber, his valet, Argyle, was all set to prepare the master for his wedding night. Steaming bowls of water for shaving sat next to his best silk dressing gown and the only cologne he cared for, a light woodsy scent mixed just for him at half the strength other men seemed to find necessary.

"May I offer my congratulations again, my lord? What an exciting day for us all." The valet beamed at him. Hadn't the man been present at the disastrous introductions this afternoon?

Calder gazed at the gleaming shaving instruments and wondered if perhaps those were best kept far from his new bride's hands. She was none too pleased with the situation—nor was he himself any too pleased with her—and it simply didn't seem right to embark on . . . er, nuptials at this delicate moment in time.

He cleared his throat. "Her ladyship—is not expecting me this evening." Or was she? Would she coldly go through the motions *now?* After all, by making her vows she had agreed to precisely that. He would be within his right to barge into that scented bastion of femininity and demand, well, pretty much anything he wanted.

Deirdre naked, golden hair streaming down over her full breasts, kneeling obediently at his feet—

Which would be abhorrent, of course. No right-thinking man would ever force a woman, not even—or rather—especially not his own lady wife.

She might like it.

Calder gazed helplessly at the door to the adjoining chamber. He truly didn't know. He'd married a stranger—again—and so far nothing was going quite as he'd planned.

Again.

Melinda, although apparently willing, had wept quietly when he'd consummated their union. He'd been gentle and thorough, so he knew he hadn't truly hurt her. He'd thought it merely maidenly fear and silently cursed her mother for preparing her so ill. Although she never seemed to truly enjoy it, she'd never refused him, in fact—until the night she'd left him. Up until that moment, he'd had no idea that she despised him so. She'd seemed rather wan in the months after Meggie's birth, but he'd chalked it up to womanly emotions and gone about his business.

Then, facing him down in her silken boudoir with her color high and her fists clenched, she had spilled out her hatred and contempt in a bursting dam of bitterness and gleeful abandon. She was leaving with her lover, she'd told him, leaving to board the first ship that would carry them far from him and Brookhaven, which apparently she hated as much as she hated him.

Then the lover had appeared from where he'd been secreted by Melinda's faithful maid and the battle had ensued. Calder had awoken to find himself lying on the cream-colored carpet with a lump on his skull—from a lamp wielded by Melinda herself, apparently—and had run from the room in pursuit of his beautiful, betraying wife.

He'd not stepped foot in that room since. Had the staff ever managed to get his blood from the carpet? Or repaired the chipped mantel from when Melinda had flung a vase at his head and missed? The ugly scene wore the patina of time in his memory, not as clear or vivid as it ought to have been, perhaps.

What rose more vividly in his mind now was the way that Deirdre, gloriously gowned from their wedding ceremony, had stood on the steps of Brook House and defied him openly, with anger snapping brightly in her sapphire eyes.

Perhaps . . . perhaps he'd been right about Miss Deirdre Cantor after all. He was a formidable man, he knew. Most people scarcely dared speak to him, yet the lovely Deirdre had raised her chin and called him out, on his turf, in front of his own staff yet.

He didn't let the tug on his lips quite form a smile, but he gazed at the closed door with a bit more hope. She had looked magnificent in that moment, hadn't she? Spirited and furious and arousing, if a man were to be honest with himself. . . .

Without quite realizing it, he reached out to press the latch of the door. He was simply remembering her eyes, furious and a bit hurt, now that he thought about it. He could go to her now and—well, he certainly had nothing to apologize for. Still, perhaps it wouldn't hurt to . . . to end the day on a more benevolent note—

The door didn't move. Calder looked down in

surprise at the first latch ever to be locked against him
in his own house. He pushed harder in disbelief. The
door didn't budge.

If he was a cursing man, he'd be cursing now.

He turned sharply and strode from his room, turned
a forceful left and took the distance between the doors
in a few large, impatient steps. This time the door gave
in to his ownership. He flung it open to glare at the
woman within—

Who jerked her head up in surprise and covered her
wet, naked breasts with soapy hands.

Oh damn. His imagination hadn't even come close.
There she was, his bride, immersed in a great copper
tub before the fire—bare, wet, gleaming, dripping in
scented suds and succulent flesh—

And more furious at him than ever.

"How dare—!" She halted. It was his house, after
all. Every damned stone of it, including those lucky
ones in front of the fire that supported the most fortunate copper tub in all of England.

She lifted her chin, though she blushed furiously—
her cheeks were nearly the color of the pink nipples he'd
spotted for a brief but memorable moment—and narrowed her eyes at him.

"What do you want . . . my lord?"

*You. Now. Hot and dripping all over those sheets
there and maybe a bit slippery still, just so that my
hands can slide more quickly over your beautiful skin.*

If he'd thought she was lovely when dressed, he'd
had no idea what was in store beneath the perfect, stylish wardrobe. He'd angered this outrageously desirable
creature on their wedding day? Was he completely out
of his mind?

If he'd been a smoother man—like his persuasive brother, for instance—he would have said something charming, endearing, just a tad bawdy and certain to grant him entrance to more than just the door.

Alas, he was only himself, a man without the inclination to make pretty words. How he wished he'd practiced more. "You locked me out."

No, that wasn't it.

He tried again. "This is my house and you are my wife."

All true, but hardly smooth, old man.

"I can come and go as I please." Wait, no. That hadn't come out quite right—

Let's hope she's too innocent to detect that *double entendre.*

Her eyes widened and she blinked at him, genuinely shocked now.

No such luck. Too bad. It might have been the best night of your life.

Idiot.

So be it. He ducked the flying sponge neatly and flicked suds from his sleeve. "I shall say no more on the subject. Pray take care not to lock my doors in the future."

He made his escape, shutting the door just in time to let it take the impact of a bottle of bath scent.

Chapter Eight

When the door shut on her husband—her husband!—Deirdre covered her face with shaking hands and sank beneath the water. He'd seen her naked. How mortifying!

Oh really? Is that why your nipples hardened while he stared at you?

Naked! Completely! Vows or not, she'd not been quite prepared for that. Nor for the look of stunned animal lust that had crossed his expression. How dreadful!

Dreadful? Is that why your hands are trembling and your knees are weak? Is that why you stayed where he could see you, rather than dunk or grab a piece of toweling?

There'd been something dangerous in his gaze—something as possessive and hungry and as old as time itself. It seemed that under the fine, somber clothes and cool control, the Marquis of Brookhaven was a man, after all.

And what a man! Had he strode forward and pulled her dripping from the tub, she feared she would have submitted from sheer female response to his sudden dark sexuality. With a shiver, she stood. Letting the water sluice from her body, she reached for the toweling that Patricia had left out for her.

Even after donning a shift and pulling her wrapper

over her nudity, she could still feel the heat of his gaze on her skin. How was she to look at him the same way now? How was she to walk into the same room as him and not remember the black, wicked lust in his eyes?

Not to mention the answering desire in herself.

Suddenly unable to breathe in the steamy room, she fumbled hastily at the window latch, then thrust the window wide. With both hands braced on the sill, she leaned far out into the night, taking the chill spring air into her lungs. The outside world smelled of soot and city and the acrid oil burning in the streetlamps spaced about the square.

"I cannot do this," she whispered. "Won't you turn me cool and unbreakable?"

She kept her eyes closed as she spoke, willing her plea to be carried on the night to whomever it concerned. Expecting an actual answer was mad, yet she lingered there, waiting.

"Mew."

Deirdre's eyes opened in surprise. "What?"

"Mew!"

There was no one in sight, although the great tree that grew before her window would obscure many things. She stepped to one side, peering into the tree. Light from the room behind her caught and glowed back at her from wide slit pupils.

A small kitten crouched on the largest branch whose tips waved nearly to the house. It was a hideous little creature, bedraggled and damp, its dirty black fur smeared this way and that with God-knew-what. Huge batlike ears braced each side of its skull, ludicrous on the tiny, delicate head.

It was adorable.

"Oh heavens!" Deirdre held up both hands. "Don't fall, kit-kit. I'll—I'll—"

What? Call a footman to risk his life to save a stray? Deirdre leaned over the sill and peered straight down. It was at least a three-story fall to the hard ground below. There wasn't even an accommodating bush nearby to give one false hope on the way down. Wouldn't that endear her to the Brook House staff, to kill a servant mere hours after becoming their mistress?

"Mew." The kitten started forward at her movement, walking confidently toward her along the narrowing branch.

"No! Stop right there!" Deirdre shook her finger vigorously. "Bad kitty! Er—stay?" Or was that for dogs? She hadn't the foggiest idea.

Tessa hadn't allowed animals in the house. She claimed they ruined the furnishings, but Deirdre suspected it was because no creature on this earth had ever warmed to Tessa in the first place. Even her own mother had probably wanted to put her to bed in the mews.

The kitten continued to lope easily along the branch, which was now no thicker than Deirdre's wrist. She waved her hands at the creature.

"No! Go back! Climb. Down," she said, pointing at the ground. She spoke with exaggerated clarity, as if that would make the idiotic thing understand. The kitten stopped and sat its bony little bottom on the branch, tilting its head to gaze at her curiously from blank, baby eyes.

Deirdre straightened, surprised. "Well, you seem quite at home in the tree. I suppose you're in no real danger after all—"

The kitten lifted its back paw to scratch its ear—and slithered right off the branch!

"Oh!" Deirdre squeezed her eyes shut in horror and recoiled from the window. The poor little thing! Her stomach went cold at the thought of the limp furry beastie now surely dead on the ground.

"Mew!"

Deirdre whirled back to the open window. The kitten was still there, only it now dangled from the limb by a single tiny claw. Its pudgy body writhed with the effort to get a better grip as it mewled in fear.

Before she even realized what she did—or had the opportunity to talk herself out of such madness!—Deirdre had clambered onto the sill. She stretched out her hand, but the branch was too far.

Muttering a senseless prayer under her breath, she closed her eyes and rolled onto her belly on the sill, her bare toes fumbling to find purchase on the cold stone facade of the house. At last her feet found a raised portion of the grand embellishments that ran beneath her window. She tested the sooty and pigeon-slimed ledge blindly, finding it only a few inches deep, but enough to hold her weight if she didn't lose her grip on the windowsill.

Behind her she could hear the kitten still crying. There wasn't much time. "I'm-going-to-die-I'm-going-to-die," she warned herself frantically, but she couldn't bear to stop. Taking a deep breath into lungs tight with fear, she opened her eyes and leaned outward into space, her hand stretching to the damp miniature bundle of fur that now squirmed wearily, about to give up.

The moment her hand wrapped about the rounded little belly, however, the kitten recovered its courage enough to dig needle teeth and claws into a new threat . . . her hand!

"Ow!"

That startled moment was all it took to turn Deirdre's

somewhat stable perch into a slippery trap. One yelp of dismay was all she managed before her body slammed into the stone and she hung by one hand from the windowsill, her dirty feet scrabbling at a wall gone suddenly blank and featureless.

Two hands! She needed to save herself! Her fingers began to open automatically to let the kitten fall, but she jerked him close to her instead. He gave a fierce little growl and struggled against her, suicidal little monster that he was.

She gritted her teeth against the pain in the hand that hung on and the hand that was being chewed and lifted the kitten high. "Cats always land on their *feet*," she growled as she flung the beastie through the open window of her bedchamber.

Her grip slid dangerously over the stone sill. She froze abruptly, terror hard and cold in her throat.

She was going to die after all.

On her wedding night.

To save a kitten.

The very thought of the newssheet headlines tomorrow was almost worse than the impending doom itself. It seemed there was no help for it. She was going to have to scream. Well, might as well do a good job of it.

"*Help! Help meeeee!*"

He was there in an instant. "My God!"

She started when his dark shape loomed from the window. Her slithering grip failed completely. A wail of fear rose in her throat.

Then large warm hands closed over her wrists and she was lifted easily back into the room. Once through he pulled her close in his arms. She leaned into him, shaking from reaction.

Chapter Nine

Calder held his shivering bride in his arms, his own fear startling and real. Then he quelled it impatiently. There was no need for it, after all. She was perfectly well . . . at least physically. Yet what desperation had driven her to fling herself from the window? Surely such theatrics hadn't been caused by the minor disagreement over locking her door?

He set her from him with both hands on her shoulders and scowled. *"Were you trying to kill yourself?"* He hadn't intended to bellow, but perhaps the situation called for a little bellowing.

She pressed toward him again, as if seeking his warmth, but he kept her at a distance. She wiped a shaking hand across her eyes. "No! No, there was a—" She looked about, leaning and peering around him at the floor.

"What, did you see a mouse?" He looked as well. "There's nothing here now, Deirdre." He gave her a tiny shake. "And even if there were, what were you thinking to dangle yourself three stories above the cobbles? If you're so afraid of mice, simply have Fortescue set traps."

She pressed her lips together and glared at him.

"I am not afraid of mice." She turned her face away, muttering something that sounded like "Dratted cat!"

Over his dead body! "No cats," he said firmly. "I don't care to live with animals. Traps will have to do."

The doorway was full of staff by now, by the sound of the startled murmurs. He didn't bother to turn his head to check. "Fortescue, set out rodent traps immediately."

"Of course, my lord," Fortescue replied evenly. Then, "All right, you lot. Off you go. His lordship has everything well in hand."

Indeed, Calder had his fresh sweet bride quite firmly in hand. He suddenly, abruptly, became aware of her near nakedness. Her wrapper had slipped from one shoulder during her adventures. Beneath it was nothing but a damp shift of the finest batiste. He let his gaze rove over her possessively, his hands still holding her firmly away from him.

Pull her close.

The bare skin of her shoulder was like cool silk to his fingers. Almost like something he had no right to touch, except of course, that he had every right. His fingers tightened slightly. Beneath her fine-grained skin she was firm, a woman of action—albeit mad action!—not some pasty creature of leisure.

Touch her.

He hardened at the thought. Her curves were full but supple. She would writhe in his hands. He could make her cry out in release. He could make her like it.

Take her.

His groin throbbed, leaving very little blood in his brain to think sensibly with. Normally he avoided such a mindless state, but at the moment he couldn't recall why. He wanted to be mindless, longed to be lost in her, covering her, owning her . . .

A memory . . . Deirdre naked. Wet. Soapy.

Was that astonishing tub still in the room?

She pulled away from his suddenly numb hands and tugged her wrapper closed against his gaze. "Since I'm neither dead on the cobbles or dangling from the windowsill, I suppose I should thank you." Her glare belied her grateful words.

"You're welcome," he said, before he realized that she had not, in fact, actually thanked him at all. He narrowed his eyes at her. "I do not approve of melodramatic displays."

She bared her teeth. "How nice for you." Turning away, she tied her wrapper with quick furious jerks. She muttered something he didn't hear.

"My dear," he said crisply, "I also do not approve of petulance."

She turned back to him, her damp hair whipping around to cling to her blazing cheeks. "I said 'I'm not a madwoman!' I didn't risk my life to avoid a blasted mouse!"

He waved a hand in irritation. "Nonsense. There are no rats in Brook House. You've too much imagination."

For some reason, that seemed to incense her further. She pointed a shaking finger at the door. "Go!"

He stiffened. "I am master here."

She narrowed her eyes at him this time. "I feel copious tears coming on. Absolute rivers. Are you prepared to dry them?"

Tears? Egad. He drew back. "Er . . . I'll send your maid in, shall I?" He hurried to the door.

She watched him, wry amusement mingling with the

fury—or was it frustration?—in her eyes. "Her name is Patricia," she called out as he fled.

Of course it was. How silly of her to think he didn't know the name of one of his own servants. Except that the flame-haired girl who bobbed a nervous curtsy as she joined her mistress didn't look all that familiar. Had he put on more staff lately? He must ask Fortescue.

Another matter to look into—after he'd taken a brisk walk in the chill night air to cleanse his nostrils of the scent of his delightfully luscious but quite possibly crazed bride. Yes, a short walk would do him a world of good.

Or a long one. Whatever it took.

THE MOMENT THE door closed on Brookhaven, Deirdre was down on hands and knees, searching the room for the nasty monst—er, tiny kitten. When Patricia entered, she found her mistress sitting tailor fashion on the floor, a confused expression on her face.

"Patty, did you see a—" Deirdre frowned. Calder allowed no pets.

"I'm sorry, milady. I didn't see a mousie . . . unless you should like me to tell his lordship I did?"

Deirdre looked up in surprise. "You would do that?"

Patricia looked uncomfortable yet defiant. "Indeed, milady. A man has no idea what we women put up with. If a lady wants to see a mouse now and then, why then I suppose she has as much right to as anyone."

Deirdre laughed despite her trying evening. "Patricia, I'm not the tantrum sort. It doesn't actually solve anything."

Patricia shrugged with a smile. "Depends on what a

lady wants solving, I suppose. A few tears got rid of Himself right quick, didn't they?"

Deirdre held up a hand and let Patricia pull her to her feet. "All men have a breaking point."

Patricia tsked and shook her head. "His lordship is a fine fellow, my lady. It isn't his fault he doesn't know what to do with the weepies."

The maid turned to preparing the bed while Deirdre continued to surreptitiously search the room. There was no kitty, although there were a few nasty smudges near the door. She was going to have to search the house tomorrow, for she'd not be able to meander about the dark house at this hour without inviting comment.

And when she found the kitten, what was she going to do with it?

A slow smile crossed her face. Brookhaven wouldn't like it. Then again, it had been made very clear to her that Brook House was not her concern. Besides, Meggie was so alone. And Meggie was much more practiced at battling his lordship.

Deirdre stifled a twinge of conscience at that calculating thought. After all, this war was his idea, wasn't it?

Chapter Ten

The next morning, Calder seated himself at the breakfast table at the same early hour that he always had. His plate, containing the usual eggs and ham, was centered before his place, with his coffee cup right at hand and his morning newssheet ready at his left. Fortescue stood the usual respectful distance behind him, ready to pour or serve or take away without so much as being asked.

It was precisely the same as it had been for many years. Long, peaceful, uninterrupted years of breaking his fast alone. . . .

Calder set his cup down with a bit too much force, then waved away Fortescue's forward motion almost before it was begun. Damn it, he was a married man now! He shouldn't have to eat alone again for the rest of his life!

He stared down at his plate. Ham and eggs this morning. Ham and eggs every morning. Ham and eggs when he was twenty. Ham and eggs when he was ten.

His father, the previous marquis, had been a vigorous man—a man of action, a man of deeds . . . and a very early riser.

"No man ever spent his life in meaningful pursuit if

he spent his day in bed!" The marquis would wave a finger in the air. "Get the blood pumping early and the rest of the world will have to play catch up to *you*."

"Meaningful pursuit" had been the old marquis's watchwords. Calder had spent his days in meaningful pursuit since he was a toddler—supervised, tutored, scheduled every moment of his life.

No one ate with him. Meals were fuel meant to aid him in keeping productive hours. Rafe had fallen under that particular umbrella rule as well, yet somehow he'd always managed to sleep luxuriously late. He would charm the nurse or the governess or the cook—no woman seemed able to resist him, even at that age—and his breakfast would be secretly brought to him on a tray in his room.

Calder had never protested, nor had he told his father that Rafe had not been at the breakfast table. He took part in the mass conspiracy to give Rafe the freedom that he himself had never known.

And for the most part, he'd taken comfort in such order. He'd been that sort of boy, somber and intelligent, the only child among adults—for his father was enough of a snob that while he lay with a village seamstress and begot another son, he would not allow his son to play with the children of commoners, not even the sons of the local solicitor, or the many children of Mr. Bixby, his own steward.

No, only the society of the highborn for Calder, except that there were no highborn children nearby and no one with inclination to bring any closer. There was no family to visit on holidays, there were no local gentry who met his father's exacting standards. There was only his governess and his tutor and the maid who cleaned his room and the groom who cleaned the hooves of his horse.

Rafe, when he came, had no such restrictions put upon him. He was allowed to swim naked in the river with the sons of the blacksmith, to climb trees with the swarm of Bixby brats. He used to ask Calder to join them, but Calder was too proud and too jealous to admit that he was not allowed, so he sneered and claimed he had better things to do with his time.

Rafe must have known however, for he always brought back some treasure for him—a bird's nest with one blue egg, a stone as smooth as glass from the flowing water, a ribbon teased from a Bixby girl's hair. There would be a story attached, of course, that Calder would listen to with an expression of bored tolerance, but that he waited for each day, all day.

There was a certain amount of gloating, of course. Nothing with Rafe was ever that simple. The gifts were part trophy, part sharing. The stories bragged and taunted even as they entertained. Love and envy twined through their every thought, their every reaction. Brotherhood but not equality. Bonds that held only as far as the intricacies of inheritance allowed. Rafe would fight for him, he knew that. He also knew that Rafe would fight *with* him, just as wholeheartedly. The wall of inequity between them meant that they might never truly be friends, but it could not completely sever the ties of blood and childhood.

Rafe was the other side of himself, the side that he could not seem to reach, nor even see. Like visages on a coin, never facing the same way. Rafe had all the ease and friendliness and charm.

Everyone loved Lord Rafe, as he became known.

The baker saved the best cakes for him, the store-keeper's daughter flirted with him and ruffled his dark hair, the carpenter carved him a matched set of horses—one of which he tried to give to Calder, who refused it.

It was so easy for him. Calder watched in envy shielded in scorn. He knew the successive kings and queens of England in order, could spout centuries of literature and tally sums into nine digits with ease, but he could not make a chambermaid smile, nor coax his father's booming laugh with a story about falling into the river while flying a kite.

That he outmatched Rafe in their studies was not cause for celebration, but only what his father expected of him. Rafe was quick to learn but just as quick to lose interest. Calder was the one who carried doggedly on, past the point of learning about the dashing battles won on to the politics beneath the war.

There was only one area of study where Rafe surpassed him—when it came to Brookhaven itself. Rafe soaked up the family history as if he'd always known it and only needed reminding. For Calder, giving the estate over to Rafe's care on his brother's wedding day had not been hard. Rafe would never fail Brookhaven. He would be a good master.

Yet for all his easy charm and quick likeability, Rafe had never presumed to be more than he was. Without affectation or pretense, he did not try to hide from where he'd risen. Down to the silver buttons on his coat—when most who could not afford gold tried to fool the world with cheaper brass—Rafe was without an ounce of shame for his low beginnings.

What was it like to be so contented with oneself?

Calder gazed stonily at his chilled breakfast and his

tepid coffee. He was not his brother. He did not attract people like moths to his flame. He had to pay them well, like Fortescue, or, like his new bride, marry them into submission.

He stood and tossed his napkin onto his congealing eggs. "I've work to do. Bring more coffee to my study." He stalked away from Fortescue's bow. The last thing he needed right now was the silent sympathy in his butler's gaze.

Chapter Eleven

For her part, Deirdre had the sort of morning she had always dreamed of. She rose at her leisure, put on a silk dressing gown, and reclined upon her velvet sofa in her luxurious bedchamber, drinking the exquisite tea brought by her cheerful maid.

She asked for her customary breakfast on a tray and it soon appeared. Toast and a small dish of berries. No cream, no butter, no jam.

She was weak-kneed from lack of food the previous day, but the dry toast went down hard, squeezed by the knot of unease in her belly. She picked at it restlessly, the silence of her beautiful bedchamber oppressive on her nerves.

She hated eating alone.

Woolton had been an unfriendly place under Tessa's rule. Any servant of quality had fled from her step-mother's demands and infrequent salary. Even a scullery maid liked to be paid.

That left the incompetent and dishonest ones, who resented Tessa openly—and put Deirdre into the same class. Being left with the evil Tessa when her father died, she ought to have become a sweet, compassionate survivor like Phoebe. Well, no disrespect to her cousin, but Deirdre had long ago decided upon a different solution.

She built herself a shell of poise and pretty Society manners and flinty, unrelenting determination to get as far away from Lady Tessa as the borders of England would allow.

Yesterday, she had done just that.

She closed her eyes against a powerful jolt of missing Papa. How he would have loved to have been there yesterday, to give her away to the man of her dreams, to have seen her in that lovely gown. If only he could have given her away instead of the vicar. She'd chosen Phoebe's father because he was at least someone's father, and his tall, silver good looks set off her own golden beauty nicely, but it hadn't been the same.

Then she shut that door of memory with force. Papa may have partially gotten her into this mess, but there was no one to help her get out except herself.

The letter to the solicitors had already been posted. She had only to wait out the months or possibly even mere days until she went from being the Marchioness of Brookhaven to the Duchess of Brookmoor.

Twenty-seven thousand pounds would go a long way to fixing matters, wouldn't it?

STICKLEY AND WOLFE, partners in estate law, sons of more successful fathers, sole handlers of the significant Pickering fortune that was even now slotted to be bestowed upon Deirdre, Lady Brookhaven—as soon as old Duke of Brookmoor cocked up his toes and passed the title on to his nephew, of course—sat in their silent and somewhat grand office, face-to-face across the two desks their fathers had arranged four decades earlier.

I wish the blackguard would drink himself in front of the first ale cart to come along.

Stickley sat perfectly upright, of course, the very model of a proper solicitor, right down to the discreet gold watch fob and spectacles. Alas, the painful fact was that no matter how he squared his shoulders and kept his chin high, he would never approach his partner's easy masculinity. Unlike Wolfe, he could never carry off sprawling listlessly in the opposite chair as if his spine had melted into the fine leather and would never come away again. Not without looking feminine and pathetic, at any rate, like an abandoned dolly.

This only made Stickley's spine stiffer and his indignant sniffs more incensed.

"Stick," Wolfe muttered without raising his drowsy lids or even properly opening his lips. "If you don't quit your damnable sniffing, I'm going to twist your nose from your face and grind it under my heel."

"I cannot help it. You stink," Stickley responded. "You reek of cheap perfume and cheaper gin."

The reminder only made Wolfe's handsome lips curl in recollection. "Actually, I'm fairly sure the perfume was cheaper." He leered, lost in memories all too apparently lurid.

Stickley jerked his gaze away to contemplate the far less disturbing bookcases lining one wall. The spines gleamed despite the fact that no one had opened those volumes in his lifelong memory. "Say no more. I wish no accounting of your decadent misadventures!"

Unfortunately, this time Wolfe took him at his word

and sank back into his hung-over stupor without another word about the shocking but intriguing source of the cheap perfume.

Which was hardly fair, since it had been Stickley himself who had supplied the coin for it—in a manner of speaking, of course. He and Wolfe might be equal partners, but there was no illusion of who did the actual work. Why, without Stickley's efforts the Pickering fortune would not have grown so vast over the last two decades—which meant that Wolfe's portion of the retainer had grown as well, enabling the fellow to live out his days in the pursuit of pleasure instead of putting effort into the partnership.

The least the bastard could do—since he insisted on darkening the office door at all—was to relieve Stickley's boredom with some outrageous tales to be properly scandalized by.

"Why are you here again?"

Wolfe gusted a bored sigh and lifted his boot heels to rest on the blotter as if he could scarcely find the strength to do so. "Damned landlord locked me out again."

Stickley raised the superior brow of a man who owned his own proper little house in a respectable neighborhood. "Stinted on the rent again, did you? I paid out your share yesterday. Did you waste all of it?"

Wolfe shrugged. "Waste?" He gave a bad-dog smile. "I wouldn't say it was *wasted* . . ."

Stickley pricked up his ears, but Wolfe rumbled back to sleepy silence once again.

At that moment, a tap came at the office door. "That'll be the post." Perhaps not a great leap of deduction, since no one else bothered to come to their office. Stickley rose and dug into his waistcoat pocket for a penny to pay the postage as he crossed the room. Of course, Wolfe made no move toward paying for something.

There was only one letter, a crisp costly envelope with the Brookhaven arms embossed on the flap. "Ah, her ladyship!"

When Miss Deirdre Cantor had landed the marquis in a masterful play just after his lordship had given up his previous fiancée to his bastard half-brother in a ceremony that was still the talk of the town, Stickley had dusted off his hands, declared his meddling days over and had settled down to manage the vast fortune that the new Lady Brookhaven had promised to leave in his—their—capable hands.

After all, what need had she for it, when Brookhaven's own wealth outshone even old Pickering's? The plan had worked nicely, even though it had been Wolfe's idea. Together, they had made sure Brookhaven's first engagement had failed.

Of course, it was true that Wolfe's information had been faulty and Brookhaven's fortune was solid—and it was true that kidnapping Brookhaven had turned out to be a spectacularly bad idea, especially when it hadn't been Brookhaven after all, but his brother—and it was true that Miss Phoebe Millbury probably wouldn't have had any more use for her inheritance than did Miss Deirdre—er, the new Lady Brookhaven.

Well, however they had arrived at this point, it was a good place to be. Stickley had not nurtured and tended the Pickering thousands all these years to be happy about them being frittered away on alleged female "needs." Now he wouldn't have to be.

With relish, he opened the flap and withdrew the

thick, heavy paper within. He read aloud, although Wolfe didn't seem interested.

" 'To the firm of Stickley & Wolfe,
    Dear sirs,
    I hope this letter finds you well.' "

Stickley smiled, a brittle twist of his lips. "Lady Brookhaven is a most well-bred young woman, is she not?"

Wolfe grunted. At least, Stickley preferred to hear it as a grunt and not as some other, less savory exudation. Ignoring his partner, he went on.

" 'I have decided not to inform my husband of my incipient inheritance—' "

"Well, that is her prerogative, I suppose," Stickley said with a judgmental sniff. "Although I shouldn't allow a wife of mine to keep such a thing from *me*."

He ignored Wolfe's muttered slur on his possibility of ever being in such a position in the first place— really, just because a fellow took a bit of care with his appearance didn't mean—

He read on silently until he came to a sentence that made his hand clench the perfect paper to a permanent crease.

"Oh, no. Oh—oh—" There was no help for it. Only a curse would do at a moment like this! "Oh, *blast!*"

This roused Wolfe from his stupor as if the cast silver wolf's head on his walking stick had just risen up and bitten him. His boots hit the floor and he rose to his feet in a not-as-smooth-as-usual motion. "What? What is it?"

Stickley couldn't breathe. "F—f—" He waved the letter frantically at Wolfe. "F—"

Wolfe raised his walking stick. "Spit it out, Stickley!"

" 'Full withdrawal'!" he gasped. " 'Immediately upon becoming the Duchess of Brookmoor'!"

Wolfe went pale beneath his greenish hue and sank slowly back into his chair. "Oh." He took a long breath. "Oh, *hell!*"

Stickley nodded hysterically. "Exactly! Precisely! Oh, Wolfe, what are we going to *do?*"

Wolfe gazed into the glinting silver eyes of his walking stick for a long moment. Then he raised his head slowly. "The poor thing," he said silkily. He shook his head. "So she's realized what it means to marry the Beast."

Stickley gazed down at the brief note, trying to divine its source. "You think she wants to leave him?" He blinked rapidly. "So soon? But why?" A chill went through him. "Do you think she's *afraid* of him?"

Wolfe let out a heavy sigh. "Can it be anything else? She must have discovered his true nature right away. She is desperate now, I'll wager, afraid she'll end up just like the first Marchioness of Brookhaven."

Stickley shifted, uncomfortable with such dark imaginings. "Then, if she is truly in danger," he said slowly, "perhaps we ought to simply give her the money. It is rightfully hers, after all—or at least, it will be soon."

Wolfe nodded thoughtfully. "That might be a solution—unless he took control of it. Then she'd be helpless." He spread his hands. "And who would stop him? He's already gotten away with murder."

That had always been Stickley's personal belief as well. "What are you suggesting?"

Wolfe pondered the head of his walking stick. "I'm thinking . . . what if we do more for her? What if we help her free herself from that dreadful marriage . . . permanently?"

Stickley flinched at the hardness glinting in his partner's eyes. He suddenly recalled those alarming moments during their last adventure when he'd been almost sure that Wolfe was contemplating . . . well, *violence.* "You don't mean to—"

Wolfe sharpened his faraway focus on Stickley's pale face. The steely glimmer became shuttered and an easy smile took the place of the incipient snarl. "Don't worry, Stick. I know exactly what to do."

Stickley shook his head, more worried than ever. "I was afraid you were going to say that."

Chapter Twelve

Once Deirdre had eaten and dressed, she found herself at loose ends. There was nothing to do in Brook House. The household already ran smoothly. Other than seeking out the lost kitten, she had no plans for the day, or any day soon, so there would be no choosing of gowns or dressing of hair later.

She steadfastly refused the compulsion to look for a partner in crime in Meggie, for the act smacked a bit too much of obeying his lordship's edict that she raise his daughter. Besides, her ladyship had every right to inspect her new domain, after all. She would work her way from the cellar to the attic, she decided.

Unfortunately, the cellar was extremely dull, consisting of a rigidly organized storage area for root vegetables and the even more immaculate kitchens, where she didn't dare step foot.

The public rooms of the house, the parlors and drawing rooms and music room, she knew well already. His lordship's study remained a mystery, but Deirdre was not about to brave the Beast's very den—especially when she remembered the way he'd gazed at her last night!

She would have to face him sometime if she wished to wage her battle, but perhaps not just yet.

In the end, she found herself wandering the gallery, peering beneath the skirted tables and whispering allegedly cat-attracting noises. The hallway ran the front of the house, with inset windows looking out over the very best of London's houses perched along the street below.

Pausing in one of the window embrasures, Deirdre gazed out at the city she'd expected to own outright by now. Here she was, the Marchioness of Brookhaven, gripping the bars of her cage and staring out like the most forsaken Bedlamite.

Activity on the street below caught her attention. Three men approached the door to Brook House. They moved with the lithe bodies and easy steps of youth. After a moment, she recognized a certain gaudily striped waistcoat.

Ah, her worshipful faction had arrived. The waistcoat would be Cotter, the gray jacket would be Saunders and the dark blue . . . that would be Baskin.

The fact that she'd been wed only the day before seemed not to give any of the three pause—and why would it? It had been obvious to the world that hers had been a marriage of convenience. Why would life not go on as usual, with gentlemen callers abounding?

They were only a bunch of bored boys, anyway, with no real prospects of inheriting anything worthwhile and no real mission in life to occupy them. Flirting was their favorite pastime and, really, their only skill. Why should a little wedding ceremony slow them down a bit?

Cotter and Saunders enjoyed her company well enough, but she would guess that it was Baskin who couldn't stay away.

Baskin was the failed son of a renowned poet. Deirdre

spared a moment of sympathy for what it must have been like to grow up in the shadow of great expectations— among the artistic elite of Hampstead yet—but that pity evaporated like dew in the morning as she recalled the long hours of tedious verse he had subjected her to in the past.

Heaven help her, she almost wished Fortescue would let them in. Even Baskin's dreadfully overwrought penning of passionate devotion would be a relief from the tension and boredom she feared would constitute the rest of her life.

Or perhaps not. Baskin would insist on reading them aloud to her, until her eyes glazed over and her arse went numb. It was with mixed regret and relief that she watched them amble away, dejection in every step.

She turned from the view. Right. It wasn't as if she'd truly wanted to see any of them. After all, those days of attentive flirtation and sparkling conversation were over.

The opposite wall of the gallery hosted great life-sized paintings of every member of the Marbrook family—apparently reaching back into the days when men thought they had the panache to carry off the wearing of slashed doublets and tights.

Marbrook men did tend toward the satisfyingly muscular thigh, didn't they?

Were his lordship's thighs so well-strapped? He was tall and long of leg, and his trousers were well-fitted—though not so tightly as that fop Cotter's—so she knew that his buttocks were hard and his stomach flat, and it looked as though he might well have all the requisite family history for truly handsome thighs as well. . . .

She came to the most modern paintings to see two young men at the last. Lord Raphael and Lord Calder Marbrook, the engraved plates said.

Calder had not had his portrait painted since then, but he had apparently commissioned one of Melinda. She sat regally posed in an elegant chair, wearing a lace gown that was so stylishly advanced that Deirdre would not be ashamed to wear it tomorrow. Of course, but the young, beautiful Marchioness of Brookhaven had sparked the fashions, not followed them, hadn't she?

Deirdre knew she herself was beautiful in a bold, golden fashion, but Melinda had been something altogether rare and lovely. So slender as to approach frailty—except that on her it merely seemed exquisite and otherworldly—Melinda's dark hair and mist-pale complexion gave her an air of another time.

Her wide, heavily lashed eyes had been painted nearly violet in color—which was quite ridiculous and probably some artist's conceit, for who had purple eyes?—except that it looked entirely right, somehow.

Deirdre narrowed her eyes, not liking the feeling rising within her. Small of bosom, long of limb, achingly lovely—well, his lordship's first wife was enough to give Venus herself a nick in her pride!

"She's prettier than you."

Deirdre let out a breath but didn't turn around. "Lady Margaret, we really must address your tendency to state the obvious."

Meggie came even with Deirdre and gazed expressionlessly up at her mother's face. "She's prettier than me, too."

Deirdre glanced down at the child with a noise of impatience. "Soap and water does wonders." Then something inside her relented. "For now, perhaps—but you resemble her more than you know."

"There's no portrait of me."

There wasn't. It was as if the great line of Marbrook ended with Brookhaven's marriage to Melinda—as if she had wiped out the entire future of the family. Deirdre shivered, but pasted on a smile for the child. "Well, you're not done baking yet, are you? Likely when you're older—"

"It's because he doesn't want to look at me." Meggie turned stony eyes to meet Deirdre's gaze. "If he cannot look at me when I'm here, why would he want to see me when I'm gone?"

Deirdre didn't bother denying it. She hadn't been here long enough to know if it was true or not—and she wasn't in the mood to defend Brookhaven either way. "I'm in the mood for tea," she said. Turning, she walked a few steps before turning back. "You might as well come, too."

Meggie lifted her chin and gazed resolutely at her mother's otherworldly eyes. "I might . . . or I might not."

Deirdre nearly walked on, but after casting one more look back at the tiny, scruffy figure standing tense and alone in the great gallery, she let out a breath. "I believe I once saved some society articles about your mother . . . if you want to see them."

A quarter of an hour later, they sat side by side in the family parlor, poring over the yellowed clippings from years ago.

In her teenaged fervor, Deirdre had religiously sifted through it all to find everything she could about the young lord and his doomed lady.

There were sketches of her as well, for it seemed that

no artist could resist the opportunity to draw Melinda. Even the most meager talent rose to new heights with such a model, so there had been a great number of those to choose from.

Meggie absorbed it all, laboriously reading every word about the most talked-about young couple of the *ton*, from the first clipping announcing their engagement to the wedding, and all the Society appearances. Her grubby fingers could not seem to help but trace over every line delineating her mother's face.

Melinda didn't deserve such devotion, but Deirdre was careful not to let such bitter judgment sully the moment for the child.

After all, Meggie wasn't so bad when one got to know her. In fact, she reminded Deirdre of herself. She knew just how much a young girl could long to have someone who truly had her best interests at heart.

She reached to take the book before the next page revealed the scandal sheets. "That's all there is. I'm afraid I left London for Woolton about then."

Meggie's fingers twitched toward the book, but surprisingly she made no protest. Deirdre reminded herself that little Lady Margaret had taught herself not to ask questions she didn't want to know the answers to.

At any rate, there was no time for argument, for Fortescue announced a visitor.

Chapter Thirteen

"Lord Graham Cavendish, my lady."

Before the butler had finished the words, a pair of strong arms swept Deirdre up in a hug.

"Oof! Graham, put me down or I'll have you flogged! I have minions and lackeys now and don't you forget it!"

She was plunked back onto her feet but received an unrepentant buss on her cheek. Her cousin—actually, Tessa's cousin, but since Deirdre had grown up with him he felt much like a cousin, or even a rather useless but amusing brother—Lord Graham Cavendish, held her at arm's length and grinned widely.

"Pretty Dee. Lovely Dee. *Rich* Dee. Can I borrow a few quid? How about a hundred?" He heaved a happy sigh. "When do you think I can tap the big fellow for a loan? Is today too soon? It might be good to catch him early, don't you think, wedding night and all?" He winked. "He's sure to be in a good mood right now."

"Ahem." Deirdre elbowed the wretch in his hard middle and indicated the presence of little Lady Margaret with a tilt of her head.

Graham turned and spotted the child. "Hullo, darling,"

he said with a delighted grin. "Who're you and how do I get in line to marry you someday?"

As simply as that, Graham had another slave for life. Ferocious, bristly, little Meggie melted in a pool of feminine goo and adoration. Graham, the rotter, soaked it up.

He was nothing but the youngest son of four of the Duke of Edencourt. Without the merest chance of inheritance, unfortunately, for his three brothers were all hearty and healthy and in their prime. Without prospects or ambition to propel him to use his excellent mind and talents, Graham tended toward lazy and irresponsible.

It was too bad, really, for he was handsome enough to cut quite the figure through Society—if one preferred gentlemen of a lean ilk.

"I'm so glad you could make it to my wedding," Deirdre said dryly. "It meant so much to have all my family there."

Graham shrugged, his smile slightly guilty. "I heard you'd wound the great Brookhaven about your little finger. I figured that posh crowd would do you well enough."

"Still avoiding Tessa, then?"

Graham shuddered. "Avoiding everyone, actually. I've been hiding out in a certain lady's house for weeks, but her hus—" He glanced aside at Meggie. "Her family arrived this morning and there simply wasn't room for me any longer."

"Why there? Did you burn your house down again?"

"I never burned it *down*. It was only a small kitchen fire. The cook was out and I wanted bangers and mash."

"The cook quit because you wouldn't eat anything but bangers and mash. And the fire wasn't in the kitchen, it was in the study."

He spread his hands. "Where I was trying to make bangers and mash!"

"So why can't you stay there? It's nearly as big as this one."

For the first time something darker flashed across the unsullied green of his eyes. "Father is once again in residence . . . along with the chest-beaters."

Deirdre couldn't hide a grimace. Graham's brothers were three of the largest, hairiest, crudest men of the aristocracy, surpassed only by his father, the Duke of Edencourt himself. "All four of them at once?"

"Oh, God." Graham passed one hand over his face. "Save me, Dee."

"Did they bring home more hunting trophics?"

He sighed, still hiding his eyes. "Death hangs on every wall. Glass eyes follow one everywhere."

Fortescue brought more tea and cakes. Deirdre settled back with her feet curled beneath her on the sofa and her cup in her hand, willing to let Graham entertain her doldrums away. He soon had Meggie talking excitedly about her life at Brookhaven and regaled her in return with tales of boyish derring-do performed at his father's estate of Edencourt. Graham was a useless sponge, but he had a way of making things brighter.

Fortescue entered the parlor and bowed to Deirdre. "Good afternoon, my lady." Then he turned to where Meggie sat in the window seat. "Good afternoon, Lady Margaret."

Meggie turned her face upward in surprise. "What's so good about it?" she asked with genuine curiosity.

Graham made a choked noise.

Fortescue cleared his throat. "My lady, it seems that something of yours has gone astray. One of the chambermaids took quite a fright when she found it in the linen closet." He reached into his pocket and pulled out something Deirdre had given up on ever seeing again.

The kitten, it turned out, was of the black-and-white variety. His glossy little face was entirely dark but for the edges of his jaws where his white throat began, which spread down his little chest, making him look for all the world like a collared and ascot-clad dandy. His two front paws were also white, like tiny furry gloves. He sat on Fortescue's palm, blinking widely.

Meggie went very still. "It's mine?"

"Perhaps," Fortescue replied, "there is some other young lady in this house who lacks a kitten?"

Apparently, Meggie found this point irrefutable and reached out to take the kitten. Cuddling it high up under her neck, she gazed at Fortescue with worried brown eyes. "Does Papa know?"

Deirdre set down her cup, ready to jump to the defense of the kitten, but Fortescue only straightened. "I'm sure that such a very small sort of animal is beneath his lordship's notice . . . for the moment."

Meggie ignored the warning and smiled sunnily at the butler. "Fortescue," Meggie announced, "I am going to name him after you. After all, you're dressed just alike."

She held the kitten about its plump little body, legs and tail dangling. Deirdre had to bite her lip, for the kitten's black-and-white markings did look remarkably like the butler's elegant, begloved livery. "Fortescue, meet Fortescue."

Fortescue didn't laugh and, admirably, barely flinched. "I am honored, my lady," he said gravely, "but while this is not an issue for me, might it not cause some confusion among the staff?"

Meggie blinked and turned the kitten in her hands to consider it with a frown. "But that is the only name I can think of."

Fortescue nodded. "Naming is an important matter. Perhaps the ability to wear evening clothes with such panache does give hint of an underlying dignity—" The kitten crossed its eyes and batted little white paws at nothing at all. Fortescue tilted his head. "—that will someday emerge. A gentleman feline of such distinction deserves a very special name indeed."

Meggie gave a decisive little nod. "You're right, Fortescue. This isn't something I ought to rush into." She poured a saucer of cream from the tea tray and deposited her rakish gentleman-to-be on the table to enjoy it.

"Indeed, my lady." Fortescue turned away with a bow. He caught Deirdre's amazed gaze. "Yes, Lady Brookhaven?"

Deirdre clasped her hands on her knees and tilted her head. "Fortescue, is there a finer manservant in all of England?"

"Not that I know of, my lady, but then I am not a well-traveled man." He bowed, but not before Deirdre saw a flash of amused respect cross his expression.

No. Impossible. Fortescue would never mistake her for someone to respect, not now that Brookhaven had diminished her status to that of a disobedient child. Then again, Fortescue seemed to have a great deal of respect for Meggie.

"Fortescue, you did not inform me that we had company." Lord Brookhaven had arrived on the scene.

Chapter Fourteen

Everyone in the room froze, except for Fortescue, who smoothly dropped the domed silver cover of the cake tray over the kitten before he turned. "My apologies, my lord. I did not think it amiss to welcome a member of her ladyship's immediate family."

"Hmph." Brookhaven gazed at Graham with resignation. "I see the pattern now. You pluck one rake from the house and another simply pops up in his place."

Deirdre would rather die than laugh at anything her husband uttered at the moment, but a faint snort did escape. She covered it with a demure clearing of her throat. "My lord, would it not be enjoyable to have my cousin join us for supper?"

Graham, who had watched them both most carefully since Brookhaven had entered, stood and shook his head with a charming smile. "That's a grand offer, pet, but I must fly. There's a card game awaiting me, I fear."

Brookhaven folded his arms. "Don't let us keep you then."

Graham bowed over Deirdre's hand.

"Traitor," she muttered.

He flashed her a smile. "Give him a chance, love. He's all right."

"Great lot you know about it." There'd been no time to tell Graham about her situation—nor was she sure she wanted to. She'd worked so hard to win this man. She wasn't ready to admit that it hadn't been a good plan.

Graham bent to give her a peck on the cheek. "I wish you happy, Dee," he whispered.

Deirdre pushed him away. "Get off. You're not my brother, Graham."

He grinned as he straightened. "I couldn't love you more if you were my very own sister, pretty Dee. I'll visit often, I promise."

Sister. As if she'd have him. She watched him saunter out past Brookhaven with a reluctantly fond smile on her lips. It would be nice to have at least one person about who didn't despise her or think her mad.

Brookhaven was gazing at her. She let out a breath. "Did you wish to speak to me about something, my lord?"

He pulled an envelope from his pocket. "You have a letter. It's from Phoebe."

Her temper flared. "You've read it? Am I to have no rights in this house?"

He flushed. "Of course I have not read it. I recognized her handwriting. I am not an ogre, you know."

Beside her, Meggie made a dismissive noise. Bolstered by such solidarity, Deirdre glared back at her husband of one day with complete disdain. "Well, what must I do to receive this letter—wash the windows? Or is it last evening's display you wish me to repeat?"

He darkened, but it was not simple anger that flared in his eyes.

Calder gazed at the woman he had chosen above all

others and wondered how in the world he could have made such a drastic mistake. She was impossible!

Oh, she was capable of charm and laughter. He'd stood in the doorway, watching her with her alleged cousin—that fop was no blood relation, he well knew!—all smiles and graceful ease.

But none for him.

Graham was just like Rafe—pretty words and entertaining manner, but where was his character? He had nothing but his name, so whose money would he be losing at the card table tonight?

Yet Deirdre, whom he had somehow managed to allow himself to believe was attracted to *him*, spent all her pretty attention on useless boys like Lord Graham Cavendish!

Jealousy and old doubts twined within him. He stalked forward and thrust the thrice-damned letter into her hands. "Do be sure to let me know if my brother sends me word as well."

Then he walked away from his bride . . . again.

Deirdre pressed the letter between her hands for a long moment and allowed her heartbeat to settle. She'd had the sudden, wild impression that he was coming to pull her into his arms just then. It was just like her contrary heart to be disappointed.

The letter from Phoebe was precisely as Deirdre had expected, a surprised and delighted reaction to the announcement which had followed her wedding journey through Spain.

When Phoebe had won Brookhaven's proposal merely by standing across a crowded room, it had been difficult for Deirdre to like the cousin she'd not seen in many years. She hadn't behaved all that well at the time, actually, reminding herself more of Tessa every day as the wedding date had grown closer.

Now, she was able to think quite fondly of Phoebe and smile as she read.

"You've done it now, Dee. Rafe is sure his brother will never forgive him—and why would he think otherwise when he chooses to set his wedding while we're gone?"

Oops. To be truthful, Deirdre hadn't given her cousin's presence much thought and none at all for Lord Brookhaven's bastard brother. Turned on its side, the matter looked much worse than it was.

Or did it? She had no idea how Brookhaven felt about his brother's actions—actions that in anyone's book played out as betrayal. True, he'd taken part in securing Phoebe for Rafe, and hadn't that been romantic in the end?

Calder had chased Phoebe down when she'd run away with Rafe and brought her back in the middle of the night, her gown torn and ruined, pale and silent after Rafe had left her alone at that inn. Yet, he'd been kind after, protecting Phoebe from Tessa's wrath.

Deirdre sighed. A complicated man was Lord Brookhaven, that was for certain.

She brought her attention back to the letter in her hand.

"I'm happy for you, Dee, and I'm sure you'll be a better Marchioness of Brookhaven than I ever would have been . . ."

Hmm. Phoebe hadn't known about Lady Margaret either, Deirdre wagered. There was some comfort in knowing Calder had kept her in the dark as well, that his hideously inconsiderate plan had not been some sort of personal judgment of Deirdre herself.

No, the man was simply an idiot when it came to the feelings of others. Deirdre had lived with someone else like that for most of her memory. She knew supreme self-involvement when she saw it, but with Calder it was something else. She knew he did not lack in feeling, like Lady Tessa. It almost seemed that he feared to care.

Looking at Meggie's smudged little face, however, only firmed her resolve to break through to the man. He might have a heart where Tessa lacked one, but if he didn't use it the end result was much the same.

Graham's visit and Phoebe's letter helped. She did not feel nearly as alone as she had this morning. At least Brookhaven didn't intend to deny her family . . .

A smile teased at the corner of her mouth. She must ask Sophie to visit immediately. And if Sophie came perhaps a few others could ride in her wake . . . and wouldn't Brookhaven find that extremely annoying?

Chapter Fifteen

Calder spent that afternoon secluded in his study, staring at ledgers that refused to add up. The records were accurate. It was his attention that disobeyed him. After sufficient hours of uselessness, he rose to dress for supper. If he wished Deirdre and Meggie to obey the niceties, he could hardly skirt them himself.

Supper was perfect, as usual. He would not have stood for less—but it all tasted of sawdust to him.

She looked so beautiful, seated across from him, bathed in candlelight. Her hair was different, softer. She'd pulled back the front, but the rest poured down her back like a waterfall of summer light. There was something softer in her eyes as well—as if she might be thinking more kindly of him this evening.

Heat flooded his body at the thought of what a fellow might expect from more kindly thoughts. Forcing down that sudden disquieting lust, he spent so long trying not to stare at her that the meat course was served before he realized that she wore the same gown she'd had on earlier, a simple muslin fit for receiving a cousin in a parlor but nothing fine enough for supper.

"You didn't think it necessary to dress for supper?"

His abrupt question cut the silence too harshly. She

visibly flinched, making him feel like the ogre he'd denied being earlier.

She swallowed the bite of beef she'd been chewing delicately. "I did not know you wished it."

He was surprised. So simple a response? Where was the fiery defiance? Where was the bristling pride?

She leaned forward and inhaled deeply to say something else, but the roaring in his ears blotted out every word. A long fair curl fell forward over her shoulder only to become tightly lodged between her full breasts. Didn't she realize it? Didn't she know that his hands were shaking with the desire to reach across the table and free it for her?

Deirdre smiled to herself. *It's working.* He couldn't take his eyes from her. Unfortunately, when his eyes darkened hungrily and fixed upon her bosom, she ought to have been satisfied with her victory—but satisfaction was not to be had when his hot gaze only ignited a new heat within her. Her thighs dampened and her nipples tightened. It ought to have been mortifying.

It wasn't.

Men had wanted her before, both obviously and subtlety, and it had had no effect at all. This man with his flaming gaze and his silent slow burn was about to turn her into a bonfire without so much as touching her!

She had said something, hadn't she? She couldn't remember. He had not replied anyway. There was no point in attempting conversation anyway, not when her mouth had gone dry with need and her throat tightened with aching anticipation. He might come to her tonight, if she unlocked the door . . .

"*Dee!*"

Abruptly Deirdre realized that Meggie had been trying to get her attention for several minutes with a very obvious stage whisper—and of course, the little vulgarian had picked up on Graham's ridiculous nickname for her.

"Dee!"

She tore her gaze from Brookhaven's. *"For pity's sake, what is it?"*

"My kitten's gone missing!"

Brookhaven cleared his throat. "I ordered Fortescue to give it to Cook."

Deirdre turned to gaze at him with concern. If he tried to get rid of poor Meggie's only friend, she was prepared to—

"Kitty for *supper?*"

The volume was deafening and the shrill pitch made one want to crawl under the table. Meggie's rising wails drowned out any attempt of Brookhaven's to correct the impression that he had served her pet to her topped with gravy and roast potatoes.

At first Deirdre was concerned at the hysterics—until Meggie flashed her an evil grin from behind her napkin. They'd planned on doing something upsetting at supper tonight, but this far outshone their debated plate-in-his-lap scheme. Deirdre had to grant silent applause. Such thoroughness and dedication to duty in one so young! Heavens, the child was quite professional!

Then, grabbing up her own napkin, Deirdre pretended to gag into it. "Oh, how *could* you?" she cried at her husband's confused scowl.

Finally, the man hit his limit. He threw back his head. *"Enough!"*

Despite her worst intentions, Deirdre found herself

silenced by the male authority in his bellow. She'd never heard him raise his voice before, however, so perhaps she ought to count some sort of triumph.

Meggie halted with a last damp wail and a muffled hiccup. Deirdre shot her a sympathetic glance. She had worked herself into quite a state, however deliberately.

He placed both palms on the table and stood very slowly and deliberately. "Since neither of you seem to have any appreciation for Cook's fine meal, you will both go to bed without any supper," he growled.

Deirdre might have bristled under such a childish punishment, but after all, she richly deserved it. On the whole, she'd had enormous fun. She rose with complete composure. "Off we go, Lady Margaret."

Meggie sniffed and complied. At the door, she turned back. "I want to sleep with my kitten."

No one had ever said the child lacked fortitude. Outmanned, Brookhaven sank back into his seat and dropped his head into his hands. "We'll discuss the kitten's future tomorrow, Lady Margaret. Cook will take care of him well enough until then."

At which point they beat a wise retreat from the ground of battle, considering themselves the victors of the day.

"HAVE YOU EVER tasted bonbons?"

Deirdre and Meggie had fallen back to regroup in her ladyship's bedchamber. They lolled dully before the fire, their stomachs rumbling in earnest now. The last thing Deirdre wanted to think about was food. "Of course."

Her tone must have been a bit too offhand, for Meggie went silent, her gaze on the coals. Deirdre set down the book she'd been reading aloud. "You've never tasted sweets, have you?"

Meggie shook her head without looking away from the fire. "Papa ordered that I wasn't to have any."

"Ever?" Wasn't that just like the man, to ban sweets entirely with no thought to simple moderation? "One would think we were prisoners in the Tower," she grumbled.

Meg turned to her. "What did you say?"

Deirdre slid her feet off the settee and leaned forward. "I said, 'I have a special power.'" She grinned. "I know how to make toffee!"

Meg's eyes widened. "You do?"

Deirdre strode to the bellpull and gave it a decisive yank. "My father taught me. We used to make it on snowy days."

Fortescue, with his usual speed, tapped at the door, then entered. "My ladies?"

Deirdre waved her hand grandly, playing the great lady for Meggie's amusement. "Fortescue, I require two small pots, butter, sugar, chocolate and walnuts—immediately!"

Fortescue glanced at Meg. "His lordship has ordered that Lady Margaret not be given sweets."

Deirdre crossed her arms and raised a brow. "And has his lordship also ordered that I be so deprived?"

Fortescue's lips twitched. "Indeed not, my lady. I shall send a tray up directly."

As he departed, Meg sat up straighter. "We're going to eat sweets?"

Deirdre flung herself down onto the settee with a

laugh. "Lady Margaret, we are going to get revoltingly *sick* on sweets!"

The tray arrived, nuts already chopped and chocolate shaved to precise tiny bits, perfect for melting. There was even a pitcher of milk and two glasses. Apparently, she wasn't the only one who thought it was high time his lordship eased the reins a bit.

They sprawled on their stomachs before the coals and Deirdre showed Meg how to melt the butter and stir in the sugar until the mixture turned the perfect color of brown. Then while that cooled on the windowsill, they melted the chocolate and sweetened it to smooth perfection.

"Can we just eat this?"

Deirdre laughed at Meg's eagerness. "I used to say that, too. And my father would say, 'Patience, dear heart. It will be rewarded.'"

She poured the chocolate over the cooled butter mixture, sprinkled the nuts and set the pot back on the windowsill to cool again. "One really needs snow to cool it quickly—" She turned to see Meg's face filled with sadness, her gaze lost again in the coals. "Lady Margaret?"

"Papa doesn't like me at all." Her eyes were wide and glossy in her little face.

Deirdre couldn't very well deny it, when she'd seen no sign of any such affection. "How do you know that?"

"Your papa called you 'dear heart.' Papa never— He used to call me 'Meggie' and pat me on the head when he came to Brookhaven. Now he calls me 'Lady Margaret' and he never—he never pets me at all."

Deirdre shut her eyes briefly. *Damn you, Brookhaven.* Then she slid to her knees next to the child and put an awkward arm about her bony shoulders. "Your father loves you. He—he went out and found me, didn't he, just for you!" Which was something she hadn't wanted to admit to herself, but Meg's pain was larger and older than hers.

Meggie hesitantly leaned her head upon Deirdre's shoulder and together they gazed into the coals, but therein lay no answer to the mysteries of Lord Brookhaven's heart.

Then the toffee was ready. Meggie's expression at her first bite was priceless. For a while, contented silence reigned. Deirdre did see Meggie secrete a large chunk in the pocket of her grubby pinafore but said nothing. Little children deserved silly treats once in a while.

Chapter Sixteen

From outside the bedchamber, in the darkened sitting room, Calder watched them lying side by side on their stomachs, heels waving in the air. He might tell himself that he was upset at their lack of deportment earlier—

Is it that or the fact that they're in there and you're out here?

Then Deirdre smiled, and although it was quite clearly not at him, his heart thudded. She was so beautiful this way, uncomplicated and relaxed, the poised lady stripped away to reveal the playful imp beneath.

What was that like? To be able to be easy with others—it had always been a mystery to him.

He'd never understood women in particular, for they made even less sense to him. Men were rather closer to machines. They had a limited number of responses— aggression, cowardice, aggression to mask cowardice— and one simply ran the possibilities through one's mind to calculate what response one ought to make. Calder had found that an attitude of arrogant dismissal covered any number of possible expectations with men.

But not for Deirdre. She swept aside any intimidating pose of his to reveal the emptiness behind it. She forced him to reach deeper than anyone had ever done—even Rafe.

He forced himself to raise a hand to knock, knowing that his appearance would kill the candid mood. It usually did. He entered at Deirdre's word to find that Meggie had hidden herself. No matter. After all, he *wanted* the two of them to be company for each other.

Deirdre rose from her casual lolling, smoothly stepping before the dismembered dish of something probably forbidden. Calder had intended to politely request that she join him for breakfast.

"You will rise early tomorrow. One does not spend the day in meaningful pursuit if one spends the day in bed." He halted abruptly. Had he truly just uttered those words?

Of course, her chin rose and defiance flashed in her eyes. "Indeed? And why is that?"

"You will come to breakfast," he said gruffly.

Oh, very nice, you ass.

Damn it, he couldn't think straight with her standing there, golden-haired goddess of disdain that she was, reigning over his beastly hulk with a superior derision.

"I'll do precisely as I please," she said, "for you won't be here to see anyway. Aren't you vastly overdue at one of your factories?"

He was as a matter of fact. The requests for his presence were growing more urgent by the day. "I will be breaking fast at home. You and Lady Margaret will join me."

She raised a golden brow. "I don't take orders, my lord."

He gazed at her without easing his intensity a jot. "You

will rise and come down to breakfast tomorrow, after which you will spend every moment of the day with Lady Margaret. I've told Fortescue to make sure of it."

She folded her arms. "Poor Fortescue. Do you always make him play the enforcer? A braver man would do it himself." She smirked. "Or at least try to."

He refused to be baited. "You will rise early and come to breakfast with Lady Margaret and myself. You will dine with me every evening and you will dress for supper." He narrowed his eyes at her, stopping her retort. "You will do these things, my lady, or you will find there are a great many more things to lose than a few gowns and parties. I need not allow you to come to London at all."

She paled then. It did not satisfy him to see it, but Society-bred that she was, it was the worst threat he could muster. He would never lay a cruel hand on her, nor would he lie to frighten her. He did not want her afraid, he wanted her to grow up. He wanted an adult to share his life with, not a petulant child. He already had one of those.

"You don't seem a cruel man, my lord," she said calmly, though her eyes shot sparks. "So it must be that you don't truly realize what you are saying. To banish a wife to the country would only cause endless gossip. I would be reputed as mad or deathly ill. You would be accused of making me so, or even of killing me off— you know how tongues wag on."

She was quite right, damn it. He'd not thought it through. She had that effect on him, making him erupt in impulsive ultimatums.

Deirdre clasped her hands behind her back to hide the fact that they were shaking. She'd run from Tessa so that she could be free of oppression and tyranny. Damn Brookhaven. "Unfortunately, my lord, I know you to be a man of your word. Even now that I have pointed out your mistake, you will feel compelled to do precisely as you have threatened should I disobey.

"Since I am not a cruel woman, I will not force you to go through with such a scandalous mistake." Her slight smile was as cold as ice. "I shall see you at breakfast, my lord."

He bowed shortly, then turned on his heel and left without another word. Only when the door was closed behind him did Deirdre ease her aching fingers apart.

Meggie crawled out from under the bed. "If he thinks I'm coming to bloody breakfast, he really is mad," she announced furiously.

"Perhaps . . ." Heavens, it was becoming quite clear to Deirdre now. He didn't want to eat alone. This insight broke her heart just a tiny bit, but she could not allow him to jump off the hook quite so easily. She matched Meggie's earlier smile at supper. "That is too bad," she said, "for it should be most amusing."

OUTSIDE HER LADYSHIP's bedchamber, Calder stopped to run a hand over his face. As he had thought so many times in the last two days . . .

That did not go well.

Except of course for the fact that he'd won. Hadn't he? She'd agreed to do as she was told, this once, anyway. So why the shamed ball in his gut? It was a simple enough request, to breakfast and dine like a family.

But you didn't request.

He blew out a frustrated breath. He didn't have the

time or inclination to wrap every damned sentence in
pretty words. He was a very busy man. He'd spent
many years now accustomed to issuing—

Barking.

He felt a growl rise in his throat. *Issuing* commands
and having them carried out forthwith. There was no
reason to change his ways just because some female decided it dented her tender sensibilities.

He retreated to the masculine haven of his study. He
had matters, important matters, waiting for him to
arrange. He could not allow this madwoman to deflect
any more of his attention from them.

A short time later, Calder looked up from his papers
when he heard something slide under his study door.
He saw a quickly moving shadow against the light in
the hall and heard light running steps. He crossed the
room and knelt to retrieve a small paper-wrapped package from the floor.

On the outside were scrawled the words "For Papa."
He quelled a sigh at the deplorable penmanship and unfolded the scrap. Inside was a chunk of something
brown with . . . were those nuts? And a bit of lint, apparently. It looked like something his groom might
clean out of a hoof, but it smelled . . . wonderful.

He considered the possibility of poison, then decided that Meggie, being Meggie, would never be so
obvious. Then it occurred to him that Meggie, being
Meggie, might realize he would think that and therefore
would—

He shook his head against the cascade of suspicions
and decided to take the gift as a gift. If Meggie wanted
to harm him, all she had to do was to continue in her
current rebellion.

He took a tiny, careful—he wasn't a fool, after all—bite of the concoction. Buttery chocolate pleasure filled his senses. It was only the best toffee he'd ever had, not that he'd indulged often. It tasted like it came from London's finest confectioners—yet he knew that none of the staff would defy his rules to buy such a thing for Meggie.

But *she* would.

He tossed the package onto his desk and stalked back to his seat. The bloody-minded females in this house were going to be the death of him, poison or no! He forced his attention back to the matter at hand, refusing to waste one more moment on those fomenting rebellion right under his nose.

After a long moment and several unread pages, he allowed his gaze to slide back to where the toffee sat so innocently in its crude wrapping. His fingers twitched. No. He would not be sweet-talked by sweets! He would not be manipulated. *She* had obviously put Meggie up to such an endearing act in hopes of wheedling something from him. He could not encourage such behavior.

The scent of decadent pleasure teased at him. Abruptly, he snatched the toffee up, blew off the lint, and popped it into his mouth. Leaning back in his chair with a sigh of ecstasy, he let the delicacy dissolve slowly on his tongue.

After all, he was a man who despised waste.

Chapter Seventeen

Calder sat down to his breakfast at precisely the same time he always did. And, as always, despite the specific instructions he'd given his bride last night, he sat down alone.

He drew a deep breath. "Fortescue, where is her ladyship?"

"I believe her ladyship is still—"

"Her ladyship is right here, my lord."

Calder's head jerked up at that husky purr to see that Deirdre was indeed standing in the doorway—or rather, was lounging sleepily against the doorjamb as if she didn't quite have the alertness to stand.

She rubbed the back of one hand across her eyes, then blinked hard. "God, Brookhaven, who in the world eats this early? I can scarcely stand to look at the food."

His breath stuck in his throat. "*What* are you wearing, my lady?"

She blinked at him with wide eyes. "You said 'dressed for supper.' You never said 'dressed for breakfast.'"

Clad in a hastily tied wrapper and something lacy and diaphanous beneath, she was a mess—a luxuriously half-dressed erotically tousled mess drawn straight from his darkest fantasy of damp and tangled bed linens. She yawned with catlike delicacy, her lacy sleeve slipping halfway up her arm as she covered her mouth with the back of her hand, then blinked sleepily at him. "I might as well eat, since I'm here."

That was it. No greeting, no husky "Good morning, my darling," no sleep-warmed arm twining about his neck to pull him down for a soft-mouthed drowsy kiss . . .

The lack of such was no oddity—but his sudden aching longing for it was. She was his wife. She should be waking in his arms, her smooth limbs tangled in his, her soft breast weighing heavy in his palm, her sleepy blue eyes seeing only him—

She flopped into the chair Fortescue pulled out for her. The damned butler got a smile and a husky-voiced thanks, of course. A plate appeared before her—toast and a sliced apple. She drank only tea with no milk.

Calder frowned. She ought to eat more. Her figure was lovely, but he had no objection to a bit more of it. He opened his mouth to protest her diet—then halted. The bloody-minded creature would only do the opposite and starve herself. So instead, he eyed her plate with feigned approval. "I see you're very disciplined with your figure. Good. You wouldn't want to get fat."

That lit a spark behind her drowsy gaze. "Fortescue, eggs and ham," she snapped.

Calder hid a smile behind his napkin.

At that moment, Meggie wandered in. The fact that his daughter had obeyed him stunned him, but the fact that she was somewhat clean and dressed and more or less groomed—in a summer-in-the-country manner— left him entirely speechless.

Her dark hair was shining and combed and braided,
albeit lopsided. Her dress showed not a dot of mud or
food or soot and her face, pink and freshly scrubbed.

She was a beautiful child, just as anyone would expect a child of Melinda's to be. Her mother's face, softened by the childish lack of angles—her mother's hair,
gleaming nearly blue-black, her mother's shy smile
that had hidden so much loathing for so long . . .

Pain twisted within him. Not for the loss of
Melinda—at least not for *his* loss—but for what he'd
done and not done and what he'd cost the child before
him. He looked away, frowning, and missed the way
that Meggie's wistful smile faded slowly away at his
lack of greeting.

Deirdre didn't miss a thing. *Idiot man.* "You look as
though you're going out today, Lady Margaret. What
are your plans?"

Meggie, her mood obviously now as foul as her father's, only shot her a disdainful glare from beneath
long lashes. "Don't be ridiculous. I have to stay in all
day with you."

Deirdre sighed. They were a pair, the two of them.
Meggie even sounded like her father. She glared at
Brookhaven in renewed fury. "You're no help at all, do
you know that?"

Fortescue slid her new plate before her at that moment. "Small victories are still victories, my lady," the
butler murmured under the cover of arranging a fresh
breakfast napkin for her.

Deirdre sighed. It was true. In the breakfast battle,
she thought she'd scored rather highly off her husband.
And he'd looked directly at his daughter for once, at
least for a moment. That was something.

She glanced up to see Brookhaven's dark gaze fixed upon her bodice. The nightdress she still wore was not terribly concealing and her wispy wrapper wasn't much help.

Good. Let him see what he was missing with his idiotic tyranny. She put down her own fork and breathed deeply, dropping one shoulder so that her neckline came dangerously close to falling down. It wouldn't, of course, but she'd flirted enough in her life to know that the anticipation of even a tiny possibility of such a thing was enough to keep most men riveted for hours.

His eyes darkened and his sculpted jaw clenched. She could feel the heightening lust burning off his skin like the heat of a black coal fire.

Unfortunately, when he looked at her like that—as if the only thing stopping him from sweeping the table clear and debauching her upon it was his own rigid control—she went a bit weak in the knees herself.

Her mouth went dry at her own vision and her breath seemed harder and harder to catch. To distract herself, she blindly cut a bite of food and forced her trembling hands to carry the fork to her mouth.

Then the first bit of salty-sweet ham dissolved on her tongue, diverting her lust for her husband into something far more attainable.

Oh, *bliss*. She closed her eyes to enjoy the taste to the fullest, then hurriedly cut another, larger bite. She hadn't had ham in years—and why not?

Now that she thought of it, the strict diet was Tessa's idea. Deirdre had been banned from indulging anything resembling a normal appetite since she was fifteen years old.

To be truthful, it wasn't all Tessa's doing, for nothing

would have stopped Deirdre if she'd decided to rebel. Such rigid protection of her figure had made sense when she was duke-hunting. Yet, she was a married woman now. She could grow as fat as a cook and Brookhaven couldn't do a thing about it.

She wriggled more comfortably into her chair and prepared to eat until she couldn't breathe.

Calder watched his lady wife as she tucked into her breakfast like a field hand. The sight was oddly satisfying. She was unguarded in her enjoyment, for just this moment in time, and he relished the genuine pleasure on her face.

Now if only he were the cause instead of his staff's excellent cooking. It was all he could do not to stare boldly at her bosom in that loose and lacy nightdress thing she wore. He couldn't even taste the food he was chewing!

Still, progress was progress. His wife had begun to take his daughter in hand, despite early signs of rebellion, and he had a full table at breakfast.

Not bad for his third day at the job of husband. Perhaps he was a bit rusty, but he'd soon have everything running smoothly enough to return to touring his beloved factories—

Good God, it had been days since he'd given them more than a passing thought.

He ought to leave at once. He needed to take a tour of his properties, involve himself in something real and concrete and entirely devoid of breasts. Yes, absolutely. It was time to leave this madhouse and lose himself in the comfortingly dry and uniform world of manufacturing again.

Reluctance pulled at him and he struggled to explain

it. It was too soon. She was too unpredictable. Meggie wasn't accustomed to her yet. The staff wouldn't know to keep a tight rein upon her.

Yes, that was it. He didn't dare leave. He wasn't blind to the way she'd seduced Meggie to the dark side. Even Fortescue, whose heart was made of such dependable ice, was clearly becoming smitten by her. At the rate she was going, she'd take over the world before he made it back!

No. It was best to stay—to stand his ground. She must learn that he would not be swayed from his course.

Besides, even though he wouldn't have admitted it under the vilest of torture, he was rather curious to see what she would do next.

Chapter Eighteen

The tension in the breakfast room didn't ease until his lordship gruffly excused himself and tossed his napkin to his plate. Deirdre smiled brightly at her husband. "Are you leaving us today?"

He gazed sourly at her. "There's no need to sound so hopeful."

She fluttered her eyelashes. "I don't know what you mean, my lord."

"Hmph." He turned away, then turned back. "By the way, my dear, you *will* dress for breakfast tomorrow."

Deirdre smiled sweetly. "As you wish, my lord."

That confused him. "Er . . . well. Good morning, then." He strode away, minus just a bit of his previous smolder.

Once he was gone, Deirdre's smile faded. As amusing as it was to tease the man, "annoyed" wasn't precisely the eternal emotion she had in mind.

"That wasn't so bad," Meggie said thoughtfully. "I think Papa sort of liked having us here."

Deirdre sighed. "I certainly hope so." She pushed her plate away. "Fortescue, could we have some tea in my sitting room?" She smiled at Meggie. "We have some plotting to do."

Soon they were ensconced in private comfort in the beautiful suite. Hot fragrant tea in fine china, next to a cozy fire on a damp spring day—and no Tessa. Truly more peace and comfort than she'd ever experienced.

"Fortescue—"

He looked up from the tea tray. "Yes, my lady?"

Deirdre studied her hands. "I wish to thank you, Fortescue. Despite this—this childish war between myself and his lordship, you've treated me with great respect."

"Of course, my lady." Fortescue made to move on, but Deirdre held up her hand.

"Wait. I'll not let you brush this off, Fortescue. After living in my stepmother's household, I know perfectly well how the staff can make a mistress's life miserable if they wish it . . . and that tone is usually set by the butler." She glanced aside to where Meggie played with her kitten by the fire, then gazed earnestly up at the butler.

"It seems silly indeed to refuse his lordship's wish that I raise Lady Margaret, especially since she so clearly needs it. I simply wanted you to understand, it isn't what Lord Brookhaven asks of me that I find impossible—" She shrugged helplessly, spreading her hands. "It's the *way* he asked—or, rather, didn't ask. Do you think I'm being ridiculous, too?"

Fortescue gazed very carefully at a spot somewhere over her head. "My lady, I have often noted when integrating new staff into the household that how they begin is how they will go on, if not corrected immediately."

Deirdre laughed shortly. "That argument could go either way, Fortescue."

Fortescue bowed, his eyes shadowed by the angle of the light. "My point precisely, my lady."

Deirdre considered the man for a long moment. "You're on my side, aren't you, Fortescue?"

Fortescue met her gaze directly for a fleeting moment. "I hope that we can all win, my lady." Then he bowed again. "If you require nothing else, my lady?"

Deirdre laughed and waved him. "Go strike fear into some hapless coal-boy then. You don't alarm me anymore."

"Oh, dear," he said mildly. "I've so enjoyed it."

Deirdre was still laughing when the door closed on the butler, but her amusement faded as she gazed at the lonely little girl before the fire. Meggie's happiness depended on winning more of her father's hesitant new attention—and Meggie's happiness had somehow become very important to Deirdre.

Then she slid to kneel beside the child and coo over the kitty. Mischief-plotting could wait until after tea.

"WE COULD PUT boot black in his hairbrush."

Deirdre gave the notion polite consideration. "I should like to see that—although such a plan might be more effective if he were fair-haired, don't you think?"

Meggie's face fell. "Oh." She sighed. "Ink in his tooth powder?"

Deirdre grimaced. "What if it never came off?"

"Oh, it comes off eventually," Meggie reassured her brightly.

Deirdre sent her charge a wary look. "Remind me not to make you angry."

Fortescue brought in a fresh pot of tea. Deirdre smiled her thanks and went back to her evil master plan.

The butler lingered. After a moment, he cleared his

throat. "My lady, if I might have a moment of your time?"

Deirdre looked up to see Fortescue standing even more stiffly than usual. Goodness, if she hadn't known better she would have thought he was nervous! She leaned to whisper in Meggie's ear. "Lady Margaret, run up to the schoolroom and fetch more paper while I help Fortescue pry the iron bar from his arse."

Meggie snickered and obeyed with speed. Fortescue looked surprised at such willingness as Meggie dashed past him with a wide smile.

"You've done wonders with her young ladyship, my lady."

Deirdre frowned. She wouldn't want something like that to get back to Brookhaven. "I haven't done a thing. Lady Margaret makes her own decisions."

Fortescue bowed. "Precisely, my lady."

Deirdre gave the butler a half-smile. "What may I do for you, Fortescue?"

He cleared his throat. "I thought perhaps now that you've settled into Brook House . . . somewhat . . ." His words faded delicately away, for that was most certainly not true. "Perhaps you might consider making Patricia's appointment as your lady's maid permanent— that is, if you have found her work satisfactory?"

Deirdre blinked. "I hadn't realized that wasn't already the case."

"No, my lady. His lordship asked that I find someone on the staff to fill in until you selected your own maid."

Patricia was a lovely girl and very skilled, far beyond what one would think, what with her lack of education . . .

Deirdre straightened. "She is a very intelligent girl,

but her speech?" Deirdre waved a hand. "I worry that she will never be able to pursue possibilities outside of this house. It would also aid me if she could read and figure."

Meggie strolled back into the room with a stack of paper, a smudge on her cheek and one braid rapidly coming undone. Without thinking, Deirdre tugged the child into her lap and began to rebraid it. Meggie seemed to think nothing of it, but Fortescue's eyes widened in surprise. Deirdre went on. "If Patricia is willing, I should like to engage an instructor for her immediately."

All tension eased from Fortescue's handsome features and he nodded briskly. "I shall take care of it at once. I know precisely who to engage." He left with what might have been described as a jaunty step—that is, if one were not speaking of Fortescue.

"How is Fortescue's arse?" Meggie asked curiously.

Deirdre smiled as she used her handkerchief to absently dab at Meggie's face. The butler and the lady's maid? She found herself rather envious. "Oddly enough, I think it's better now."

Chapter Nineteen

Miss Sophie Blake had managed, despite her habitual clumsiness and inability to fade into the woodwork due to her height, to escape her aunt's house unseen and un-chaperoned. Not that Tessa was terribly diligent, but she did seem to have the most uncanny ability to detect someone about to have a bit of fun, just in time to spoil it for them.

It was odd to stroll down the London streets by her-self. Perhaps it ought to have been alarming, but it seemed her unfashionable garb and obvious lack of wealth put her somewhere amongst the great servant class and therefore rendered her nearly invisible. This was rather freeing, in fact, and she thoroughly enjoyed the long walk to Brook House.

She even smiled at Fortescue when she entered, but missed his blink of surprise because she was looking about for Deirdre.

"Her ladyship is in her sitting room, Miss Blake. If you'll wait in the parlor, I'll inform her that you are here."

Smiling slightly at the reminder that she was now a visitor instead of a member of the household, Sophie handed over her bonnet and gloves and made her way down the hall. Just as she approached the door of the parlor, she turned in response to an uneasy sensation that she was being watched.

Fortescue remained standing where she'd left him, a bemused expression upon his face as he gazed after her. At her questioning glance, he caught himself and dipped a respectful bow before striding off to find Deirdre.

Whatever could the man have been staring at?

Then she caught her own reflection in a small hall-way mirror as she passed. Her reddish hair was escaping her cap and the bump in the bridge of her nose caught the light just right and her long neck looked like a plucked chicken's rising from the ruffled neckline of her ridiculous gown.

Oh, that's right. I'm plain.

As usual, her mind instantly veered away from that thought, heading instead to her project. Whenever she could, she escaped from Tessa's social obligations to work on it. Having completely translated the first of the stories of German folklore to her satisfaction and to the thorough enjoyment of her cousins, she was now in the thick of the second translation, a magical tale that promised to be even more thrilling than the first.

Her mind on the delightful prospects of finding out what happened next, she sauntered through the music room on her way to the parlor with none of her usual care in entering a room. The sunny chamber was not empty, however.

Sophie stopped short just inside the door. There was a man seated at the small pianoforte, absently running through scales with one expert hand. The notes lilted up and down, melodic for simple scales.

She wondered what it would sound like if he truly tried to play. She adored music, though there'd been precious little at Acton, but she'd come here to see Deirdre, not be confronted with strange men.

She couldn't pass through to the parlor without him seeing her—and if he saw her he would speak to her—and then she would have to speak to him—

Panic rose within her. No, she would turn around and find Fortescue—who had already disappeared to fetch Deirdre, blast it! Perhaps if she bustled right by the fellow, he would mistake her for a maid and simply keep playing. She might even be able to muster a curtsy without catastrophe—

"You're going to scorch the hairs off the back of my neck if you keep staring that way."

With a gasp, Sophie looked up to see that he was gazing directly at her by way of the mirror above the fireplace. From the relaxed posture that hadn't shifted since she'd entered the room, he'd been watching her the entire time.

"Do you always dither that way? It was like watching a cat decide between a dog and a dunking."

Sophie opened her mouth to respond but nothing came out. He was handsome—too handsome by far. His narrow face was creased with sardonic humor and his green eyes twinkled at her knowingly—oh, yes, he knew he was a delicious devil.

Sophie's palms went damp and panic welled up within her, and even though she was standing several feet away from anything breakable, she knew it was only a matter of time. She would shatter something valuable, or knock over something loud and clattering, or spill something—oh, God, not that—and then he would gaze at her with sympathetic confusion and then he would look away—forever—because to stare at someone so pathetic would be rude—

"Are you planning to combust or some such?" His gaze was curious and amused, not pitying. "I don't think I've ever seen anyone go from white to red to white again in the course of a breath." He turned smoothly and stretched his long legs out, leaning one elbow insouciantly on the pianoforte.

If Sophie thought being watched in the mirror was bad, it was nothing compared to the full force of this attractive man's attention. She stood there, frozen and feeling entirely naked, while his amused gaze went from the top of her head to her toes and back again.

"You certainly are a dress length and a half. Did your parents decide to buy by the yard?" He stood and moved nearer. "I'm still taller, so I win."

He was indeed several inches taller than her, which gave her the oddest feeling, almost as if she were, well, *not* a towering tree. She had to tilt her head back slightly to look him in the eye, which required her to straighten from her usual posture. How . . . unusual.

Oh, he was fine indeed! He wasn't heroically handsome, like some steel-jawed, iron-thewed knight of old. He was leaner, with a long, chiseled face and eyes like seawater in the sunlight . . .

His eyes began to twinkle further, his grin broadening. "I'm quite the looker, aren't I?"

"What?" Oh, God, she'd been staring at him, ogling him like a lovesick maiden! Horrible—any moment he would say something kind to let her down easy. No, how unbearable! She stepped back jerkily, almost stumbling, not caring, just wanting to get away from the look that would momentarily rise in his eyes—

One long-fingered hand flew out to wrap about her upper arm. He pulled her back quickly, drawing her against him for a mere instant.

It was long enough to find out that his languid ease hid a lean body that was hard as granite against hers. What small bosom she had was crushed against a muscled chest that gave not at all at the impact. She gasped as much from that unexpected discovery—and the instant effect it had upon her—as she did from the surprise of his motion.

He let her go as soon as she had her balance and stepped back easily. "Door," he said with a grin. "Those cost money, you know."

Sophie glanced behind her to see that, indeed, she'd been about to turn and run directly into the closed door. Still turned away, she shut her eyes. Idiot! What was wrong with her?

He moved around her, his head tilted in order to look into her face. "I think you must be Miss Sophie Blake. Deirdre said you were tall and plain."

He thought she was plain—that was no surprise. The fact that he said it so naturally—that was new. Most people either avoided saying it with such determination that their very silence had humiliating emphasis or felt it was necessary to offer her a sort of gleeful encouragement.

"Don't worry, pet. Somewhere out there a man is looking for a no-nonsense, skin—er—slender sort."

This fellow wasn't pitying at all. She lifted her head a little to look back at him, curious.

"Well?" He grinned. "Are you the elusive Sophie or not?"

"Do you see any other tall, plain ladies about?" Good heavens, was that her voice, so tart and crisp?

He laughed, then gave an insouciant minimal bow. "Hello, Sophie. I am Lord Graham Cavendish. Lady Tessa is my cousin."

Sophie relaxed slightly. He was family—or at least, he was Tessa's family, which very nearly counted, didn't it? Still, the way he was looking at her—right at her, no less!—was making her rather twitchy. Almost family or not, he was incredibly attractive.

"I am pleased to meet you, Lord Graham Cavendish, Tessa's cousin." Did that sound childish? She'd meant it to be light and worldly.

She absolutely reeked at being worldly.

Lord Cavendish seemed to think so as well. "Where have you been all these years? Living in the bottom of a well? I suppose that explains your height. You've spent your life trying to grow your way out of it."

He was laughing at her, but it was entirely in fun, without the slightest cruelty. Sophie found her own lips beginning to curve. "Indeed. And every year they would hand me a spoon and ask me to dig it deeper."

His smile widened. He bent close to her. "That's my girl," he said approvingly.

His breath was warm on her cheek. Sophie jerked back in surprise. Again, he caught her arm and dragged her away from a bruising confrontation with something architectural.

He released her a bit more slowly this time. "Are you a little bit insane?" His tone was conversational. "Or is something physical awry?"

Damn it! Sophie closed her eyes miserably. "It's—I'm—" She hunched. "I only get this way around . . . men."

"Hmm." He crossed one arm over his chest and tapped the fingers of his other hand on his chiseled jaw. "All men? Does the butler send you spinning into solid objects?"

Sophie writhed. "No . . ." Oh, what did it matter. She opened her eyes and gazed at him miserably. "It is mostly around handsome, eligible men."

He nodded sagely. "Well, then, you need not gain any more bruises from my availability."

"What do you mean?"

He smiled, his expression almost gentle. "I mean that I am not in the market for a wife—ever!—and furthermore, I, handsome bloke that I am, am entirely out of your reach. So you see, we might as well be friends, for there isn't a chance in hell that we will ever be anything else."

In a strange, skewed way that thought actually helped. Sophie looked at him—God, he was beautiful—and then down at herself. He was right. They were not even the same species. The idea of them together was as odd as mating a tiger to a giraffe.

Relief flooded her, lifting her hunch and lightening her mind. She smiled easily at Lord Graham Cavendish. "How lovely to meet you, my lord."

Chapter Twenty

Calder tossed aside the ledger he was pretending to read and leaned his head back on his chair. Inhaling deeply, he let out a minor experimental groan. It helped a little.

Deirdre was driving him mad, and she wasn't even in the room! He'd just spent half an hour staring at columns of numbers that made no sense while his mind was filled with her hair, her breasts, her eyes . . . but mostly her breasts, if he was honest with himself.

What was she doing right now? She might be bored, or even a little lonely. He could seek her out and tweak her powerful pride just a little, just enough to make her cheeks pinken and her blue eyes flash haughtily . . .

It was a marvelous plan. Being a man of deeds, not words, he jumped up to put it into action immediately.

Unfortunately, as he entered the front hall of the house he heard the sounds of company in the house— company that was having far too good of a time!

"Fortescue!"

As usual, his butler materialized as if he'd rubbed a bloody lamp. He scowled at the man. "What is the meaning of this?" He waved at the parlor door. "I was very specific in my orders!"

Fortescue inclined his head. "Indeed, sir. Very specific. However, is it my understanding that I have your permission to knock milady down in order to beat her to the door?"

Calder drew back. "Of course not!"

Fortescue folded his gloved hands before him and gazed at Calder serenely. "Then might your lordship suggest by what means I am to accomplish said task? Other than grappling with milady on the foyer floor, of course."

Calder gazed furiously at his highly paid, once-slavishly-devoted-but-now-openly-traitorous butler, but Fortescue remained unfazed. Calder threw his arms wide. "Corrupted! She's corrupted you all!" He swung about and glared at the hallway, where the sound of tinkling laughter and male guffaws infiltrated his once peaceful home.

Peaceful? Or dreary?

"I should have chosen the other cousin," Calder muttered. "Miss Sophie Blake would never carry on so."

"No, my lord. Although . . ."

"What?"

"I do believe Miss Blake is in the parlor as well, my lord."

Unbelievable. His beautiful bride infected everyone she met! "I should have married Tessa herself," Calder growled. "At least then I would have known what to expect."

Fortescue raised a brow. "With respect, my lord, if you had wed Lady Tessa, you would have been obliged to hire an entirely new staff. Myself included."

Since he himself would rather run naked through Westminster Abbey than spend ten minutes with demon-spawned Tessa, he could hardly blame his butler for such an insubordinate statement. "Like begets like," he muttered.

Fortescue cleared his throat. "My lord, if I may be so bold to say—*milady* is nothing at all like her step-mother."

The odd emphasis didn't escape Calder. "But I am, is that what you're saying?"

Fortescue only bowed deeply. "If there is nothing else, my lord, there are guests to be attended to."

Calder gestured sharply. "Oh, get out of here, you turncoat. I never would have thought a head of fair hair and a fine bosom would warp a man like you, Fortescue."

Fortescue bowed. "No, indeed, my lord. I think it might have been the mind and the heart beneath."

Calder looked away, for he'd not been privy to nearly enough of either and it didn't behoove a man in his position to be envious of his butler! "Fortescue," he forced out between gritted teeth. "Pray, ask her lady-ship if she would excuse herself so we could speak for a moment."

Fortescue entered the parlor, then left, followed after a moment by Deirdre. She walked past Calder quickly, forcing him to follow her. Not that he minded—the view going was nearly as attractive as the view coming. Once they turned the corner in the hall, she turned on him in a rustle of silk and indignation.

"My lord, I am surprised at you! How could you do that to poor Sophie?"

Calder blinked. "I'm quite sure I've done nothing to Sophie. You, on the other hand, likely have a great deal to answer for."

Her eyes narrowed. "Well, that shows what you know. Tell me, now that both Phoebe and I are out of the house, do you imagine that Sophie gets many callers there?"

His frown eased. "Ah. So this is how you intend to keep Sophie in the social circle? By captivating every man within a mile and keeping him from so much as glancing her way?"

She folded her arms, her chin lifting. "I am trying to teach her *by example.*"

"Hmm. Actually, that notion has some merit, I suppose." *Damn it.* "She certainly won't learn how to hold a conversation with a man if she never leaves her studies."

Her forehead cleared in surprise. "Yes, precisely. I hadn't thought you would—"

He let out a breath. "My lady, I am not a complete block, you know." He glanced back toward the parlor door. "Poor thing, all alone there with Lady Tessa." He turned back to Deirdre. "You should invite her to come often."

She tilted her head, a tiny crease appearing between her brows. "Brookhaven, are you actually being *nice?*"

She needn't look so astounded. "Of course not. Anything that troubles Lady Tessa is sure to be a good investment in time, that is all."

An answering glint appeared in his wife's beautiful blue eyes. "Indeed."

He curled the corner of his mouth. "Indeed."

They stayed that way, each unwilling to do anything to end the rare moment of accord between them.

Calder could feel her close to him, as if the air between them was charged with incipient lightning. Her near smile faded slowly as her eyes softened to a summer blue. She grew sweeter, softer, warmer with each passing second.

His for the taking, hanging ripe and inviting on his very own vine—why was she not in his arms? He could not recall at that moment. She ought to be.

He could reach out right now to stroke that lock of hair that she let curl just over her ear, or perhaps allow his fingertips to trail softly over her cheek to those pink, full lips . . .

He shifted in her direction. She swayed toward him, her eyelids drooping in willing surrender—

From upstairs came a crash and furious shriek from Meggie, then a string of words no seven-year-old girl ought to know.

Calder shot a frustrated glance up the stairs. "What a menace. I ought to pack her right back off to Brookhaven—" He turned his gaze back to Deirdre to see that she'd stepped back, disappointed anger in her eyes.

"You would, wouldn't you?" She folded her arms. "Why don't you just bundle her up in brown paper and send her through the post? Or me, for that matter— where will I be bundled off to if I don't behave?" She was really working herself into a spitting rage now. It looked good on her.

Damn. He sighed wearily, knowing it would annoy her more than anything else would. "I don't have time for this nonsense now. I'll be in my study."

She narrowed her eyes. "Go on. Hide. It is what you do best, after all."

He shook his head and turned away from her, flushed cheeks, bright eyes and all. He must remember what he was about here. He would not get anywhere if he let her bait him into reacting.

When Brookhaven turned his broad back to her and walked away, Deirdre nearly pounced on him in her frustration. Oh, how she'd like to pound some sense into that thick head!

With no available projectiles in her path, she had to satisfy herself with a noise of frustration and misery.

Score: Brookhaven one, Imprisoned Bride nothing. Nothing but a belly full of the fiercest desire she'd ever experienced mingled with loss and ache and plain, ordinary, bone-deep *mad*. She stamped her foot, for being childish didn't count when no one could see.

"Brookhaven, one day you are going to kneel at my feet and beg me to love you forever," she vowed. "And then I'm going to—to—"

What? Deny him? Reject him?

Love him right back for the rest of his life?

The fight seeped from her body and she let out a sigh. Yes, she probably would.

Damn it.

Chapter Twenty~one

After clashing with Brookhaven in the hall, it was a relief to return to the parlor and the uncomplicated admiration awaiting her there. Perhaps she was shallow, but what was wrong with a bit of innocent flirtation? After all, it wasn't as if his lordship cared—at least, he didn't care as long as she wasn't having too much fun.

Well, drat him, she would have more fun than she could stand, beginning right now.

She sailed into the room with her very best smile for her admirers. Sophie looked up with a rather wearied glance, obviously twitching to disappear back into her stuffy books. Deirdre felt a twinge of guilt for using her cousin so.

She settled on the sofa next to Sophie, discreetly turning her best profile to the three young men on the opposing one. Graham, who was sprawled in the chair by the fire, shot her a wry glance of appreciation. She raised an admonishing brow and turned to Sophie.

"Cousin, do tell us about your latest translation. I've been simply dying to hear." Actually, the stories were rather intriguing, but it would have been worth the transformation in Sophie even if they hadn't been.

Instantly, her drab, restrained cousin brightened. "Oh,

yes—this one is called 'The Summer and Winter Garden.' There is a spell, you see, that causes snow to fall on one half of the garden in the summer and roses to bloom in the other half of the garden in winter. One day, a man journeying by sees the roses blooming in the snow and stops to pick one for his youngest daughter—"

"I hope this isn't about gardening," one of the young men, that dreary poet-in-his-own-mind Baskin, drawled.

Quelled, Sophie lowered her gaze. "I haven't yet told you about the beast—"

Graham leaned forward, spurred from his languishing sprawl. "I want to hear, Sophie."

Deirdre sent Baskin an arch glance. He was not so endearing this way. "I, as well."

But shy Sophie had lost her tenuous nerve. It was best to let her stop before she tripped Fortescue with the tea tray or demolished one of Brookhaven's art treasures in her distress.

Baskin must have realized his mistake. In an obvious attempt to change the subject, he turned an adoring gaze upon Deirdre. "Why don't you tell us about the first ball you're going to throw here at Brook House?"

Oh, dear. She ought to have known that letting people in meant that her humiliating secret might get out. Playing for time, she waved a hand. "Oh, I'm not ready to announce anything yet."

Baskin leaned forward. "But you must have chosen a theme? You were so looking forward to it the last time we talked."

Deirdre blinked at him, touched that he'd actually remembered what she'd spoken of more than a week ago. She rewarded him with her most blinding smile. "When I'm ready to announce my plans, you shall be the first to know." She leaned forward and patted his hand. "After all, only my *dearest* friends will be invited."

The silly fellow actually glowed. Honestly, it was like having a faithful hound, if a hound wrote excruciatingly bad poetry. She added even more intimate warmth to her smile. Sweet, faithful Baskin—a certain guarantee against husband-induced doldrums.

Now that she'd reduced one admirer to a puddle of longing, she turned her attention back to the rest of the party. She was determined to enjoy this respite from Brookhaven, whether she liked it or not!

FORTESCUE STOOD BEHIND the desk in his small but precisely neat office. He'd taken this room, which was once meant for a lady's morning room, as a private workspace when he'd first succeeded his mentor. Since her ladyship didn't seem inclined to ask for it back, it would do as a classroom for Patricia as well.

The fact that it was a charming room with a delightful aspect of the garden had nothing to do with it—unless perhaps it was the fact that the large window provided good light.

Then again, he'd planned the lessons for evening, so the only thing one would see might be moonlight on roses . . .

You're a bad fellow, John.

True. He'd honestly never realized he had such a calculating streak, but he refused to allow shame or propriety to stand in his way. He could not bear a day without Patricia in it.

Now he waited, showing not a fragment of his

quivering anxiety as he waited for a response to his proposal—er, *her ladyship's* proposal.

"Me, Mr. Fortescue? Learn to read?"

Fortescue kept his hands folded before him and his gaze properly on Patricia O'Malley's face. Her own gaze had been properly downcast—saucy she might be, but Patricia knew the proprieties—until her startled green eyes had risen to meet his.

As green as the hills of Ireland itself . . .

He cleared his throat and nodded. "You, indeed. Her ladyship believes you more than capable of learning—as do I."

She blinked. "You do, sir?" Her cheeks grew slightly pink.

Was she blushing from his compliment—as if he'd concocted rhymes about hair like fire and eyes like emeralds and spoken them aloud?

Not that he would. Ever. Particularly not to a pert lady's maid who worked under him—er, beneath him—er, oh damn. He cleared his throat again.

"I have a spare hour every evening after supper." Actually, it had taken an entire afternoon to rearrange his strict management schedule. "Her ladyship has no engagements scheduled . . . for the moment. We will work in here."

She fixed her gaze upon him sharply. "Here, sir? In the evenings? Alone?"

"Did you expect her ladyship to ship you off to school?" He raised a brow. "I appreciate your hesitation, Patricia. It shows you possess a modest bent. However, I am old enough to be your father—"

"A bit older, actually, sir. Me da's not yet forty years of age."

Her blasted da must have had an early start indeed. Well, it was a good thing to remember, wasn't it, when he thought too hard upon the way the curve of her waist was revealed beneath the proper black gabardine when she moved? "Then there is nothing to worry about, is there?"

She still gazed at him doubtfully, a tiny wrinkle between her auburn brows.

"What is it, then?" He hadn't meant to speak sharply, yet she did not so much as flinch at his terse tone. She had a spine, this one.

"I'm sorry, sir. I don't want to disappoint her ladyship, but I don't think I can do it. It's not right, is it, that you take so much time away from your duties, when I likely won't learn a thing, big country cow that I am."

He begged to differ. "Patricia, I have worked in the houses of the nobility for many years. If you vow never to quote me, I will swear to you that many a child, much stupider than you, has mastered reading and arithmetic and gone on to make us all miserable with their idiocy."

She tried to press her lips together but the smile won out. "Yes, sir. I see what you mean, sir." She took a breath and nodded. "All right, sir. If you think I can do it."

"Very well, then. We shall start tonight, immediately after the family has finished supper."

She bobbed smartly at him and left, her face glowing and her eyes bright.

A clever girl. No, better than clever. Brave. She had the heart of a lion, to step from her tiny Irish dale into such an unfamiliar world as London and try to better herself the way she had.

"You'll do fine, my Patricia," he whispered to the empty room, his tone a caress. "Just fine."

Chapter Twenty~two

When the guests walked down the steps of Brook House, the cousin, Miss Blake, boarded the Brookhaven carriage with that Lord Cavendish, who was some sort of relation, and that drove away, leaving the three young men behind to make their own way home.

From a doorway down the street where he watched the house, Wolfe could clearly see as two of them, the bright-colored dandy and the one who smiled too much, began to stroll away, their expressions already becoming bored once more.

Only one lingered. He was a mournful-looking bloke—not long of face so much as having a lost look about the eyes. He was the sort who searched for artistic inspiration in liquor and opium but never seemed to find it.

The fellow stared longingly up at Brook House for quite a bit longer than was proper for a "friend." Wolfe smiled. This one would do. He was good-looking in his melancholy way, and his love was pure—that was written all over his face, the pathetic sap.

It had taken Wolfe a while to sober up enough to conceive this particular plan. After all, the marriage had already taken place. The trick now was to end the damn thing before the old Duke of Brookmoor gasped his last. An annulment might do the trick, if the marquis could be provoked into it. But how? A woman would have to embarrass a man like that nearly to death—

Runaway wife. Runaway fiancée. And now perhaps a runaway bride. . . .

"Well," Wolfe grunted with a coarse chuckle, "they do say the third time's the charm."

Finally the lovelorn man turned to amble reluctantly away from Brook House. Wolfe followed. It took far too long for the fellow to reach his destination, due to him taking many dramatic pauses and deep sighs. Good God, the bloke had it bad!

At last, he turned to enter a decent if not top-drawer gentlemen's club. Wolfe increased his pace to match his target's just as the fellow drew even with the doorman, who bowed.

"Good evening, Mr. Baskin."

Perfect. "Baskin!" Wolfe called out. "May I have a moment of your time?"

Baskin turned and blinked at him. "Do I know you, sir?"

Wolfe put an expression of desperate concern across his face. "I thought she might have mentioned me—did you see her? Is she well? I worried so when I was turned away—"

Baskin's brow cleared at the introduction of his favorite subject. "Ah, you are acquainted with Miss—with the Marchioness of Brookhaven?"

Oh, someone was having a bit of trouble accepting the marriage, was he? Wolfe nodded, letting just a touch of frantic seep into his voice. "We are great friends—or at least, we were. Tell me all is well with her! I cannot bear to think of her alone in that house with that—"

Baskin cast a worried glance at the doorman, then grasped Wolfe's arm to draw him into the club. "Be careful!"

Wolfe suppressed a sneer and allowed himself to be dragged to a private corner of the main room within. Once seated, he leaned forward. "Pray, do not prolong my worry! Tell me you saw her!"

Baskin nodded. "I have seen her. She admitted me only this afternoon. She is holding on tolerably, but she is not happy."

Wolfe shook his head. "Oh, woe! She ought not to have given in to that demon's coercion . . . yet how could she have resisted such a powerful man?" He shook his head. "I warned her, but what could she do?"

Baskin blinked. "Coercion? What do you mean?"

Wolfe sat back in feigned alarm. "Oh, dear. I have said too much. It was all in confidence—"

Baskin narrowed his eyes. "I flatter myself that I am in Miss—in her ladyship's confidence."

Wolfe shrugged helplessly. "I'm sure, I'm sure. It is only my long connection with the family, you see. My father was quite close to her grandfather. I have been involved nearly all my life."

Baskin nearly glowed green with jealousy. "And you wanted her for yourself."

Wolfe blinked rapidly, doing his best imitation of Stickley. Next time he ought to adopt some spectacles to clean. "What? Me? Heavens, no. I am not nearly worthy. If I were, I should never have let her wed that monster! I would have stolen her away, but I feared him too much . . ." He jabbered on in that vein for a while until the suspicion faded from Baskin's eyes.

Baskin leaned forward. "You must tell me of this coercion. How could Brookhaven force her to wed him? She is not without friends."

Wolfe shook his head sadly. "I fear he has no reason when it comes to his obsession." *Much like you, my useful friend.* "Once he lost Miss Millbury to the brother he hates, he became fixated on Miss Cantor. Why else wed so quickly? A man with enough influence to slide a swift ceremony past the bishop—why would he let a bit of feminine objection stop him?"

Baskin frowned. "She objected? I thought—"

Wolfe waved a hand, being sure to include Stickley's limpness of wrist. "She is so brave. She could not bear to let her family name endure more scandal, as he threatened—" He clapped a hand over his mouth. "Oh, in my worry I do run on!" He blinked wistfully at Baskin. "Yet you, too, seem so concerned for her. Perhaps . . . perhaps I have finally found a champion worthy of—" He gave a nervous laugh and leaned back, visibly turning off the waterfall of words. "I daresay you think me mad—"

Just as he'd ensured, Baskin was hooked hard and fast.

"No!" Baskin glanced around, then lowered his voice. "Please, sir, you must tell me everything. I want to help her—I *need* to be . . . be near her . . ." The fellow's voice faded away, choked with emotion.

Oh, brass balls, the twit was nearly in tears! Wolfe suppressed the powerful urge to slap the young man. Women were for one thing and one thing only—and that stuck-up Brookhaven bitch probably wasn't even any good for that!

Bored now, Wolfe twitched with impatience to be on his way. Baskin was a goner. Better to let the information sink in so that when he elaborated on the lie later, it rang even more true.

Besides, he needed a drink. All this sugary shite was enough to make a real man gag.

"I—I cannot break her confidence—I'm sorry—" Dragging his arm across his eyes, he bolted from the table and was gone before Baskin realized he wasn't coming back.

Give the pathetic sod a day to get righteously worked up on milady's behalf. Then aim him at Brookhaven. If he was truly fortunate, he could get the blighter to duel the marquis. Baskin would die, of course, but Brookhaven would be hanged for it— *before* he ascended to become the Duke of Brookmoor.

Wolfe checked his gold watch and sneered. Not bad for an hour's work, by God. Not bad at all.

Chapter Twenty~three

Calder made sure the house was quiet before he emerged from his study at last. His patience was to no avail. Deirdre was lurking outside his door like a hunter in a blind.

"My lord, you are a dodo."

"How unfortunate for me." Calder forced himself to bow briskly and keep moving. "Good afternoon, my dear." It was a handy little maneuver he'd happened upon years earlier with his mother and then perfected with Melinda. Usually, it had the effect of leaving an irksome woman sputtering in his wake as he made a smooth getaway.

Deirdre, it seemed, was made of sterner stuff. She darted lightly to stand before him again, blocking his progress. He automatically repeated his bow. "I shall see you at supper." He stepped smoothly to the right, intending to slip past her.

She matched his movement instantly, popping up before him once more. He halted, momentarily perplexed. He could hardly bob his head again, mouth another meaningless greeting and then lunge past her like an escaping wildebeest!

She folded her arms and smiled wryly at him. "Penned you."

He attempted hauteur. "I have no idea what you mean." Her smile widened. He could have sworn the hallway warmed instantly.

She leaned forward. "I'll give you a hint. The same trick rarely works twice on me."

He caught her scent. Sweet jasmine and warm, clean woman. She'd bathed again. *I missed it? I missed the suds and the gleaming creamy skin and the pink nipples?* "I . . . ah . . ." What the hell? He'd meant to retort with something dignified and imposing. She had him stuttering like a lad with nothing more than the thought of her in the bath!

Bath. Soap. Breasts.

Pull yourself together, man! She was gazing at him with one perfect brow raised in amused patience. "I forgot what I was going to say." Except he hadn't meant to say *that!* "What I mean is . . . I . . ."

Now her brows drew together in a frown. "My lord, are you unwell?"

Yes, I am unwell! I am about to burst my trousers from a mere whiff of your skin!

Please, God, don't let her look down.

She didn't, but kept her sapphire gaze locked to his. Her eyes were so beautiful. He'd seen bluer, although not many. He'd even seen the most fascinating shade of aquamarine—but he'd never seen eyes so perfectly clear and direct. Truthful eyes.

A ridiculous notion. Eyes were simply eyes. Blue or brown or green, eyes showed nothing more or less than what a person chose to see in them. He'd chosen to see purity and affection in Melinda's, simplicity and propriety in Phoebe's. He'd been wrong on both counts, hadn't he?

"My lord, is there something amiss with me?"

He yanked himself back to the moment. "Of course. I mean, no, of course not." She was frankly frowning at him now. Who could blame her? He was acting like a lunatic.

"You are the oddest man sometimes."

You have no idea, lovely Deirdre. And he had no intention of letting her know it. Letting out a gust of air, Calder forced his thoughts into something resembling logical order. "You had something to say concerning a dodo bird?"

She blinked. "Oh. Yes."

He could almost see the clockworks rewinding in her head, gearing up for speed.

"You lay your eggs in other birds' nests and expect them to raise your young," she stated triumphantly.

"Cuckoo."

She blinked. "I beg your pardon?"

He sighed, for he was in no mood for a lecture on his paternal shortcomings. "The cuckoo bird is the one who lays eggs in another bird's nest."

"Oh." She waved her hand negligently. "An insignificant detail. The point is—"

"I grasp your point." He held up one hand to forestall further harangue. "You believe Lady Margaret's misbehavior is an attempt to corral my attention. You think she would settle down immediately if I took her for rides on my horse and read storybooks to her at bedtime."

That stopped her in her lovely tracks.

He went on. "Your brilliant, life-changing proposition is that I abandon my responsibilities in order to be at the beck and call of the same small, willful being who has frightened off more than a dozen nurses and half again that many governesses—grown women, mind you—experienced professionals with astounding credentials and impeccable references, none of whom made it more than a week—most less than that."

He folded his arms and gazed down at his stunningly beautiful, gobsmacked wife. "Why in the world do you think that I—a man completely lacking experience and aptitude with children—could possibly do better for Lady Margaret than those many intelligent and accomplished women?"

It was a brilliant argument delivered in his best high-lordly manner, one that had swept the rug out from under many an interfering governess and sent several of the above-mentioned hardened nurses sniffling piteously from his presence.

Beauteous Deirdre, Lady Brookhaven, gently reared and indisputably ladylike, looked up at him with limpid blue eyes . . .

And blew an incredibly crude noise through her lips.

"What a cartload of horse-apples," she said, and rolled her eyes.

Then she stepped forward until she was close enough to wrap into his arms, to pull hard against him until she felt his desire press into her, to kiss that damp mouth until she lost the power of speech. He felt a dull pain and looked down to see her index finger poking him in the chest.

"Lord Brookhaven, you are a coward. What's worse, you are a liar, as well."

Anger flared, mingling with the lust. "You tread dangerous ground, my lady."

Another roll of her eyes. "What will you do, lock me in my room and forget to feed me? I've already survived that, thank you very much. You would have to go a long way to outdo Lady Tessa's punishments, and I don't think you're that kind of man."

Calder frowned. Could that be true? He truly ought to look into Lady Tessa further. That decided, he filed that tangent away and focused on the real issue at hand—his bride's defiance. "Be careful, my lady." He fixed her with his most baleful gaze. "Are you quite prepared to toss away every single social event until next Season?"

He thought she'd quail or at least hesitate. Instead, she matched his menacing gaze and raised him another poke in the chest.

"Brookhaven, you can chain me to the battlements and I'll just shout you to sleep every night about Meggie. You claim to have responsibilities? What in the world could possibly mean more than your responsibility to your own child?"

"My father was the Marquis of Brookhaven as well. He was far too busy and important to spend time sprawled on the floor playing with toy soldiers with little boys. Yet somehow I managed to grow to adulthood without attempting to ride a washtub down the stairs or setting fire to the draperies or any other of Lady Margaret's latest offenses."

She looked perplexed. The expression was delightful sketched upon her features. "Did that work?"

She'd lost him. "Did what work?"

"Riding a washtub down the stairs. It seems to me that the bottom of the washtub has the wrong sort of configuration to handle the unevenness of the stairs." She looked thoughtful. "A copper bathtub now—that ought to do the trick."

He blinked in surprise. Actually, a bathtub might indeed work—

"Ah!" He pressed his fist to his forehead in a vain effort to keep his brain from exploding. "Enough about tubs, bath or otherwise! My point is—"

She fluttered her fingers dismissively. "I grasp your point. You think since your father wanted nothing to do with you that all proper fathers behave in such a manner." She folded her arms. "My father was a busy man, yet not only did he take me for rides on his horse and read stories, he did indeed sprawl on the floor with my toys. Moreover, I truly believe he enjoyed it." She tilted her head and narrowed her eyes at him. "I dare you to try it."

"Oh, be serious."

She gazed serenely at the ceiling. "Yellow," she sang softly.

He straightened, deeply offended. "Don't be ridiculous."

She shrugged. "I fear there is no help for it. You're a yellow-bellied cuckoo bird, my lord. Brought to his knees by the thought of reading to a little girl." She sighed. "What a waste of a great, manly, handsome fellow like yourself."

While he sputtered for some rational answer to such an outlandish statement, she turned and walked away, her skirts swaying with self-satisfaction.

However, the truly galling part of it all was that he kept watching until she turned the corner of the hall. Damn it, if he couldn't keep his head in a disagreement with his own bride, then it was clear it was time he got the bloody hell out of Brook House!

Chapter Twenty~four

Deirdre hadn't actually expected Brookhaven to heel obediently and appear in the parlor with a storybook in his hand—but she certainly didn't expect him to call for his horse in a bellow the entire house heard clearly. She watched from the window as the dratted man threw himself upon his stallion and pounded away down the drive and into the city streets as if the hounds of hell were behind him.

Frowning, she hurried to the front hall.

"Fortescue, where is his lordship going?"

The butler clasped his hands behind his back. "His lordship said to inform you that he will be back by supper, my lady."

"Fortescue, that was not my question."

"Indeed, my lady, but that was the answer I was provided with."

Deirdre gazed at the butler for a long moment. "He didn't tell you where, but you know, don't you?"

Fortescue focused his gaze somewhere over her left shoulder. "I wouldn't presume to guess, my lady."

She narrowed her eyes. "Fortescue, I like you." She folded her arms and tilted her head. "That being said, you are by no means safe from my wrath. Do you take my meaning?"

"Of course, my lady," he replied calmly. "You are implying that if I withhold information from you that I shall find hay in my bed linens and soap in my shoes."

Deirdre smiled falsely. "If you're lucky."

Fortescue nodded. "However, if his lordship believes me—of all the staff in this household—to be unreliable, I shall find myself without employment." He didn't seem terribly worried. "What a pickle."

Of all the staff in this household.

Ah. Deirdre smiled more sincerely. "Then by all means keep your own counsel, Fortescue. I've no more time for this discussion. I'm on my way to speak to . . ." She waited.

Fortescue pursed his lips for a moment. Then he met her gaze for the first time. "I believe Cook awaits your instructions as to the menu, my lady."

Cook, of course. Brookhaven might have ordered a noon meal packed to take with him. Moreover, Cook adored milady's healthy appetite. "First I've seen a fine lady who don't turn up her nose at good plain food!" she'd announced stoutly.

Lovely, loyal Cook. Marvelous Fortescue. Deirdre smiled benignly upon her favorite butler in the entire world. "Fortescue, you are a marvel of diplomacy and discretion. How lucky we are to have you."

He bowed. Then he straightened and favored her with a shadow of a smile. "The regard is mutual, my lady."

In the kitchen, Deirdre found Cook busily preparing something large and pink and dead. A great knife that could behead a king swung down with such a thwack that various departed beast parts on the tabletop jumped like obedient minions. Swallowing, Deirdre looked away but managed a smile.

"Dear Cook, how delicious dinner looks! I do hope his lordship won't be too late home this evening to enjoy it. I'm sure he has quite the journey ahead of him on his way to—"

Cook looked up, her flushed round face puzzled. "His silk-weavin' factory in Southwark, milady? Why, it don't take but an hour to get there on horseback. He'll be home in plenty of time for my special roast, don't you worry, milady."

"Why didn't he take the carriage, I wonder?" Deirdre idly toyed with a pile of greens in a bowl.

Cook smiled. "Well, milord's not one to wait on traffic, is he, milady? Says the carriage is 'inefficient,' he does. So he takes a groom with him and rides across the bridge in half the time." She pointed the gory knife riverward. "What with all them mad carters drivin' like the devil's after them down Weston Street, I expect milord just likes to be able to get out of the way!"

Deirdre smiled and avoided looking at the crimson blade. "Weston Street, yes. Of course." She waved a vague hand at the grisly battlefield of beastly bits. "Well, carry on, then. It all looks so very . . . appetizing."

She wasn't going to be able to eat a single bite this evening, but at least she'd learned where Brookhaven had escaped to. She smiled to herself as she left the kitchens. "You won't escape us that easily, my lord," she murmured.

Once informed of their destination, Meggie didn't waste a moment getting dressed to go out. The carriage was waiting before the front steps, although Deirdre hadn't actually ordered it.

Fortescue bowed as he helped her into her spencer. "Do take care in Southwark, my lady. The manufacturing district can be a rough place. I've attached young Trenton to be your personal footman, just to be safe."

Deirdre looked up . . . and up . . . at young Trenton. The lad was a burly giant with a round face and bland eyes who made the Brookhaven livery look positively military. "Good heavens," she breathed. "Are we expecting to face an army?"

Fortescue nodded. "It might seem so when you arrive, my lady. It would not be wise to become separated from Trenton." He glanced down at Meggie. "Are you listening, Lady Margaret?"

Meggie grinned up at him. "Don't be soft, Fortie." She reached up to take the giant footman's enormous hand. "Trenton's my friend."

Fortescue seemed overly alarmist to Deirdre as well. "We're only going to visit a factory," she reminded him.

He gazed at her with a slight crease between his brows. "The factory is safe enough, my lady. It is the journey there and back that worries me."

Half an hour later, Deirdre gusted a great sigh as she stared at the unchanging scene out the carriage window. Traffic had come to a halt just on the city side of the London bridge as what seemed to be half the carters in England converged on the one path to cross the Thames to Southwark's acres of factories.

Carriages and carts lined up in ragged queues that seemed to stretch forever before and behind them. How frustrating when one could see the other side of the river perfectly well from here.

Meggie was grumbling already. "I'd rather swim it."

Deirdre peered down at the filthy river and shuddered. "I'd rather die. You'd not get the stink from your hair for years."

However, after another thirty minutes of Meggie's whining and groaning, Deirdre was seriously contemplating tossing the child in and letting her try. At last the carriage began to roll, eliciting cheers from Meggie and great relief from Deirdre, who'd narrowly been saved from the gallows for murder. This matter of motherhood was even more annoying . . . er, *taxing* . . . than she'd previously realized.

Once across the river, Deirdre began to see the reason for Fortescue's concern. The factories were huge ugly buildings, some of them more than four stories tall! Her eyes had become used to the ornate and graceful facades of Mayfair, making these grimly undecorated edifices all the more intimidating.

Not only did the buildings seem foreboding but the streets themselves were unswept and filthy. Dark alleys pierced the rows of stone walls, dank tunnels full of furtive movement and the occasional alarming noise. The inhabitants were the worst, however. Nearly everyone entering or leaving the buildings seemed underfed and shabby—all except for the occasional relatively well-dressed fellow with prosperous equatorial dimensions who gazed suspiciously at the fine carriage and shooed and shoved the lesser citizens from his path.

"Overseers," thought Deirdre.

"Bullies," muttered Meggie.

Belatedly, Deirdre tugged the curious Meggie back from the carriage window and pulled the shade. Kidnapping and ransom weren't as common as they had been twenty years ago, but it didn't serve any purpose to advertise the presence of the wealthy and vulnerable Brookhaven ladies.

At last they arrived before the gates of a factory that made the others appear even shabbier and filthier in comparison. Brookhaven's crest was painted upon a sign above the gates, but there was no other indication of what lay within the high walls. When Trenton helped her out of the carriage into the spotless, bare courtyard, Deirdre hesitated. What had seemed a daring and amusing way to get under Brookhaven's skin now seemed rather childish and dangerous.

Meggie, however, felt no compunction at towing Deirdre directly to the door and opening it wide. They stepped through it to find themselves on a small platform before a large open room full of machines.

Chapter Twenty~five

The noise that met their ears was astonishing. Great clangings and bangings of metal on metal from the immense looms, the roar of a furnace somewhere unseen, the shouts of people used to communicating over the din, all in a great hot blast that made Deirdre long for the filthy street outside.

Then she saw Brookhaven standing partway up an open staircase that ran up one high wall. There were other rooms, of course. Someone must keep books and records and . . . she hadn't the faintest idea actually. She'd worn woven fabric every day of her life and never once wondered how it came into being. Someone must have shouted something to Calder, for he turned from the man he was speaking to and spotted them standing there. He stared for a long moment. Deirdre wondered if he was contemplating ignoring their presence, but then he began to descend the crisscrossing stairs, running lightly down them with great familiarity.

As he approached, she breathed deeply and raised her chin. She was lady of this factory, too, blast it, and she could visit any time she wished!

Surprisingly, Calder did not seem all that displeased

to see her. "Good afternoon, my dear. Would you care for a tour?"

Having girded her loins for argument, she could do nothing but sputter and nod at such a mild greeting. Soon she found herself at the far top of that staircase, close to the ceiling, attempting to ignore the spindliness of the railing while Calder explained the goings-on below them. Meggie, having flatly refused to climb at all, sat on the distant bottom step, gazing with fascination at the nearest loom.

"So you see," Calder was saying, "by consolidating all the processes beneath one roof, we are able to operate at much higher efficiency."

Deirdre gazed at him with fond exasperation, wondering how many times this afternoon she was going to hear that word. He continued, giving her expression no notice. "Before, the spinning and then the weaving would have been done by the workers in their homes. That made the quality very difficult to assure—not to mention that some workers were not as dependable as others."

Truly, everyone did seem to be working hard. They seemed cheerful, she was glad to see, and more prosperous than many she had spotted on the way down Weston Road. Of course Brookhaven would pay well. He would also demand the best from them all, which they were obviously glad to give him.

So why should you be any different?

She felt a moment of shame at that thought—yet she did not wish to be simply another employee, after all. She might make a fool of herself with this ridiculous battle, but winning the war would be worth it.

She gazed at the magnificent man next to her with concealed longing. *So very, very worth it.*

"Now if you'll look up, you'll see what makes this factory so superior to all the others."

The fierce pride in his expression captivated her for a moment more, then she turned her gaze obediently upward.

Above them all ran a crisscrossing of lines drawn by no plan that she could fathom. Her eyes adjusted to the gloom and she realized that the lines—no, belts!—were moving. Like a strange reproduction of the warp and weft of the looms below, they were strung between and among each other. Then she realized that all tangents seemed to meet above where the great huffing steam engine was housed. A single steel rod as thick as her thigh rose from that housing, rotating and winching all the belts where they wound over it at different altitudes.

It looked like something a madman would arrange but Brookhaven gazed up at it with intense satisfaction in his eyes.

"You see, by attaching all the individual machines to the primary gears of the steam engine by this system of belts and pulleys, the entire factory runs as one." He almost smiled. "Almost as if it is alive."

Deirdre saw the set of his jaw relax and his near permanent frown unfurl. In that instant, she realized something very important about her husband. Calder was a man who had lost faith in everything but the mechanical, in what he could see and repair and that would never leave him. This, then—this great, wheezing, whirring, clacking organism of a factory—this was the true home to Calder, the man, not the marquis . . . although perhaps also the clever lonely boy within.

Enfolded within its mechanical outlandish arms, he was as unguarded and happy as she'd ever seen him.

She gazed back at the factory floor and—just for an instant—she grasped the harmony of the seemingly random movements below her. Like a great, nightmarish merry-go-round ride, the entire place rose and fell as one beast, as if it inhaled thread and power and exhaled the finished woven fabric. Then she blinked and all returned to chaos beyond her comprehension.

"It's very . . ." There was no help for it. She had to say it. "Efficient."

A high compliment in Brookhaven's estimation, for he nodded with brisk satisfaction. "Thank you."

This was all very enjoyable—at least she was at his side—but she had a reason for coming here today. She didn't simply fight for Meggie, she fought for herself. After all, if his own child couldn't get through to him, what chance had a not-quite-perfect wife?

Knowing that her words would dissipate the truce between them, she raised her chin and assumed an arch expression. "So these machines take the place of people?"

He blinked in surprise, but he was still in the role of good teacher. "In a way, I suppose they do. It takes less manpower to run my factory than to piece the work out."

Less manpower—or less emotion? He even kept his workers to a minimum so that he could have as little interplay as possible with humanity. She leaned over the railing and pretended to observe the workings. "So you buy them—"

"I have them built especially."

She nearly sobbed at the affection and eagerness in his voice. "So you have them built and you bring them here and . . ." She waved her hand vaguely at the ceiling, "and you wind them up like tin soldiers and they spit out fabric?"

"*Superior* fabric."

Of course, superior—because who would want the imperfect, the flawed . . . the human? She straightened to look him in the eye. "What happens to them if you neglect them?"

Ah, now he began to be suspicious. "What do you mean?"

She folded her arms. "What happens if you leave them out in the rain? What happens if you never oil them? Or check those belt things?" A bitter laugh escaped her. "What happens to them if you leave them out at Brookhaven until they are seven years old? What happens if you lock them in a house and refuse them a Society life?"

He was glowering now, but she went on, her voice rising. "What happens if you refuse to speak to them for days at a time or to say *one bloody kind thing*— ever!—and they begin to blame themselves that they will never, ever be good enough—!"

"Enough!" The sharp blade of his command sliced through her tirade. He glared at her with eyes like glowing coals. "I haven't the faintest idea what you're speaking of. I am nothing like that."

"Oh! You are the stubbornest, most arrogant, irredeemable—" God, she was without words to describe him to himself. She gave up. "You . . . you *sod!*"

Then she whirled in a flutter of skirts and ran from him, flying down the narrow wooden stairs without a thought to falling, until a hard hand came about her elbow and jerked her hard against that chest of iron.

Chapter Twenty~six

"You little fool." Calder's voice was harsh in her ear. "You'll kill yourself."

She would not deign to struggle for his amusement. "Let me go," she bit out. Though she teetered with one foot still in space, she would not cling to him.

"If I let you go, you'll fall to your death on this staircase." His voice was but a growl. It reverberated through her, ensuring that the tremors in her body were not of fear.

"What would that matter to you?" A plague on him, for making her voice break so!

His hand tightened on her, tugging her fully against his body. He bent his head until she could feel the heat of his breath on her ear. "If I should come up with yet another dead wife, I fear my reputation would never recover."

That he could be so cold, at that moment, with her body plastered to his and her desperate tremors obvious to his senses—whether he thought her afraid or aroused, either meant he was nothing but solid ice within!

In which case, she refused to allow him to freeze her as well! Slowly, she raised her gaze to meet his cold one. Then her free hand lifted to stroke tender finger-tips from his brow to his rigid jaw. She traced the corner of his mouth with one feather-light touch. "Then you must stop provoking us to flee you, my lord," she whispered.

His expression did not change, but she felt his body harden against her belly. His gaze dropped to where her bosom pressed to his chest, swelling high and creamy and full. She drew in a deep breath, just for his benefit.

His gaze locked once more with hers and his jaw worked slowly. "Then should I lock you in a tower to keep you?"

Oh, yes. She melted into him, letting her gaze fall to his lips. "Would you promise to visit me every night?"

He swallowed, hard. She ignored that small triumph, for arousal was easy. What she wanted from him was much more difficult. Oh, to be loved, truly loved, by a man like this one—could mortal woman survive a night in his arms? What about a lifetime?

She was dying to find out.

"You dare to toy with me," he growled.

She raised her gaze to his, allowing the heat and longing within her to flare into her eyes. "I do not make promises I will not keep."

His dark eyes turned black. With one movement, he turned them both until the banister pressed against the small of her back and his hard body pressed into her lower belly. She was trapped there, pinned tightly against his arousal. She realized that his abrupt motion had caused her to slide her free hand into his coat to grip at his waistcoat. She left her hand there, spreading her fingers over the muscles of his chest, feeling his great heart beat against her palm.

This was progress, certainly . . . but that heart was still not hers.

Would it ever be? Was she woman enough to win it?

She scarcely knew what that meant, much less how to prove it to herself. Her character had not yet been tested . . . or had it? Had all her years under Tessa's influence done more harm than she knew? Would she even recognize a character-defining moment of choice, or had she faced them again and again . . . and already failed?

"I want to be a good woman, a good wife to you," she whispered to him uncertainly.

His hot gaze did not alter. He did not hear her. He was already lost in lust, when she'd wanted him lost in love.

His gaze dropped to her bosom and one large hand came up to cup her breast. "You are so lovely." His voice was husky and strained. Tessa had once commented that when a man's blood engorged his member, his brain suffered the loss. Yet his touch was something else she wanted—had longed for, in fact. A man dizzy with lust was not such a bad thing, when her own body throbbed in response!

So she went supple in his hands, shutting off that part of her heart that cried "Too soon!" and allowing her own longing and need to boil into her blood. She closed her eyes and gave her body over to him, for it was something, was it not? Something better than a long, cold life alone?

His hand was hot on her breast as he hefted it. He slid his thumb across the bare upper portion in a forceful caress that made her knees weak. The neckline of her gown slid aside as he pushed her breast high, freeing her hardened nipple to the chill air.

They were in full view of the factory, though it was very dim up so high and those below them were concentrating on their work. She shivered into him, too vulnerable and too achingly eager to care who might see. Let him strip her naked on the stair if he wished, so long as he did not stop touching her!

He released her arm at last in order to wrap his about her waist, supporting her as he lowered his mouth to her breast. Her own hands freed at last, she buried them in his thick dark hair as he drew hard on her nipple with his hot mouth.

Such sweet pain! It shot through her body—oh, heaven, she'd never known—how could she have known? A burst of answering heat came between her thighs, wetting her there, making her press her knees together in pleasure. She fisted her hands in his hair and moaned.

He growled in response and yanked her sleeve down over her shoulder to free her other breast to his burning mouth. The first nipple, hardened and inflamed by his suckling, then fell prey to his seeking fingertips. Deirdre arched back over empty space, her breasts bare, rising and falling with each gasping breath, as her husband ravaged them. His hard fingers pinched and slowly twisted, just to make her mew in pleasure and pain, while his lips and tongue and teeth sucked and nibbled and rolled her other nipple in counterpoint.

His hand dropped then, leaving her poor nipple alone, to slide down her body and dip between her thighs. He pressed her there, his hand outside her gown and petticoats, rubbing the flat of his fingertips in a circular motion over the hottest and wettest part of her. The first layer of fabric dampened instantly and she knew he must be able to feel the soaked heat of her there.

He moved his mouth to her neck. "You're wet for me?" he rasped into her skin.

She nodded frantically as she wrapped her arms about his neck and held on to him tightly against the pleasure roiling through her. "Yes—oh, yes—I want you so!"

His hands fell away, leaving her to grab at the banister in sudden fear of falling. He backed off a step and gazed down at her as she clung there, shaking and gasping in her arousal and confusion.

"What—?" She tugged hastily at her gown.

Calder was shaking with lust, dizzy with it, his vision gone nearly gray with the throbbing ache in his loins. Oh, dear heaven! So sweet, so soft, so fervent—

You're a fool. A real man would have carried that eager, exquisite creature off to that great cold empty bed and rogered her unto mutual death!

He forced his breathing to steady.

Her passion for him was stunning, outrageous, and perhaps a bit . . . unbelievable? He'd made a grievous mistake in marrying a treacherous beauty once. Had he been the classic fool and allowed his judgment to be overruled by his cock?

Fine. Your cock won. Now award it accordingly! She's still quivering for you. Beg her forgiveness and then bend her over that damned banister!

He passed a shaking hand over his face—and caught the scent of her that still lingered on his fingers. Instantly, time spun back to when his arms were full of wet, hot, willing woman. She'd given over so easily, yet he couldn't bring himself to believe that she was so bad.

Yet, to behave as though his merest touch drove her senseless with desire—as though she'd been waiting her entire life for his slightest caress? That was so unlikely as to be laughable.

His cock throbbed in favor of the idea and suggested that it bore further testing. Immediately. At length. Exhaustively, even.

Sternly and mercilessly, Calder choked the life out of that voice and stuffed it deep, deep inside until he couldn't hear it anymore. Finally, only cold, logical silence ruled his thoughts.

Excellent. Now he could think clearly.

Then she raised her eyes to his, her blue eyes swimming in tears and anger and . . . love? His throat released a low, fervent sound he didn't recognize and his hand reached out to her without thought—

At that moment the factory below them exploded into chaos.

Chapter Twenty~seven

Meggie gazed at the giant, shuddering loom in dismay. She hadn't meant to kill it. She'd only wanted to see what made the wheels turn within—and if when sticking a long wooden weaver's shuttle into the spinning, meshing gears, if they would chop the wood. The gears had sucked the shuttle from her hand as if she'd no grip at all and pulled it deep within. She'd had to jump back as the shuttle had nearly smacked her in the skull as it vibrated wildly back and forth.

Now it quivered like a spear in the guts of a dying beast.

The man operating the loom stared at it in disbelief, at least until he spotted her. With a wild howl of consternation he lunged at her. She turned in a panic and ran for her life. Ducking behind a machine that wound thread, she peeked behind her. The man wasn't following, he was desperately trying to pull the shuttle from the gears. His cries brought others who gathered to help him. Some then scattered, racing back to the other machines while gazing upward in apprehension.

What were they looking at? Meggie leaned forward to see past the thread-winder's bulk. She saw her father and Dee up high on the stairs, coming down, the marquis shouting something. Had she ever seen him run so fast? She almost pulled back into her hiding place, but something was creating the most horrendous whine, like an injured hound—no, more like a nest of angry wasps, rising in rage. The noise was coming from above the dead loom, which had apparently breathed its last. The long shaft that came down from the ceiling to power the gears had stopped rotating—but the belt that turned it had not. Now smoke was wisping up from where the band stretched over the rod . . . and then the wisp became a cloud . . . and then the band snapped with a sound like a Chinese rocket.

Shouts and screams came from the dismayed workers as the belt's smoking charred ends floated to the floor—and the wasp nests multiplied. Meggie crawled out farther, appalled fascination overcoming fear. Sitting on her heels, head tilted back to gaze upward, she watched one belt after another smoking and snapping as the rods froze—or worse, *bent* under the uneven pressure of several snapped belts. Like ripples in a pond, the destruction spread out from the loom she'd killed, as contagious as disease. The workers clung to each other in a frightened clump, cowering beneath a maddened sky, as sparks fell from the flaming belts and tilting rods loomed threateningly. Groans and clanks crescendoed with the rising anger of the wasps until Meggie clapped her hands over her ears.

Then a single mighty groan rose to outdo them all. There was a painful rending of steel that shouldn't bend as the central steam engine's mighty rod gave beneath the torque, the final aching death rattle as an entire model of a modern factory died—murdered in a matter of moments by the curiosity of a child.

Awed, Meggie rose to her feet and gazed at what she had wrought. "Bloody hell," she whispered.

"It were *her!*"

Meggie whirled to see a crowd of angry faces—first and foremost her father's!—glaring at her. She wet her lips nervously. "Ah . . . I think it was an accident, Papa."

The loom's operator pushed forward in the crowd. "She did it apurpose, my lord!"

Papa's face froze in that look she hated so much—the one that made her feel like he wished she didn't exist. "Papa, I didn't mean it." Her voice sounded so small against the cloud of blame.

Dee pushed through the crowd then. Meggie saw her stepmother pale as she looked into Papa's stony face.

"Calder, don't," Dee said. Then she looked at Meggie in despair. "It was an accident." But even she didn't sound as though she believed it.

"Lady Margaret, what did you do?" Papa's voice was as cold as the frozen lake in Brookhaven's winter.

She swallowed. "Papa, you can buy more machines. I can sell my pony."

"What. Did. You. Do?"

"I . . . I opened a little door in the side of the machine."

"And?"

She squirmed. "And I looked inside."

"And?"

Meggie felt as though she might need a sick basin. "And it was grinding and grinding . . . little metal teeth, like my pony's teeth on a carrot."

And? He didn't need to speak. His eyes said it plainly enough.

She bit her lip. "So I fed it something." Papa's gaze was so frozen. It made her feet feel numb.

He waited.

She didn't want to say it. All she wanted in the world was to go home to her kitten and make toffee with Dee. She glanced up quickly. Papa's eyes were as black as coal.

He was a big lump of coal! Alas, just like a rock, he could wait forever, she knew. Finally, she lifted her hand and pointed at the long smooth stick-thing the loom man was still holding.

"I fed it that."

"Aye, my lord!" The loom man shook the gnawed and splintered shuttle at Meggie like a man brandishing a torch at a nocturnal predator. "Stabbed it with the shuttle, she did, right in the gearbox!"

Calder's heart sank. He'd so hoped it had been some sort of accident. What could he do now but punish the child?

Why? Why had she done such a thing? He would never have committed such a clearly wrong act when he was a child! He'd been a calm, studious boy—a child who knew precisely what was expected of him at all times. Rafe had been the wild one. Rafe had been the one to do bold, mad things—

Interesting things.

Things you never dared do.

Unfortunately, just as he'd once lacked the necessary scope of imagination to commit such misdeeds, he also lacked the wherewithal to conceive of an appropriate consequence for this vast and hideous crime. How could the child even grasp the damage she had done? His own mind whirled!

There was the equipment wreckage, the orders that would not now be met, the well-trained and valuable people who quite rightfully deserved to be paid, who would leave him for more immediate work—people he might not be able to tempt back!

His mounting frustration must have become obvious in his face, for Deirdre leapt between them with her hands held out in placation. She abandoned subtlety, instead physically placing herself in the path of his fury.

"My lord, this is all my fault. I brought Meggie here. I ought to have kept a closer eye on her."

Fine. Deirdre made a much less disturbing target anyway. "Indeed," he said coldly.

She exhaled in relief. "Yes. I don't know what I was thinking," she continued in a soothing tone that made his own teeth grind like a gearbox. "I'm sure you're furious with me."

Over her shoulder, Calder watched Trenton scoop Meggie up and swiftly remove her from the building, presumably back to the carriage she'd arrived in.

Did they all think him a monster? He focused on Deirdre's beautiful face. Even his wife?

He gazed at her for a long moment, reading the tension in her shoulders, the way her eyes slid sideways to follow Meggie's exit, the way she then watched him, as if he was an animal prone to striking tiny children and women alike.

Yes, she did.

Why shouldn't she? Everyone else in London does.

She ought to know him better than that. She ought to have looked deeper than the rumors and the gossip. He raised a hand toward her, reaching without realizing it. He'd thought—

She flinched, ever so slightly.

So.

Icy inside, he drew himself up. "You should not blame yourself," Calder said slowly. "It is my own fault that I find myself disappointed in marriage once again."

Deirdre's head snapped back at his words. It was as if he had slapped her. No, worse, for it left no mark that the world could hold against him, but only bled agonizingly within. She swallowed down the cry of pain that longed to fly from her throat. Instead, she lifted her chin and sneered. "Likewise," she snarled.

That surprised him. "You claim yourself to be disappointed? In *me?*" Absently, he took a clean cloth from one of the workers and wiped his hands.

She folded her arms against the hurt and the lingering wash of heat from their earlier episode on the stair and raised her chin. "I'm not going to deliver Meggie back to Brook House until I know what your intentions are."

His jaw tightened. "My intentions are to send her packing. She'll be off to Brookhaven in the morning and there she'll stay." He looked away then, down at his hands that were already as clean as they were going to get without soap and water. He rubbed the cloth over them, over and over. "I think you ought to accompany her," he said slowly.

That sent a spear of agony through her, but she forced aside concern for herself. "You realize that if you banish Meggie now, she'll spend the rest of her life convinced that you love your factories more than you love her."

He raised his gaze to meet hers. "Don't be ridiculous. My factories keep Brookhaven prosperous, nothing more."

She raised her chin. "Your factories are your life. You adore them. They are your friends, your family, your very self. Meggie knows this, but until today I think she harbored some hope that she mattered to you as well." *As did I . . .*

"Don't be ridiculous. I am a gentleman. I would never neglect my dependents!"

"You think being a gentleman means adhering to dry, lifeless absolutes."

"I believe in a strict code of ethics. If that is what you mean, then yes."

"What of compassion? What of understanding—sympathy—even pity? Can you not concede that sometimes it is necessary to do the wrong thing for the right reason?"

"That is ridiculous. If a thing is wrong, then it is wrong. The reason does not excuse a single thing."

"Let me ask you this then. Today Meggie was fascinated by the moving parts of a machine—even to the point where her curiosity was provoked to dangerous experimentation! That's nothing like Melinda, at least not that I've heard. It doesn't even seem particularly like Rafe. Who do you think that resembles?"

He scowled. "I haven't the faintest idea what you mean."

"You're the clever one." She glared at him. "You figure it out."

He wasn't stupid. It was obvious what she was getting at. Calder simply didn't see it. He was an orderly, unemotional, self-possessed man. He was a *calm* man, damn it! Meggie was a mess, a wild, uncontrollable criminal riot in a grimy pinafore and unraveling braids. "My child is nothing like me, not in the slightest!"

Her jaw dropped slightly. She stared at him in amazement for a long moment, then threw up her hands and left the factory, muttering to herself.

Calder watched her go, his entire body atwitch with a combination of leftover lust and indignant fury. She was entirely mad and was apparently determined to take him to Bedlam with her!

Yet, wasn't she lovely when nonplussed, when the usual glint of calculation faded from her stunning eyes and her lips softened from their firm determination? He would have liked to have kissed those lips just now.

Her hands and face still bore traces of factory soot. She was probably going to bathe once she reached the house . . .

Wet, bare, slippery skin. Damp tendrils of golden hair trailing between full creamy breasts. Rosy nipples crinkled in the chill . . .

The memory dried his throat and tightened his trousers.

Damn, he'd just ruined another wedding night, hadn't he?

Chapter Twenty~eight

Back at Brook House, Meggie, bathed and brushed and pitiably subdued, climbed listlessly into her bed and allowed Deirdre to tuck her in without so much as protesting the early hour or the extra grooming. Patricia, who had taken on maid duties for Meggie as well, stood to the side, worry clear in her green eyes.

Deirdre sat carefully on the edge of the bed and gazed at the child whose fighting spirit she'd thought nothing and no one could shatter. She sighed and smoothed the covers yet again. "I've done it now, haven't I, Meg?"

Meggie's gaze slid away to fix blankly on the glowing coals in the fireplace. Deirdre brushed a dark curl back from the child's forehead, but there was no response to the tender touch.

It was difficult to remain calm when she was filled with such stunning guilt. All that had transpired today was completely and entirely her fault. True, she hadn't made Calder into what he was, but she'd brought Meggie to the factory, where she clearly didn't belong, and then left a seven-year-old girl unsupervised while she . . . ah . . . allowed herself to be distracted.

"I fear I'm a wretched excuse for a mother, little one."

She'd gone too far, using a child's heart for her own purposes. Now she'd driven the two of them even further apart and she hadn't the slightest idea how to fix it.

She started to sit up and take her hand away, but Meggie's gaze flickered back to hers. "Don't go," the little girl whispered.

Deirdre felt something inside her melt and soften, completely and without reservation. Her eyes stung as she nodded acquiescence. "Patricia, you may go."

"Will you be wanting your own bath, my lady?"

Though she went weak in the knees at the thought of washing away this awful day, Deirdre shook her head. "Later." She bent to remove her shoes and then pulled the covers aside to slide in with Meggie. When the little girl snuggled into her, her heart broke completely. How could she have involved Meggie in her battle of wills? What sort of monster used a child so?

The sort raised by Lady Tessa, apparently. Well, she wouldn't do it. Meggie was out of this little game, as of now. Stroking the hair back from her small brow, Deirdre closed her eyes against the guilt. *I will fix this, little one. I promise, I will make him see.*

But how? How to teach a man who'd never known love that it would save him forever if he'd only allow it?

MORE THAN EVER, Calder regretted setting eyes on Miss Deirdre Cantor. His factory was in ruins, his workers angry, his unruly child promoted to a menace beyond compare—his bride had certainly accomplished a great deal in these few days of marriage!

Even his anger had an unfamiliar edge to it, one prompted by unresolved lust. What was happening to him? He wasn't an ill-tempered man, yet he found himself growling at his groom and snapping at Fortescue when he entered Brook House at last, filthy and exhausted and minus one once satisfyingly progressive and profitable factory!

Argyle had his bath steaming and ready in his bedchamber, but Calder couldn't drum up so much as a grunt of thanks. He stripped off his things and flung them to the floor, all the while recounting his wife's multiple offenses to himself. Sinking into the heat without taking a moment to accustom himself, he yelped in surprise, then snarled Argyle away when he tried to assist.

Gripping the edge of the tub until his knuckles turned white, Calder took the punishing heat and let it melt away his deep frustration. When at last the burning eased from his skin, it took the worst of his fury with it. With a long sigh, he leaned back in the tub and tried to turn his mind to more pleasant things.

Brookmoor would be his soon. It was beautiful there, quite wild still. Very refreshing after too many weeks in London.

He let his mind rest on that peaceful view. The hills were softly rolling there, just the beginnings of the range known as the Pennines. The air was as clear as water and the wind would whip Deirdre's blond hair into a golden flag, streaming out behind her. Did she ride well? He'd have to find her a gentle mare, but one that could keep up with his own fine stallion. They would gallop over Brookmoor until the wind pulled the color into her cheeks and she laughed with joy, her exquisite smile only for him . . .

Abruptly he sat up, sending a tide of bathwater onto the floor.

Bloody hell!

Opening his eyes, he glared across the room at the door in the opposite wall. So close he could reach her in a few steps, his nemesis resided behind that door, doubtless plotting new and more exciting ways to ruin his life.

His gaze fixed on the latch. If he tried it, would it open? Or had his outburst today guaranteed her refusal once more? He was master of this house, master of her, damn it! Why did she have to make such a simple matter so bloody complicated?

What did she want from him?

Well, he wouldn't stoop to pressing that latch, begging for admittance like a supplicant before the queen! She could lock it or not—he wouldn't trouble himself to find out either way!

He shut his eyes and sank beneath the water, shutting out the world. Unfortunately, Deirdre wouldn't leave him alone. Her constant testing kept him engaged, her beauty kept him on the edge of torturous arousal, and her quick mind kept him interested despite his doubts. Between the outrageous pranks and her ruthless beauty, he was having trouble maintaining the icy distance that had served him so well for all these years.

Bloody hell!

AFTER HER OWN late bath, Deirdre avoided the great silken-hung bed and remained by the fire, brushing out her hair, clad in her nightdress and wrapper. It had been, quite frankly, one of the worst days of her life— and that was claiming quite the contest!

She was exhausted, but far too upset to even think of

sleep yet. Shame over her own actions chased doubts and regrets through her mind again and again. What was she fighting for? She could scarcely remember. Could she and Calder not simply stop this war? Hadn't they done enough harm to each other yet?

Across the room, the firelight gleamed on the brass latch on the door she'd never opened. Her gaze slid to it again and again. It was still locked, she was sure, though he'd not tried it again.

Was he in there, wide awake as she was, too rigid in his pride to reach out yet longing for this madness to end? If she was so righteous to demand him to change, could she not relent a little as well?

Before she could talk herself out of doing the one thing she'd longed to do, she rose to her feet and strode across the room to turn the key. The door opened on a scene that took her breath away.

The room was dark but for the golden radiance from the coals. The fine dark-finished furnishings disappeared in the gloom, leaving only the great bed like a bright island, the snowy bed linens vivid in the fire glow.

Across the wide bed, arms outstretched, hands limp in sleep, Calder looked like a weary knight stripped of his armor. His big body was bare to the glow of the coals—and to her hungry gaze. Her fingers twitched with the urge to stroke her hands all the way down his great, cat-like frame—to start by running them through his thick dark hair and down his tanned throat, over his powerful chest and down over the ridges of his stomach, following that narrow trail of dark hair that arrowed down, down . . .

Her knees struck the bed frame with a faint *thunk.* Oh heavens, she'd crossed the huge room without even realizing her feet moved over the carpet! For a long moment she stood frozen, waiting for the noise to wake him. He would open his eyes and see her there, looming over him, staring at his thick . . .

She covered her face with her hands. Now, if she just moved her index finger slightly she could keep his male organ in clear view. Much better. Now if he awoke, he wouldn't think she was either a wicked voyeur or a lecherous trollop obsessed with his body.

He might quite like to wake up to that. You would.

Well, yes, but she wasn't the one who was so angry, was she? He didn't want anything to do with her, remember?

He shifted, stretching one leg slightly. Her eyes locked on the flexing muscles of his thighs. He was tanned all over . . . how could that be? Did he swim naked somewhere on the Brookhaven estate? The very thought of Calder's big body skimming lightly through the water nearly knocked her to her knees. The sunlight would gleam from his rippling muscles, the droplets running down his golden skin as he walked from the water towards her, reaching out one powerful hand to her with a knowing smile on his face—

There the fantasy came to an abrupt halt. Calder didn't smile. Ever.

Nor would he if she gave in so soon. As difficult as all this was, there was a reason. A lesson that he must learn. She had learned hers . . . at least she hoped she had.

Now she must hold strong until he learned his. She turned resolutely away and left the room immediately— well, that last long wistful look didn't count if no one was looking!

For pity's sake, Calder, hurry up and fall in love with me! I don't think I can stand this much longer!

Chapter Twenty~nine

The next day, Calder did not appear at breakfast, although Deirdre kept the appointment, properly dressed this time. She ate alone, for Meggie was still refusing to do anything but gaze listlessly into the fire or out her bedchamber window. Deirdre was worried that the girl's spirit might be permanently crushed. She hadn't the slightest notion how to heal it, so she'd left Meggie in Patricia's brisk and cheerful care, resolutely not listening to any of Patricia's progressively more hilarious stories about her younger siblings. If that didn't bring the old Meggie back, Deirdre was quite without other ideas.

After she'd pushed her food about her plate for sufficient minutes—well, she did manage to choke down a bit of ham—she gave up on Calder and went looking for Fortescue. She found him polishing something that didn't need it in the front hall.

Frustrated, she folded her arms. "He's hiding from me when we've so much to discuss."

Fortescue said nothing and kept polishing.

Deirdre sighed and continued, "So many things to apologize for, so many things to regret . . ."

Polish, polish, polish.

"Well, I can hardly chase after him, not after yester-day. I'll only make things worse again. I suppose I'll have to let him come to me this time."

Fortescue straightened and snapped his cloth. "Excellent idea, my lady."

Deirdre smiled then. "Well then, I suppose I shall dress, just in case I have any callers today!" She certainly wouldn't want Brookhaven to find her pining away for him. It would be lovely if Sophie stopped by. Or Graham. Blast it, today she'd even be glad to see that idiot Baskin!

WASN'T IT A pity that of all the wishes she'd made lately that Baskin's appearance was the one chosen to come true? Later that morning, Deirdre sat through yet another paean to her unworldly beauty and timeless . . . duty? Oh God, the execrable rhymes were worse than usual today!

This particular piece was an ode to the day he'd first seen her, riding in an open carriage, looking "like Bodicea charging the Roman army." It was a tribute to his lack of talent that he made such a connection, since she wasn't driving that day and she didn't have red hair, and while she might have the wish to trample Tessa occasionally, she wasn't the sort to charge the Roman hordes.

Sophie, now . . . Her gaze drifted to where Sophie stood gazing out the window. The light glinted red-gold in Sophie's hair and there was something in her irritated posture—Sophie thought Baskin the rankest fool—and the height of her frame that seemed . . . commanding?

Deirdre blinked. Heavens, she must be addled by her

lack of sleep lately. What a thought—mild, bookish Sophie, a warrior queen?

At last the poem ended—less than an hour this time, thankfully—and Baskin gazed at her with worshipful anticipation. "What did you think?"

Ah, therein lay Baskin's primary charm. He actually cared what she thought. He didn't bark orders, he didn't run roughshod, he didn't glare at her with hot, black eyes . . .

Shaking off the rush of heat caused by that memory, Deirdre smiled warmly at Baskin. A bit too warmly, to judge by the avid gleam that appeared in his washed-out blue eyes. His rounded face flushed darkly and he shifted closer to her.

"Er . . ." Deirdre managed to move away by smoothly reaching for the closely scrawled pages clutched in Baskin's fist, then rising to her feet. "I shall treasure it always!" She stepped aside swiftly, leaving him to nearly fall into the place where she'd been seated. The window was the point farthest from his ardor. She made her escape—too bad she couldn't flee *out* the damned thing! "Look, Sophie! Baskin has given me his poem!"

Sophie, who still had her back to the room, crossed her eyes rudely. " 'Tis indeed thrilling," she murmured. "How happy you must be."

Still smiling brightly, Deirdre whirled to show the pages to Graham, who sprawled in a high back chair, sleeping most soundly. "Graham, is it not wonderful?" She woke him with a kick to the ankle, her crime concealed by her skirts.

He jolted awake. "Ow! H—how excellent!"

Graham had always been quick. Now Deirdre wiggled her brows and flicked her eyes in Baskin's direction.

"You look tired, Graham. Are you sure you're not *ill?* Sophie, does Graham not seem a bit *ill* to you?"

"Goodness me." Sophie was practically snoring with boredom. "Graham, you must conserve your strength. I'll see you home myself."

Fortunately, Graham wanted escape as badly as Deirdre did, and although Baskin might want to linger once the others left, it would be the height of bad manners to stay on unless expressly invited to.

Sophie burst from the front door as soon Fortescue stepped aside. She didn't know how Deirdre could bear to be polite to that fawning idiot. The fellow was lucky that she herself was shy around men, for she'd spent most of his everlasting poem creating detailed scenarios where she'd either suffocated him with her reticule or dismembered him with a very dull pair of garden shears!

Graham was a close second behind her as they made their way to where one of the Brookhaven carriages awaited to transport Sophie home. "Give me a ride, will you? It's a long way back to my rooms," he wheedled. "I want to put miles between myself and that smarmy little pip." He glanced back over his shoulder to where Baskin was now descending the steps. "I don't like that bloke. He's . . . twitchy."

Despite her own dislike of Baskin, Sophie found herself defending the fellow. "I suppose it is hard loving someone who doesn't love you back."

Graham scoffed. "Love? I never knew you were so sentimental. You're above such girlish nonsense, aren't you?"

She looked away, her blush rising. Graham laughed. "My, my. Pray tell, whom do you love, Sophie Blake?

Give me his name so I can kidnap him and force him to the altar for you!"

She swung on him then, gray eyes stormy with fury. "Thank you, but if that's what it takes for someone to wed me, I think I'll pass on tying myself to such an unwilling victim! As for giving you a ride, the walk will do you good! If you didn't gamble away every penny you have, you could take a hack home!"

Leaving him stunned and blinking at her sudden vehemence, she hopped nimbly into the carriage and departed down the drive toward the street.

"Bloody hell!" he muttered. "You'd think I'd said something wrong!" Shrugging, he shoved his hands into his pockets and ambled off.

He didn't notice that Baskin lingered behind, gazing longingly at the door to Brook House.

Chapter Thirty

After the bustle of footmen and hats, Deirdre was alone once more. As the front door closed and silence descended, Deirdre closed her eyes to let the stillness leach the tension from her shoulders.

It didn't work.

Calder. She opened her eyes. Of course, the real source of her unease was still here, avoiding her, hiding out behind his study walls when they had so much to settle between them. Coward.

And you're not, sitting here flirting with that pup and then tricking him into leaving so you don't have to tell him you don't like his poetry?

She still had the pages in her hand. Heartfelt words from someone she didn't care for, cold silence from the man whom she loved. Suddenly angry, with herself, with Calder, with Baskin, she crumpled the sheets and tossed them into the cold hearth.

She didn't want poems and pretty words. She wanted her husband, damn it!

BASKIN DITHERED ON the steps of Brook House. He hadn't actually meant to *give* the poem to Miss—er,

Lady Brookhaven. Or at least, not until he'd made a copy of it. It was, if he did say so himself, one of his finer works.

Pounding on the door again so soon might seem a bit desperate, and then there was the prospect of telling his beautiful Deirdre that he wanted the poem back . . .

Perhaps if he simply entered quickly to see if by chance she'd left the pages in the parlor? It would save him considerable embarrassment and then he could present her with a beautifully penned copy of the poem tomorrow!

Reminding himself that he was a welcome guest, privy to visiting along with family, he opened the door and entered. Moving quickly, he walked down the hall toward the parlor door.

Voices close by made him halt. Past the parlor, he could see the butler's back just around the corner. If the man saw him, there would be a great deal of explanation—

"Then the door between his lordship and my lady is still locked?"

Baskin stopped backing away. Instead, he crept forward until he could see around the corner.

The pretty maid standing before the butler nodded. She looked miserable about it, whatever it was. "Milady won't go near it. She even had me put one of the wing-backed chairs before it, as if it were just a bit of wall!"

The butler shook his head. "This is not a good beginning to a marriage. The previous Lady Brookhaven managed to go several years before she chipped her bedchamber mantel by flinging a vase at his lordship."

"I—I wanted to ask you—should I say something to

her? If she is merely afraid of . . . relations with a man, I could—well, to be true, I couldn't, but perhaps Cook could speak to her?"

Baskin felt hope surge throughout his body. Deirdre was fending off her great lout of a husband? Had done so since the wedding if he interpreted correctly!

If she is merely afraid . . .

Deirdre feared the man they called the Beast of Brookhaven! Damn, what unnatural practices had he asked of her, for her to lock and barricade the door between them?

Or—dare he hope?—perhaps she was saving herself for true love? For him?

She was alone here, surrounded by Brookhaven's faithful minions who even now plotted to pressure her into unspeakable "relations" with her fearsome husband. There was no one to help her.

Resolve stiffened Baskin's spine.

No one but him.

DEIRDRE SAT IN the silent parlor, slippers off, feet curled up next to her on the sofa, feeling rather listless without some sort of plan. From the first moment she'd read that Brookhaven had reappeared in Society, she'd had direction. First to attract him, then to wed him, then to teach him a lesson and now—now she only wanted an end to this endless plotting and conniving.

Lost in her mournful thoughts, she barely noticed the door opening. When no one came to remove the crumb-filled tray on the table before her, she glanced up.

"Baskin!" She sent a guilty glance toward the crumpled pages in the hearth. Standing quickly, she distracted him by approaching him with a smile. "I thought you'd gone."

He stared at her intently. "But you're glad I'm not, aren't you? You're glad not to be alone in this house."

Uncomfortable, she halted and veered toward the door with a light laugh. "I'm always glad for good company," she said. Hoping that opening the door would prompt him to step through it, she reached for the latch.

He caught her back with a fervent hand on her arm.

Startled, she stared at him. "Mr. Baskin!"

His grip did not abate. "My lady, you must know I would be your devoted champion . . . should you need one." He gazed into her eyes. "Do you need one?"

He was standing so close she was overwhelmed by his cloying cologne. She tried to step back. "Sir, I'm sure I don't know what you mean."

"You mustn't pretend to me! Not to *me!*" He moved closer. "Before I met you, my life was like that foul fog, the London particular. It surrounded me, suffocated me, tainted every breath—I did not want to live. I couldn't see my way—I was lost and alone and everything made me ache—I couldn't bear the world itself— can't you see? It was you who made it go away! You smiled at me and I could breathe for the first time! When I am with you it is as though I walk in the sun, even when it rains!"

It was the finest poetry he'd ever written, had he but realized it. Yet the desperation in his eyes, the near lunacy of his pleading—she pulled away, alarmed. "Baskin, I am not so extraordinary. You ought not to paint me in such a light—"

He lunged forward to wrap both hands about her upper arms. "You *are* the light! Don't you see—without you the fog comes back—the dark descends—!" He dropped to his knees, wrapping his arms about her waist and burying his face in her stomach. "You must save me—you *must!*"

Dear God, he was truly mad. Fear jolted through her. She put both hands on his shoulders and shoved him away with all her might. He fell backward, catching himself on the edge of the sofa, and stared up at her in surprise.

"Deirdre, my love, my light, my lodestar—"

She backed away several steps. Her hands and gut were shaking. "I am *Lady Brookhaven*, Mr. Baskin," she declared as sternly as she could. Heavens, her voice was shaking as well!

His expression cleared. He slowly pushed himself to stand before her, apparently unashamed by his outburst. In fact, insanely enough, he seemed pleased by what she'd said.

"Yes, of course." He smiled, his new calm eerie and nearly as alarming as his former frenzy. "Absolutely. I know precisely how to handle the matter."

He reached out a hand. She took another step back at his movement. "You must leave *now*, Mr. Baskin."

He nodded calmly. "Yes, you're probably right. We wouldn't want to cause suspicion. Keep the door locked, my lady." He gazed at her, something new simmering behind those bland blue eyes. "*I shall return.*"

With that he swept her a grand bow and turning smartly, strode from the room as if he swept a cape behind him.

Deirdre wrapped both arms about her chilled stomach. "Too bloody right, I'll lock the door, you madman!" Baskin had always seemed so harmless, so ineffectual—yet his strength when he'd captured her made her realize precisely how vulnerable she was against even a stripling like him. Abruptly, she felt unsafe alone in the pretty parlor.

She left the room at a near run, hefting her skirts high with one hand as she ascended the stairs at top speed. It was not until she'd pressed her back to the closed door of her own bedchamber that she breathed an unfortunately familiar sigh of relief.

There had been times in the past when one or another of Tessa's lovers had left her bed to come wandering down hallways where they didn't belong, into bedchambers where they weren't wanted.

The first time it happened she was fourteen. Fortunately, the fellow was too drunk to do much more than grapple clumsily with her, pinning her to the bed until she struck him directly in his perversion with a flying knee. While he groaned helplessly on the floor, she had nimbly climbed out her window and down to the one below.

She began to sleep in that room whenever Tessa's lovers spent the night, for it was her father's study, dusty and locked tight. She would curl up on the velvet sofa, wrapped in his smoking jacket that still hung on a hook behind the door, dreaming that he watched over her with indignant fury in his eyes.

Now, like then, she'd had no one but a ghost to turn to.

Chapter Thirty~one

Baskin made his way from the parlor carefully, keeping a watchful eye out for Brookhaven's lackeys.

"Are you still here?"

Whirling in surprise, Baskin nearly stepped on the small figure standing before him. "Wh—what?"

A dark-haired child glared at him, skinny arms folded before her in a stance of pure disdain. "You're always here," she said flatly. "You must be very stupid. Don't you know Dee is married now?"

Who was this nasty little beast? *Dee.* Lord Graham called Miss—er, Lady Brookhaven that. So did Miss Blake, on occasion. It was a hideous slashing of a lovely name, which Baskin loathed, but now he smiled silkily. Anyone who was permitted to say "Dee" must be someone very close indeed.

"I'm her ladyship's dear friend," he said smoothly. "From before her marriage."

The child didn't seem impressed. "I listen at the door sometimes. Your poems are boring." She made a face. "Love, blah, blah, hearts, blah, blah."

Baskin hid a snarl of his own and smiled condescendingly. "One could not expect a child of your tender years to appreciate the finer aspects of the great art."

She scowled but said nothing. Baskin counted the point as his. Then a horrifying thought struck him. "You listen at the door?"

She shrugged indifferently. "Unless your poems make me sleepy."

She made no sign that she'd heard an instant of Baskin's impassioned plea a few moments ago. That was a relief. Then his eyes narrowed. "People can hear many interesting things listening at doors. Things about other people . . . things they ought not to know."

The child smirked. "I know things. I know more than you."

Baskin decided to test her. "I'll tell you a secret if you tell me a secret."

She twitched, scratched her nose, then nodded quickly. "All right. What's your secret?"

He put his hands behind his back. "You first," he cajoled.

She grimaced. "Well, I know that our neighbor, Lady Barstow, sleeps in the same bed with her lady's companion. I heard her servants talking about it over the garden wall."

Baskin blinked. That was a hot bit of gossip! Lady Barstow was a clever widow, much respected, who waltzed immune through the artistic set. Knowledge like that could gain a talented fellow like him entrance into the elite! It seemed the child listened very well indeed.

Feeling entirely magnanimous now, since her knowledge clearly did not extend to his business, Baskin bent to whisper to her. "I know that your mother," for he'd figured out her identity in a flash of insight, "once threw a vase at your father and chipped the mantle in her bedchamber."

The girl drew back. "That's a lie," she said flatly, although there was doubt in her eyes. "My mother adored Papa."

Bristling, Baskin straightened with a shrug. "Suit yourself. Though you ought to check it and see, don't you think?" Anything to get rid of the little brat and get out of this house so that he could think of how to rescue his lady! He turned to go.

"Wait!"

He turned back with an irritated noise. "Yes?"

The girl frowned up at him. "If I do check and it is broken . . ." She hesitated, then spoke in a rush. "Will you come back and tell me more things about my mother? No one tells me anything. Papa doesn't want to talk to me at all." She hunched and looked away. "I can't even find the bloody book," she muttered.

Egad, what a little vulgarian! Baskin waved a hand and turned away again. "Of course, I'll tell you whatever you like."

He made his escape and strode purposefully down the drive. There wasn't much time! His dearest Deirdre couldn't keep her door locked forever!

IT HADN'T BEEN hard to learn where Baskin kept his rooms. Wolfe had only to linger outside, just far enough down the street to keep a casual eye on the door. When Baskin jogged down the steps of his not-quite-shabby boarding house, Wolfe casually began to amble away from him along the walk, head down, hands in pockets, the very picture of dejection.

It didn't take long.

"Ah . . . sir!" Baskin caught up with him easily. "My apologies, I cannot recall your name at the moment—"

Wolfe looked up dolefully. "My name? My name is coward!" He sniffed. God, how he hated Stickley's constant sniffing! "I fear I have not been able to bring myself to do what must be done."

Baskin tensed. "You speak of her ladyship's predicament."

Wolfe nodded miserably. "You've seen her. You must help her! She's so alone . . ."

Baskin nodded, his face set like marble. "I know." Wolfe nearly smiled. Baskin was so true in his motives, pure in his obsession. Wolfe had seen it before, in more intelligent fellows than this annoying pup. He wanted Lady Brookhaven, and he believed deep down she really did love him and that she would cure all that was wrong in his world. He was a drowning man, clutching at sticks and willing them to be rafts.

Wolfe knew just what to do to send that man over the edge.

THAT NIGHT, SUPPER was subdued. Calder actually did appear and did eat, but Deirdre was too upset over the episode with Baskin to take on her husband's grim and unsubtle snubbing.

Even Meggie ate silently, her gaze on her plate. The child was obviously still upset from yesterday's debacle at the factory.

Unable to do anything about that at the moment, Deirdre's mind returned to her predicament with her most ardent admirer. What should she do? She could ban Baskin from the house, but what had he done that was so bad? Declare undying love? Wasn't it just a bit of youthful dramatics?

Yet she felt ashamed and a little soiled by the incident. She only wished she could figure out why.

Across the table, Calder's mood grew darker by the moment. All day he'd been disturbed and confounded by the smallest things. His freshly ironed shirt had a burn mark on it, his tea was undrinkable, and his dinner had been served ice cold! The female members of his staff had rebelled suddenly and he suspected he knew why.

He hadn't behaved well yesterday. He knew that. He wasn't a complete idiot, after all. He simply didn't know what to do about it. The right apology required some thought—and a bit of practice before a mirror, since it wasn't something he was accustomed to. Still, the last thing he needed was to endure the petty vengeance of his own highly paid servants as they championed his bride while he tried to mull that matter over. The hell of it was that Deirdre was so preoccupied it was as if she wasn't even aware that he was in the room!

A thumping sound snagged his attention. "Lady Margaret, young ladies do not kick at their chairs!"

The thumping halted. Calder returned to his current occupation of working up a legitimate head of steam over his bride's behavior. She ought to be angry—she ought to demand that he apologize for his actions yesterday. She ought to be trying to confuse or tease him into complying instead of behaving as if he were a piece of bloody dining room furniture!

Thump. Thump.

"Lady Margaret," he bellowed, "stop that kicking!"

Meggie started so violently that her glass of milk

tipped onto the table, splashing over most of Calder's untouched meal and spilling over onto his lap.

"*Damn it!*" He sprang back from the table, knocking his chair to the floor by accident.

At his roar and the ensuing crash, Meggie burst into tears. At the sight of her pale, crumpled little face, guilt and frustration combusted to fury. He turned on Deirdre. "What the hell is wrong with the women in this house!"

Meggie wilted further, then slid from the table and left the dining room at a run, her fading wails headed in the direction of her room.

Deirdre stood. "I'm sorry, my lord, but I seem to have lost my appetite." Her expression was neutral but disappointment and tension radiated from her like a chill. She left in a rustle of skirts and quickly fading steps, also in the direction of Meggie's room.

The mess was cleaned in moments and a fresh plate was placed before Calder's newly uprighted chair, but sometime in the last few moments he'd lost the will to put fork to food. "I think dinner's over, Fortescue."

"It would seem so, my lord."

Chapter Thirty~two

Dinner's early and abrupt end only gave Fortescue more of what was now his favorite time of the day. At the moment, he was secluded in his office, leaning over a luxuriously fiery head of hair, breathing in the softly warmed air that rose from pale, northern skin, keeping his mind on his task with the most iron of wills.

"That's quite good," he said evenly. Madness when his pulse pounded like a racing horse! Then he pointed at one error in the row of figures. "But there, do you see?"

She bent closely over the tablet. "Oh!" She corrected it quickly and leaned back with smile. "Sure and I ought to have known that one was wronger than a six-toed cat!"

Fortescue didn't laugh. "Patricia, there's something I've been meaning to say." He rounded his desk and took his usual seat. "You're very quick to learn, but you'll rise even higher once you wring the last of the Irish from your speech."

She drew back at that. "Would I, then? And what would I be usin' for a heart if I did such a cowardly thing?"

Fortescue leaned back in his fine butler's chair, nearly as fine as his lordship's in the study. "Is it cowardly to want to improve oneself?"

"Improve to what? To be a liar?" She shook her head. "I've no argument against speakin' proper, mind, but there's no shame in bein' an Irishwoman." She swallowed, glancing away to hide the abrupt shine in her eyes. "Sometimes me own voice is the only thing that makes home seem real, here is this fine city of yours. Seems more than a week's journey away amid all these stone walls and fine-dressed folk . . ."

Patricia drew a breath and forced herself to calm. Himself didn't want her tears wasting his valuable time. There he sat, that look on his face like he'd sat on a pin in church. If he were a man from her world, she'd tease him now until he laughed large and free. And wouldn't he make a fine Irishman, with those shoulders and those blue, blue eyes—black Irish, they'd call him here, with night-dark hair and a wicked white smile . . .

He moved to speak, and for a moment she fully expected a smooth deep brogue from his tongue—Mary help her, she'd kiss him full on the lips just to hear the sound of home!

Instead he spoke perfect, cold, clipped Brit—each hard word like a hailstone to her ear.

"No one will force you to do anything, of course," he said stiffly. Heaven help the man, he knew no other way to speak, it was sure. "I only meant to offer you some valuable advice."

Now he'd shamed her, as she ought to be with that outburst against his generosity.

She smoothed her skirts and sat as ramrod straight as he. "I'll think about it then, sir," she said, keeping her tone as cool and businesslike as his was. "Should I finish the readin'—I mean, the *reading*?"

He nodded, his expression even and calm—yet she

could tell she'd damaged the easier air he'd come to have during their evenings together. She suppressed a sigh. The British were a touchy lot, easy to offend and slow to forgive.

You'd best watch out, Patty-girl, and not get too high on yourself, or this one'll see your big feet back on the street.

She would do well to remember that it was only on her ladyship's request that she had this opportunity— and her ladyship's standing wasn't all that high in Brook House at the moment.

Poor milady.

CALDER PACED THE length and breadth of his enormous bedchamber and found it not large enough to contain his edgy mood.

For a brief, bizarre moment he longed for his brother's company. Rafe would know precisely how to charm the hurt from a woman's eyes, to win a smile over a frown . . .

Then again, Rafe had a habit of winning a bit more than a smile from Calder's women. Never mind. He didn't need Rafe's charm for this. He had something his brother didn't—unlimited resources. Money couldn't buy love, but it might purchase a cessation of hostilities, at least long enough for him to figure out where everything had gone so bloody wrong.

What would make a woman like Deirdre smile?

His mind wandered over every moment he'd spent with her this last month: the suppers at Brook House with her cousins and her beastly stepmother, the way she'd proposed to him as smoothly as he'd ever been offered a partnership in business, the way she'd looked walking down the aisle to stand hand in hand with him, her usual stylish beauty exalted further by that Lementeur wedding gown—

He took a breath, then let it out slowly. He let his mind rest wistfully on the few smiles he'd seen since the day he'd ordered no parties, no balls, and no new gowns.

Oh yes, that ought to do for a start.

THE NEXT MORNING Deirdre woke to find herself in a silken heaven. She blinked and rubbed at her eyes, then looked again.

Gowns. Gowns piled high upon every surface. Jewel tones in silk and lace, ribbon and pearl. Even the air in the room was perfumed with that particularly heady scent of expensive fabric!

She sat up slowly to find that gowns had even been draped over her sprawled limbs while she slept. She reached toward a lovely confection of pleated silk of midnight blue, just the tone to set off the gold in her hair!

The fabric whispered beneath her touch. *I'm real,* it said. *Stroke me. Ruffle me.* Wear *me.*

"All right," she whispered back. "If you insist."

A soft chuckle sounded from somewhere in the room.

"Hello?"

An angel popped up from beneath a cloud of creamy organza—that is, if angels were small, neatly attired men with sparkling eyes and puckish features. "Good morning, my lady."

She gasped. "Lementeur! Whatever are you doing here?" Waking to find her bedchamber full of stunning gowns was rather magical, but waking to find their designer himself come to deliver them? That was miraculous!

She smiled at London's most sought after gown maker. She felt no unease at all seeing him in such intimate circumstances, for hadn't he seen her in much less during all their fittings before the wedding?

Besides, Lementeur just wasn't that sort of fellow.

He grinned back at her and spread his arms wide. "Ali Baba's cave, yes?"

"Ali Baba's cave a dozen times over!" Deirdre laughed and scrambled out of bed, running from the piles of gowns to the piles of hat boxes, and then on to the piles of glove boxes. "And shoes! And combs! And matching reticules!"

It was heaven, pure heaven, manna to the shallow, fashion-hungry part of Deirdre's starved little soul. Then she halted, multicolored ribbons slithering from her fingers to ripple to the floor. "But . . . his lordship won't allow it."

She looked around, aching for the beauty surrounding her, then calmly put her empty hands behind her back. "I'm sorry, Lementeur," she said with all the dignity she could muster through such a humiliating moment. "You've brought all this for nothing, I fear. I assumed you knew that his lordship canceled all my orders."

Lementeur smiled, his eyes crinkling in delight. "Oh, I knew. I kept making them, of course, for I knew you'd bring him around in time. Sure enough, there he was, banging on my door in the middle of the night, the great Brookhaven himself, pacing back and forth in my entrance hall, doubling the order and paying thrice the amount to have most of it delivered first thing this morning!" He winked at her. "Repentant husbands always make it a very good month for me!"

"Calder did that?" Deirdre gazed about her, the bright colors and sumptuous fabrics now worth more to her than ever. Her lower lip began to tremble and the brilliant shades began to blur before her eyes.

Lementeur offered her his handkerchief with practiced speed and led her to a free chair. "There you are, pet. Sit down. Let me pour you some tea."

Through her upwelling of emotion, Deirdre had to snort. "This happens often, then?"

Lementeur handed her a steaming cup of tea from where the tray was nearly hidden by hat boxes, then he perched on the chair arm beside her. He had to, for there was nowhere else in the vast gown-draped chamber to sit!

He patted her gently on the shoulder while she damply sipped at her tea. "The more generous the man, the more handkerchiefs I bring. Lord Brookhaven rated a full dozen. That's a record!"

Deirdre laughed and dabbed at her eyes. "Then I hope you put in a fresh supply for me, for he's an unpredictable fellow."

"Nonsense," Lementeur said briskly. Though he sat higher than her, their eyes were nearly level. "There's no such thing. Men are as simple as wind-up clockworks. Turn the key this way, everything works smoothly. Turn the key that way, you break the spring and it never works properly again."

She let her cup settle to her knees and stared at him breathlessly. "*What is the key?*"

He smiled mysteriously at her for a long moment, then leaned forward and tapped her affectionately on the nose. "Love, of course! Love is always the answer."

"Oh." Deirdre wilted, hope deflated. "I don't know how to make him love me. I think he wanted someone sweet, like Phoebe."

Lementeur tsked. "You can't make a man love *you*. All you can do is love *him*." He stood and tugged his cuffs into perfection. "You may not be amiable or un-complicated, my lady, but what you are is strong. You've had to be. After all, it requires a will of steel to survive Lady Tessa!" He crinkled his eyes at her. "Give it a go. His lordship is a good man and no denser than most. He'll catch on."

Then he sketched a neat little bow and left her there, surrounded by piles of Calder's generosity, holding a cup of tea in her hand and a fresh bloom of hope in her heart.

Chapter Thirty~three

Calder waited in his own front hall like a twitchy suitor, his restlessness prompting even the staid Fortescue toward drawn-out exhalations of exasperation. The gowns had gone up with Lementeur, with his heavily laden underlings following him like baby ducks. Now Calder had nothing to do but wait for the dressmaker to leave.

Waiting on a blasted dressmaker! Yet, the little fellow knew women like no other man in London and he'd insisted that Calder remain downstairs until he'd been given permission to go up.

Just when Calder was about to cast that advice to the wind, the dressmaker came tripping lightly down the stair, one hand on the banister, a satisfied smile on his face. First, however, he turned to the butler. "Mr. Fortescue, if you would send that lovely flame-haired creature up to her ladyship now? I'm sure she's ready to try some things on."

Then he grinned up at Calder. "My lord, please wait precisely fifteen minutes before you present yourself." He winked. "I'm sure it will be worth the wait."

He took his hat from Fortescue and placed it upon his head, pausing to add the slightest tilt with one practiced tap of his forefinger. Then he bowed. "Good day, my lord." He left with a jaunty step.

Calder ignored him, his eyes on the tall clock in the hall. Fourteen minutes and counting. He didn't know why he was following Lementeur's orders without question. Perhaps it was because his own methods had worked so well for him before?

At last the minute hand flicked to the fourteenth minute. Calculate one minute to climb the stairs—although he thought he might have taken much less in his hurry—and to march down the hall to the marchioness's chambers—and to tap upon the door—

Patricia opened it, curtsying quickly when she saw him. "Yes, milord?"

Deirdre's voice came from behind her. "Let him in, Patricia."

The maid swung the door wide upon a vision in midnight blue. Calder's throat went dry at the lovely woman standing before him. How was it that he sometimes forgot how stunning she was?

The gown was Calder's particular favorite—had she somehow known that? It was pleated and wrapped around the bodice, arrowing in upon the best parts of her sumptuous anatomy and accentuating them without that obvious sort of display that he scorned. The rest of the shimmering silk fell straight to the floor with no distracting ruffles or bows. There was only rich blue silk encasing lovely, luscious woman.

Then the smile she gave him dazzled him further. Freely offered, delighted and real—he felt awash in light from a summer sun. He opened his mouth to speak, but it seemed he'd forgotten how.

She spun about in delight. "Isn't it beautiful? I love them all but I think this is my favorite!"

So beautiful. He cleared his throat, mastering speech at last. "I'm glad you like them."

She stroked loving fingers over more silken offerings as she walked toward him. "I must thank you. You've been most generous . . . Calder." Her eyes were on the floor now, her tone shy.

It was the first time she'd called him by his given name. He'd had no idea how he'd hungered for that until this moment. Something eternally tight seemed to unwind within him.

"Well." He swallowed. "You've been good to Meggie. She's very fond of you. I—thank you."

Deirdre lifted her gaze to meet her husband's. It was rather bare and naked, that "thank you." It was not the stuffy mouthing of "appropriate things to say" she'd come to expect from him. It was the simple wording of a man who felt more deeply than he could express.

All you can do is love him.

It was certainly worth a try. She reached for his hand and slipped hers inside. "For someone to do what you did for me today . . . no one has ever done anything like that for me before."

She saw Patricia slide out of the room, but not before the maid cast her a roguish smile of encouragement from behind Calder's back.

Deirdre took a breath and went on. "It is especially kind after the way I've treated you."

He blinked. "The way you've treated me?" His voice was deep and low, as soft as velvet, as dark as coffee. His hand warmed around hers, his fingertips smoothing a near caress. "I thought I was the one who needed to apologize."

She tilted her head, unable to resist teasing her somber lord. "You certainly have a great deal to apologize for."

He nodded. "I know. The way I touched you at the factory—"

She flapped her other hand. "Not that. I loved every moment of that. Hope to do it again sometime soon."

He gaped. "What? But—I—"

"I do think it was rather bad of you to stop, however. Rather like breaking a promise, don't you think?"

"We were exposed, in front of the entire factory. You didn't want me to stop?"

She let out an exasperated sigh. "I didn't want you to stop," she said slowly, as if to an idiot.

That startled a short bark of laughter from him. "I'm fairly certain you're half mad."

She grinned, encouraged. "What I am is disappointed. It isn't gentlemanly to let a lady down that way."

Something like a smile crooked the corners of his lips. She rejoiced to see it.

"I don't think you are anything at all like I thought you were."

She gave an indifferent shrug, but her gaze slid away. "Sorry to disappoint you." She tried to keep the hurt low and the self-mockery high. "However, the complaints office is next door, to the right."

He leaned one shoulder on the bedpost, never letting loose her hand. He looked unbearably handsome like that, gazing down at her with those dark eyes, with just the tiniest smile at the corner of his lips.

I will not melt. I will not melt.

"How did someone so beautiful become so completely peculiar?"

She stiffened. So he thought she was beautiful. That was pleasant, but since most men thought she was beautiful, it mattered less than the fact that he found her peculiar. "I hardly think insulting me is the right tack to take at the moment."

"Oh, really?" His voice deepened. Her belly quivered in answer. "What is the right tack to take, do you think? Should I get on my knees and beg forgiveness for being rough with you?"

"No."

"Should I flatter you and tell you that you are the most beautiful woman I have ever seen?"

She shuddered. "God, no."

He tilted his head, regarding her with something new in his eyes. "For all your primping, you aren't a bit vain, are you?"

She grimaced. "The primping is for your benefit, not mine," she retorted in a grumpy tone. "I long to run about in uncombed hair and ragged nails and greens in my teeth."

He snorted in disbelief. "Surely not."

She fought down a grin. "Oh, very well. I do like clean teeth."

He sat on the high bed, bringing his gaze nearly even with hers. "As do I."

He was so large before her. Something ancient and female responded to his size alone. *Strong male, will protect.* Except she didn't want protecting, not really. What she wanted was far more complicated and necessary.

She loved him, everything about him—dark and

brooding, hesitantly kind, lonely and broken and hers, if she hadn't already ruined everything.

I want you to love me—all of me—not just the pretty exterior.

He raised his hand to brush back a loose strand of hair from her temple. "I like that you are beautiful," he said softly. "I like that your eyes are just that shade of blue, and that your figure is just this shape." He wrapped his hands about her waist, his fingers spread as if to measure it. "Although I do think you could do with a bit more of it—"

Breathless from his touch, she gazed at him in surprise. "You said you didn't want me to get fat!"

He raised a brow. "And then what did you do?"

She opened her mouth to answer, then halted. *I ate everything in sight, even the ham!*

Her toes curled in memory. She had to swallow before she could speak again. "So, let me see if I understand you correctly—you think I'm too thin?"

He shrugged. "I think you work too hard at being thin. I would rather see you eat and enjoy yourself. I like you as you are. I would like you just as much if you ate ham every day of your life."

She tilted her head and let her smile grow until he blinked, as though he were just a bit blinded. "That, my lord, is a bargain."

He let out a long breath and dropped his forehead to rest on her bosom. "I am not a glib or persuasive man. I don't know how to make pleasant conversation or pretty apologies, no matter how much I wish to."

She tentatively raised her hand to rest it in his thick dark hair. He made a low noise at her touch, like a wounded beast finding respite at last. She let her hand slide, feeling the silky crispness of his hair over her fingertips, until her palm rested on the back of his neck. She felt his muscles relax beneath her touch and saw the pride and arrogance seep from his broad shoulders. His hands tightened about her waist, not in desire or at least, not entirely, but as if he silently clung, unable to tell her of his need.

He was so good at being the great Lord Brookhaven that it was easy to forget that he was only a man, subject to the same doubts and isolation as anyone else in this world.

"You can't make a man love you. All you can do is love him."

In that moment she realized that she'd not given once to this man. She'd blamed him, called him arrogant and unfeeling, yet he had been the first to give. She'd demanded his attention, fought for his respect and ached for his love—and not once had she offered hers.

She'd lived her life guarding herself and her pride and her very safety—perhaps too well. That was her old life. It was time to let down that guard.

Good-bye, Tessa.

Hello, Calder.

Chapter Thirty-four

Deirdre took a single step forward. So very simple. That step brought her to stand between his knees and caused him to raise his head from where it rested. He drew back immediately, the moment of his surrender past.

She smiled at him fondly. Now was the moment for her surrender. Wasn't he going to be surprised?

He blinked at her expression, wary hope rising in his own. Deirdre did something she'd longed to do for so many years.

She took both hands and energetically mussed his perfect hair.

Now his expression framed complete confusion. She threw her head back and laughed.

With a growl of damaged dignity, he started to push her away and stand up. She put her hands on his wide shoulders and pushed him back down. "Don't even consider it," she said briskly, still smiling. "I'm not through yet." Then she put her hands into her own hair and yanked out the pins with practiced ease. After a shake and a toss that brought her long hair tumbling down over her shoulders and bosom, she looked back at him to see his eyes dark and interested and his urge to leave quite abated.

She tilted her head and raised a brow. "Staying now, are we?"

He nodded silently, never taking his gaze from hers. He waited now with the riveted intensity of a starving hound with the possibility of a steak in its future. *Poor darling.*

Overcome with regret for her own part in his loneliness, she framed his jaw in her hands and gazed into his eyes. "I am not so bad with words," she said softly, "yet I cannot tell you how sorry I am." I love you, she wanted to say, but he wouldn't believe it, not after her behavior so far. She was going to have to prove herself first.

The only problem was, she hadn't the slightest idea how! The enormity of her ignorance swamped her, quite taking the starch from her knees. She longed to play temptress for him, but her experience extended to flirtation only. After that, she was entirely unequipped!

She hesitated, then bit her lip. "Calder, I fear you're going to have to take over at this point. I haven't the slightest idea what I'm doing."

"Oh," he breathed, "I wouldn't say that."

She blinked, then chuckled despite her nervousness. "You want me to continue . . . by myself?"

His corners of his mouth curled upward. The near-smile made him so handsome that her heart began to beat faster and more steadily at the same time. *He* was with her at last, the real Calder, the man inside— present and unarmored and gazing at *her.* The few past glimpses she'd treasured were as nothing next to the blazing force of Calder fully present.

Her mouth went dry and her nipples tingled and she felt her insides quiver. "I—" *love you.* Thankfully, her throat was too tight to let the words out. Pulling herself together, she tried to think of what to do next. Kiss him, melt into him, gaze longingly into his eyes while she let her hands stray into his lap? All the years of watching Tessa's practiced, cold-hearted seductions made her shy away from anything so manipulative. She wanted only the two of them here, only to feel what they truly felt. Only truth.

She had mussed his hair at last. What else had she longed to do?

Slowly, she took his hands in hers and stepped back, pulling him to stand with her. He came readily, making her flush with power along with her nervous desire. Then she spread his hands wide and let them go. She stepped into him until her entire body pressed to his and laid her head upon his wide, iron-hard chest. "Hold me," she whispered.

She heard his heart thump at that. For a long moment, nothing happened. Then, so slowly it was as if he feared to startle her, she felt his arms come about her until she was wrapped in him, feeling the heat of his big hands press into her back, keeping her tight to him.

Astonishingly, she felt hot tears rise behind her closed eyelids. It had been so long . . . She had been alone and unprotected for so, so long . . .

He held her close, cradled so tenderly yet so completely. This man would never harm her, nor allow her to be harmed. This man would fight for her, live for her, die for her—

If she could simply make him love her.

Yet now was not the time for her need. After allowing herself one last selfish moment of being held tightly by his strength, she took a breath and lifted her head to smile up at him. "If you'll give me a moment to clear the gowns from the bed—"

Calder wasn't a man of words, but he had never been accused of lacking the nerve to take action. He wasn't about to let her out of his arms now that she was finally, heart-poundingly in them. With a single motion, he swept her from her feet and deposited her on the enormous bed, pirate's fortune in silk and satin be damned!

He fell with her, both of them sprawling entangled upon the piled gowns. She gasped and pushed at him frantically.

He went quite still. Had he misread her? Was this some sort of teasing game, a heartless manipulation?

"Get off!" She was scandalized, all right, but not by his sudden act. "Oh, Lementeur will *kill* us!"

He laughed then, a short unaccustomed bark. She froze in surprise, blinking those incredible blue eyes at him, her face so close he could kiss her without half trying.

What a marvelous idea.

He cupped her delicate jaw in his hand and lowered his lips to hers. Her mouth was so soft, so willing and inexperienced and delicious. He found that the world shrank again, just as it had when he'd first kissed his bride, the light of everything else dimming before the glory of her mouth.

Deirdre gave in, gave out, gave over, gave everything she had to that kiss—*oh God, don't stop, don't breathe, don't ever let me go*—

He moved more fully over her and his weight pressed her into the mountains of priceless fashion and she sank willingly into them, loving the feeling of his

big body pressed to hers, allowing the heat and power
of him to shelter her hungry heart.

She wrapped her arms about his neck and pulled
him closer still. When his knee pressed between hers,
she opened her thighs without thought. The layers of
gown and trousers did nothing to hide the thick erection that swelled just to one side of her belly. His want
only fired her own. When he slid his hand down her
throat, she arched it willingly to his touch. When he
covered her breast with his large hot palm, she jolted
at the shot of sensation that hit her low in her belly
and between her thighs. The tiny sound she made only
seemed to fire him further, so he tugged at the neckline of her gown with such implacable determination
that the seams slowly gave, exposing her nipple to his
touch.

She moaned, one last sane thought crossing her
mind. "The gown—"

"I'll buy another," he growled. "I'll buy a hundred.
Lementeur will retire young."

"Well, all right then," she sighed. "But there are buttons in the back, just in case you care to—"

His response was to yank the gown to her waist with
enough force to nearly lift her from the bed. She gasped
in surprise, then laughter. "Give me that!" He wouldn't
let her grab the bodice back, however, instead taking
her wrist and pressing it to the bed beside her shoulder.

He gazed sternly down into her face. "To hell with
the gown. Understood?"

Excitement trembled through her. This man—her
man—was not to be underestimated. He was, however,
not being entirely fair. Here she was, her sheer chemise
exposed to his gaze, with her hardened nipples pressing

high through fabric not much denser than a spider's web, and he remained fully clothed above her.

She licked her lips in half-nervous seductiveness. "To hell with your shirt. Understood?"

His hot eyes warmed further with humor. Tenderness rose in her to see him inching toward happiness. "Well?"

He said nothing, only rolled her over to half-lie upon him. After she caught her breath—would he never stop surprising her?—she clambered up him to straddle his hips with her costly gown rucked up about her thighs. By the size of the organ that greeted her beneath her skirts, she would not have long to play at dominance!

She fought down a shiver of natural apprehension— there must be some mistake! It would never fit!—and concentrated on evening the score. She tried to hold up her torn bodice with one hand while she struggled with his cravat with the other, then gave it up with a sound of impatience. Stripping the tiny sleeves from her arms, she pushed the ruined silk down to her hips, which left her quite indecently clad in the chemise but left both hands free.

The damned cravat took far too long and required great attention—which Calder did his best to destroy by tugging at the narrow ribbon that gathered the neckline of the chemise over her extraordinary breasts. Determined as she was, she didn't notice until he was able to do a great deal of damage. Once he had it untied, he entertained himself mightily watching the jiggle and sway of her exposed creamy flesh before she noticed the draft.

She gasped and sat back abruptly, her hands pressing the chemise high once more. Unfortunately, this brought her warm damp center in direct contact with his throbbing cock, which was already fair to bursting through his trousers. His eyes nearly crossed.

"Unfair," she cried. "I've layers to get through yet! There's your coat and weskit and shirt and . . ." Her voice trailed off uncertainly. "Do you wear anything else under that?"

Not for long. Grasping her ribcage just beneath her arms, he brought that stunning cleavage down for a quick, hot kiss, then he lifted her off him and tossed her onto the mountain of jewel-toned silk beside him. "Stay!" he ordered, then rose from the bed, stripping off his coat so fast that there was the unmistakable sound of popping seams.

Deirdre had tunneled herself under several gowns and now peeked out, primly covered up to her chin. "I wanted to do that," she protested mildly. "Ripping seams and all."

The weskit hit the floor, minus a button or two, and his shirt followed. He bent to yank off his boots when the sudden silence caught his attention. He glanced up to see that the silks had risen to just above her nose and all that was visible was a pair of very large, very concerned sapphire eyes.

Calder stopped and braced his hands upon his knees, forcing himself to breathe deeply for a moment, forcing his raging arousal under control. For all her sass and vinegar, his sensually lovely Deirdre was innocent and very likely afraid. He would not have her regret this moment.

"Calder?" Her voice was muffled. "Why are you stopping?"

He straightened when at last he could do so. Bare-chested, still clad in his trousers and boots, he eased himself to the mattress, leaning on one wrist while he gently tugged the concealing skirts to reveal her face. She gazed up at him somberly, one lip caught between her teeth.

He swept a lock of hair back from her face. "I'm not stopping. I'm only slowing down. Is that all right?"

She swallowed and took a breath, then smiled. "Yes, thank you."

Deirdre slowly let the mound of gowns slide down until he could see that she'd wriggled out of everything but the chemise and her stockings while he was busy. She hated her sudden shyness, but she couldn't seem to help it. "I'm nervous," she told him.

He nodded. "I expected you to be."

She took a breath, rose to her knees and moved toward him until she could feel the heat coming off his skin onto hers. She leaned close but didn't kiss him. "But I'm not frightened."

She felt the soft gust that was nearly a laugh. "You don't get frightened," he reminded her. "You take vengeance."

Her words of bravado had come back to haunt her. She longed to tell him that she was often frightened, often worried, sometimes even weak and helpless and needing of protection. He didn't want to know that, she was sure. He wanted the perfect portrait she'd taken such care to paint for him. He wanted strong, saucy, thorny Deirdre, confident and proud, not the lonely girl who longed to be her true self with him.

Still, if she could make him fall in love with one side of her, could she not someday reveal all?

So she smiled flirtatiously and braved putting her

hand upon his bare chest to feel the iron muscle beneath the silken skin. Struck by the difference between his taut flesh and her own, she let her doubts subside before her burning curiosity.

He was so beautiful, all giant strength and corded sinew. Without thinking, she let her curious fingers trace the beam of his collarbone to his muscled shoulder, then circled back to feel the wiry texture of the hair that covered his broad chest. Settling onto her heels, she bent her head over her examination until, without noticing it, her long hair trailed over his skin.

His rippled belly contracted sharply at that. She passed her palm down over it, only to have him react again. "Are you ticklish, my lord?"

He pressed one large hand over hers to stop her. Surprised, she looked up to see his eyes black and burning, wild lust barely held in check. "Don't," he said through gritted teeth.

Oh dear. Much as she longed to see him lose control in his passion for her—perhaps not this time! She gave up on proving her theory of ticklishness—*someday soon, my lord!*—she spread both her hands wide over the rigid plates of his chest, only to find them too small to cover much. She was not a tiny woman but he was such a fine, large specimen of a man—

Alarm twanged within her. Her gaze flew up to meet his riveted stare. "What if it . . . doesn't fit?"

"Then I'm going to kill myself forthwith," he panted. "For life won't be worth living."

She laughed nervously, unconvinced.

He swallowed forcefully. "Deirdre, I'm not going to be able to wait much longer—"

"Oh!" She was being selfish again. She reached for the buttons of his trousers. "Here, let me help—"

He moved so fast, she didn't even see it. Suddenly she was on her back again, this time with his hands pinning her wrists above her head. "Don't—" His voice was a moan into her neck. "I won't be able to stop—"

Calder couldn't think, couldn't reason. His thoughts had to fight their way through pounding animal lust, winding slowly through to his consciousness—God, her scent! Her skin—her curious touch—her sweet apprehension—

He'd never wanted someone so much in his entire existence, not even as a randy lad! Yet she was untried and nervous, a new bride. It wasn't possible that she was ready for him. She must be terrified. He feared he was going to have to leave her before he did something they would both regret forever.

Chapter Thirty~five

"Calder?" Deirdre's whisper was warm against his ear. "Take off your boots."

His boots were airborne before Deirdre had time to draw three breaths. His trousers and underdrawers followed in a single sweep. He stood before her, naked and magnificent, his powerful chest rising and falling with the breathlessness of his desire for her.

She rose to her knees and pulled her chemise over her head, tossing it to drift lightly over the gleaming leather of his boots on the floor.

She still wore her stockings, but she didn't think there was time to—

He was on her then, his hot hands on her skin, his burning mouth demanding hers. There was no more conversation, no more thought, no more time for apprehension. He lifted her and rolled them both into the pile of silk, one hand on her back, the other spread over her bare buttocks. He moved his long legs between hers and lay upon her. "Open," he groaned. "Open for me, please, my darling—"

Her heart pounded at the words. Hiding her face in his throat to conceal the sudden dampness in her eyes, she lifted her legs until her knees gripped his hips. She dug her fingers into his hair and held on, ready for the pain, willing to do anything for this wonderful man who called her his darling.

When she felt the thick head of his penis touch her softest parts, she willed herself not to cry out in surprise. He would thrust now, impaling her and taking her virginity. It would be over soon and it would never be so bad again. She was not afraid.

He did not move, but only held himself trembling above her, his breathing tight. Deirdre hesitated, then did what came naturally, using her grip on his hips to rotate her wet flesh slightly over his erection. He gasped and jolted, which forced him a little deeper into her. She went still at the stretching pain, but it never amounted to more than a minor sting and soon faded. Encouraged, she wrapped her legs tighter and brought him further within her, inch by inch, breathing into the ache as he slowly tore away the slight resistance. He allowed it, letting her set the pace, restraining himself with a white-knuckle grip on the two fistfuls of satin beside her head.

At last he pressed fully within her. She'd had her doubts there at the last! When the last ache ceased, she stroked her hands down his rigid back. "There," she whispered. "I have you inside me now."

Then her hands clenched into the muscles of his back as he swelled instantly within her. She understood now—somehow he'd kept himself from his full size until she was ready! Despite the tears of pain that dampened her eyes, she bit her lip and breathed deeply. He would not know.

Still he grew, until she had to writhe beneath him, desperate to adjust herself to him, fearing it wouldn't happen. *Heavens, he's enormous! I can't—it won't—*

At last, she felt herself fit to him. Letting out a long breath of relief, she opened her clenched fingers and eased them over his back. It was over.

Until he began to move.

With the first slow, dragging withdrawal, she cried out at the sensation. He went still instantly, making her whimper and twist against him. "More—" she gasped.

He moved so slowly, making each moment of it last an eternity of breathless pleasure. She whimpered, she moaned, she clung to him with arms and legs and lips, unable to believe she'd lived her entire life without the touch of this man!

Each slow draw, each exquisitely not-quite-painful thrust, drove her mad until she was a wicked, panting beast in his grasp. Sweat slicked their naked skin together, her lips grew sore from his ravaging kisses, her nipples throbbed from his hot, tender fingertips, she undulated beneath him, reaching for more, more—

Until at last it broke over her like a wave on a rock cliff. White-hot pleasure from somewhere deep inside her shot through her veins, burning her thoughts away, making her cling and shudder and moan into his sweat-slicked chest.

He gave in at last with a great roar, thrusting hard and fast—once, twice, thrice—until he shuddered and moaned her name into her hair, his hands tight on her, his body rigid for a long, silent moment. She felt him swell within her tender flesh, but she could only whimper softly at the new sensation. She was lost, afloat, swirling helplessly in the backwash of the deluge of him.

After a long moment, he withdrew from her. Though he'd decreased somewhat, she was so tender that she gasped.

"Shh." He wrapped her in his arms and pulled her tenderly to lie half upon him. "Shh, my darling."

My darling. She wanted to cry every time he said it. She hid her response in a soft, breathless laugh. "Heavens," she said. "I had no idea."

He kissed the top of her head. "Neither did I."

She pressed her face into his chest. "What do you mean? You've . . . you've done that before."

Calder hesitated. "Not . . . quite like that." He wasn't ready for her to know what he himself was surprised to learn—that making love to Deirdre was soul-wrenching, stunning, outrageously beautiful and deeply, deeply disturbing. He felt raw, exposed . . . *new.* Never had he gone into a woman only to find himself lost in her, unsure of where he ended and she began. He'd sunk into Deirdre like a lost ship into the sea, helplessly floundering, powerless—without a will of his own.

He stroked his hands over her back as she still quivered in his arms. He didn't know what to do with such earthshaking need. It frightened him, yet he longed to repeat it. He was parched for her already, only moments after leaving her hot, wet depths.

You're in deep trouble now.

When she finds out, she'll own you.

Perhaps. Unless . . . unless she felt it, too? He wanted to ask her, wanted to tell her, wanted to share his entire life with her, every dream, every plan, every instant of pain and joy—

He felt breathless with that desire, storm-tossed and exposed and suddenly, warily hopeful. She might understand. She might feel the same.

If he could only bring himself to tell her . . .

Deirdre lay in the warm circle of her husband's

strength, feeling like a wife for the very first time. That had been . . .

There were no words. Wonderful? Exhilarating?

Happening again soon?

She would ask Calder. No, she couldn't face him. Not after those sounds she dimly remembered making. Not after she'd clawed at him so, panting and sweating and matching his thrusts—

Her tender flesh shivered at her thoughts, knotting and throbbing anew. She wasn't going to get more of the aforementioned if she didn't brave this first conversation. She licked her sore lips, took a deep breath and pushed herself up to rest on her elbows, looking down at him. She felt daring and naughty with her naked backside exposed, although she did bunch some of the silk over her breasts. Her beautiful, gloriously naked Lord Brookhaven lay with one arm flung over his eyes.

He wasn't asleep. She knew that because he jumped when she leaned down and bit his chest.

"Ouch!"

She batted her eyelashes at his offended glare. "I believe compliments are in order," she said.

"Ah." He gazed at her for a long moment. "You were splendid."

She laughed. "I've no doubt of that! I meant that I wished to compliment you." She tilted her head. "I know that a woman's first time is usually rather unpleasant."

His face softened. "I did not wish such for you," he said, his voice husky and tender.

Her heart turned over and gave a few extra thumps. She let out a shaky breath. "Well, thank you. I can't imagine it could ever be better than that."

His dark eyes sharpened on her face. "Then your imagination is very limited."

Oh, my God. She hadn't meant to issue a challenge, but she ought to have realized that Calder wasn't the sort to rest on his laurels.

Well, it would be a short life, but she would die happy!

Then a sharp reminder of her experience shot through her, making her wince.

"Ah." She hesitated. "Perhaps later?"

He ran the knuckles of one hand down her cheek. "That, my lady, is a bargain."

Deirdre drew in a long, shuddering breath. This man could turn her dreams into golden truth . . . or he could shatter them with a touch. To be so vulnerable before another, to risk herself so dangerously—every cautious, calculating bone in her body cried out, "Take care! Don't fall!"

Too late. She had fallen, breathless and quivering, into his arms with her heart wide open. All the years of self-preservation and watchfulness were as nothing. She was raw and naked and new.

Yet, what could she be thinking? This was Calder, the most responsible, forthright man alive. He would never turn on her. She mustered a smile for him, though her feelings did not lend themselves to anything so mild. She managed, somehow, not to cling to him as he rose from the bed.

She really must get hold of herself. After all, she was a married woman. She had this man for the rest of her life!

He dressed quickly and, of course, efficiently. She rolled over onto her stomach and watched him tie his neckcloth with swift, practiced movements. "Duty calls?"

His gaze slid to hers in the mirror. "Yes, though I can scarcely hear it through a clamoring desire to climb back in there with you."

She buried her smile in the pillow for a moment. Then she lifted her head. "Should I . . . stay here?"

His dark eyes flared hotly for a moment, then he shook his head. "I'm bound to be a while. Don't forget, I have a factory to fix."

Blinking, Deirdre realized that she'd forgotten entirely about the wreckage they'd left behind yesterday. "*Merde*," she breathed.

He snorted. "Indeed. Many times over, I'm afraid."

She propped herself up on her elbows and tilted her head as she gazed at him buttoning his waistcoat. "One would have thought you'd be there at cock's crow, giving orders and bringing chaos to its knees."

He turned then and gazed at her naked, mostly uncovered length on the tumbled bedding. "One would have thought . . ." He shook off his daze. "Something tells me that I'm not going to be starting my days as early as I used to."

She dipped her head regally. "Why, thank you, kind sir!" She couldn't resist wriggling just a bit, watching his face.

His jaw hardened. "I. Am. Leaving. Now."

"Wait!" She scrambled off the bed, pulling the sheet with her to wrap loosely and not very effectively over her nudity.

He waited, as commanded, as she approached him. His gaze ran from her bare legs to the fall of her tousled hair over her shoulders. "You will be the death of me, won't you?"

She lifted her chin. "Nonsense. I only require a husbandly kiss good-bye."

A smile quirked the corner of his mouth. "Nice try. You know I won't be able to stop with one."

He moved to the bellpull. "I'll ring for Patricia.

"Heavens, no! She'll die when she sees this mess. You'd better let me see what I can salvage first."

He pulled her into his arms and kissed the top of her head. "Throw it all out. I'll pay triple to have new ones delivered by the end of the week."

She pushed at him. "These are not just gowns, O Lord Poundheavy! These are works of art. They are worth saving."

He slid his hands from her shoulders, down her arms. He loved having the right to touch her as he pleased. "Keep them then," he murmured. "Leave them right there, on the bed. I quite liked it."

She blushed and looked away, but her snicker betrayed her. "Well, perhaps the blue one . . ."

He laughed out loud, feeling free and buoyant as he never had before. She looked up at him in surprise, then she smiled slowly. He felt warmed by it, as if he'd stepped into the sunlight. There was time to talk later. They had the rest of their lives, after all!

He hadn't made it ten steps down the hall before he wanted to turn back and hold her again. How was he to concentrate on his broken factory when she was brushing that hair, dressing that body, drawing fresh stockings up those legs—

So this is why my brother betrayed me.

He didn't blame him. If Rafe stood between him and Deirdre right now, Calder would seriously have to consider a spot of bloody murder! It was miraculous that Rafe had restrained himself with Phoebe for as long as he had. The sudden understanding lightened Calder's heart further, until he grinned wickedly at Fortescue in the front hall.

Leaving the house to fling himself upon his waiting horse, Calder laughed for nearly a mile thinking of his stoic butler's dumbfounded confusion.

Hell, one would think he'd never smiled before!

Chapter Thirty-six

Deirdre sent Calder off with a caress and a smile. The caress went with him but the smile stayed. She closed her bedchamber door with a dreamy sigh, then laughed at her own smitten behavior.

After she cleaned herself and dressed in a simple chemise and wrapper, it was time to tidy up. The room was a shambles, and while Patricia certainly wouldn't carry tales, Deirdre was still too shy about all this to want anyone to see it! First, she dealt with the washbowl and the sodden cloth with its betraying blots. That went to sizzle in the hearth while the water would simply have to go out the window.

She opened the window and tossed the water high with a flourish. Was that a muffled curse from someone outside? Belatedly she thought to check if anyone was below, but even leaning out as far as she could, she saw nothing at the base of the great tree beside her window.

Leaving the window open wide, she faced the pile of ruined gowns on the bed. Blushing, she wadded up the one that had lain beneath her. There was no saving *that.* A few of the others were only badly wrinkled, so she shook them out briskly and hung them in the wardrobe.

The stunning blue one was a sad loss, though it had

been her gain. As she lifted the blue gown to inspect the damage, she reveled in the richness of it. Lementeur was a genius. This was quite the most daring gown she'd ever worn, for although there was nothing indecent about the placement of the neckline, the gown had been so perfectly fitted that her bosom had risen from it like a dockside doxy's!

Smiling as she remembered Calder's gobsmacked reaction, she held it before her and spun about, letting the heady rustle of the silk swirl around her plainer muslin skirts.

Thud.

She whirled at the noise behind her to find that someone had clambered through her window. "*Baskin?*"

He clambered to his feet, somewhat the worse for his climb. He'd lost a button from his weskit, both shoulders of his tight dandy's coat had popped their seams and he wore a leafy twig in his hair like a lopsided antler. He looked so ridiculous that her initial alarm began to fade and fury took over.

"What do you think you're doing?" She pointed at the window. "Get out this instant!"

He gaped at her. "But I've been waiting for this chance to speak to you! When you opened your window and smiled down at me, I knew you wanted me to come to you!"

Then he moved toward her, blocking her from the door, cutting her off from the bellpull. Now she remembered why she ought to fear him.

Baskin was quite mad.

With his groom riding several feet behind him, Calder rode away from Brook House and off to the factory that needed him so badly at the moment. So much to do there . . . so many problems to solve . . .

Yet, for all the urgent importance of his goal, he could not seem to concentrate upon it.

The churning city faded from his consciousness as he sat his mount, trotting a route the horse knew as well as he did. Gone were the shouts, the cries, the rattle of carriage wheels on cobbles, the clanging and banging of civilization that never seemed to ease.

He liked the city, liked the orderliness of the solid, square buildings and the linear streets that took one where one needed to go. At the moment, however, he could have been riding through the darkest forest for all the attention he gave his world.

Deirdre filled his mind. The memory of the last few hours swam through his thoughts in random sensory impressions that made his palms damp and his throat dry.

The elegant ivory length of her . . . the warm fall of silken, golden hair over his skin . . . the way she smiled, sometimes bold, other times bashful . . . her hands roving hesitantly, then urgently, over his skin.

What a heady mixture she was—innocence and sensuality, humor and strength, bravery and shyness.

Yet, despite the pull of those soft, warm, wet thoughts, he was riding away from her at this very moment.

Idiot.

Oh, yes. He was an idiot indeed.

You should go back immediately, lock yourself in that bedchamber for the next three weeks and make many more such memories! To hell with the damn factory!

All right.

Wait. No. Not all right. There was work to be done, problems to be solved, matters to put in order . . .

All of which could easily be put in someone else's hands. He had people to manage this sort of thing, competent, talented people who were twitching for more responsibility and status.

Stunned by the concept, and by the ease with which it could be carried out, Calder halted his horse on the middle of the bridge. Behind him, his groom halted as well. The tide of humanity flowed around them, giving their fine attire and even finer horses a respectful margin.

Let me get this straight. I could, quite simply, go home?

Home. Not Brook House. Home, where his wife and child awaited him.

Home . . . to his family.

Oh, yes.

With that thought ringing through his mind on a pure crystal note, Calder signaled his groom and turned his horse sharply about.

DEIRDRE STOOD CAPTIVE in the center of her bedchamber with Baskin between her and the door. Perhaps she ought to smile at him, to cajole him. After all, Baskin was a pup, a sop to her pride, a pawn in a game she wasn't interested in playing any longer. Wasn't he?

Unfortunately, something seemed to have inspired the darker side of Mr. Baskin. Far too alarmed to smile, Deirdre waited cautiously. He advanced upon her, his eyes hot and cheeks flushed as he gazed at her loose hair and flimsy attire.

"I've a plan, my darling," he said urgently. "It's so daring and outrageous that no one will expect it, least of all the Beast of Brookhaven!"

Keeping one eye on her goal, the door to the hall, Deirdre held out a placating hand. Where were the servants? Could she reach the bellpull from here?

"I must look a sight. Won't you wait for me downstairs, Mr. Baskin?" No, blast it. She lacked four or five steps yet. "I'll have Fortescue bring us some tea—" She turned in a rush.

"No!" Baskin lunged forward to pull her away from the embroidered strap that swung just out of her reach. He grabbed her arm and towed her toward the bed. "You mustn't alert his servants! They're part of his scheme!"

She tried to pull away naturally. "What scheme? Who?" His grip didn't slacken. She'd sometimes managed to slip away from Tessa by relaxing her resistance for a moment. Putting her other hand gently over where his knuckles went white with the force of his grasp, she let herself down to sit next to him on the mattress. "Please, Mr. Baskin, help me understand."

He leaned close. *"I'm going to save you from Brookhaven!"* His eyes were wild with mingled fear and excitement and his breath reeked.

Deirdre shrank away. "You're drunk, sir!" *You're mad, you idiot!*

Careful. He was on the brink of losing control. She'd fought off enough of Tessa's groping suitors to know that much. If she screamed in this vast house, would anyone hear?

"Drunk?" He wheezed a high chuckle. "No, no, just a little liquid courage, as my new friend says. He's a friend to you, as well, you know. You have many friends."

"Indeed?" She could bloody well use a few right now! Nodding slowly, she tried to peel his fingers off her aching arm. "Mr. Baskin, I fear you do not know your own strength."

He wrapped his other hand about her other arm and she found herself quite thoroughly pinned in his grip. He might seem effete, but she was no match for him still. Seated as she was, she had no opportunity to kick him anywhere useful, so she held that plan in reserve. Perhaps she was in no real danger. This was Baskin. Likely he only wanted to plead his devotion to her again.

Then why did every instinct in her body scream for her to run for her life?

She took a breath and became stern. "Mr. Baskin! Let me go at once! My husband awaits me—"

"That's my plan!" He smiled joyously. "Your husband won't want you after we've consummated our love!"

"*What?*"

"Oh, my love, my beautiful Deirdre—I know you've saved yourself for me!" And he was on her, nuzzling his wet mouth into her neck, pressing her back onto the bed with his weight until she could scarcely breathe.

"*Baskin!*" She struggled, but he simply held her arms down and rendered her helpless. She kicked now in earnest, but he trapped her limbs beneath his weight as he pressed her down. She tried to scream, but her cries were stifled as his mouth came down over hers, wet and disgusting.

She writhed furiously, but she couldn't dislodge him, could scarcely breathe—

Bite him!

Yes—

But her teeth closed on empty air as he flew away from her, landing against the nearest wall with a crash that shook the house.

Chapter Thirty~seven

Calder! "Oh, thank God!" Wiping her arm across her bruised mouth in revulsion, Deirdre scrambled up to see her husband pounding the living daylights out of her assailant, the black rage on his face dangerous to behold.

After the first few blows, which Deirdre shamelessly relished, her fury turned to fear. Calder didn't look as though he planned to stop anytime soon!

Baskin, who had seemed so powerful and dangerous just moments before, now in Calder's enraged hands seemed pathetic and weak, a victim of too much imagination and too little sense.

"Stop!" Deirdre rushed forward to wrap her hands around Calder's raised fist. "You mustn't kill him!"

Calder froze, then turned his head slowly to look at her. She shrank back from his furious, accusatory glare, her hands slipping numbly from his. He couldn't think—"Calder, no—"

"Leave her alone!" Baskin struggled to rise from his semiconscious sprawl. "This is all my doing—she had no idea I'd come up with a plan for us to run away together! She feared she was going to have to stay wed to you forever!"

Deirdre gasped. Baskin's lovestruck protestations weren't helping her case! "Shut up, you idiot!" No, blast it, that only made it look as though she had something to hide!

She turned her back on Baskin and faced Calder. "Please, Calder—you've misunderstood this completely! Baskin—" *Baskin tried to rape me.* That would only get the stupid boy killed outright! "Baskin has had a bit too much to drink. I'm sure that's the only reason why he would try something like that—here in Brook House itself!" Couldn't he see that only a drunken idiot would risk such a thing?

"As opposed to somewhere else, you mean? Your aunt's house, for instance? Haven't you been seeing him for months?"

She drew back. "Wh—what? No, Calder, don't be an idiot—"

His eyes snapped black ice. "I won't be, not any longer at least." He took her by the hand, his grip implacable but not painful. "Fortescue, toss milady's paramour into the street. I have things I wish to say to her."

He turned and strode toward his bedchamber, moving so quickly that Deirdre could scarcely keep up. She tried to pull away, or slow him down at least, but it was as though she were a feather in his wake.

Anyway, why was she struggling? She wanted nothing more than to get Calder away from Baskin and somewhere quiet so she could explain this entire hideous mess properly! So when he attempted to drag her, she simply left her hand in his and outran his long legs, reaching the door before him.

"So sorry to spoil your beastly display," she said, fighting for calm. "I have things I wish to say as well."

He ignored her grumbling and burst through the door into his bedchamber. Argyle looked up in surprise from where he was arranging something manly in some manly fashion.

"Leave us!"

The valet obeyed his lordship's barked command with alacrity and left her alone with her large, looming, furious husband who was convinced she'd betrayed him.

CALDER COULD HARDLY breathe for the pain in his chest, like a tightening band of iron that threatened to burst his heart! His hands shook with it, his very vision was clouded by it—God, she was driving him mad!

Old betrayal, old pain, threatened darkly but was faded to mere shadow by the bright and astonishingly tormenting new sense of loss that swept him.

Deirdre!

He'd thought—hoped—

But what the hell did that matter now? Just like with Melinda, just like with Phoebe, he'd proven unsatisfactory to her and she'd turned to another! It might seem ridiculous to think that puling fop could draw her—but Melinda's lover hadn't been much more than that! When he so obviously had no idea what a woman wanted, how could he hope to keep one?

I want to keep this one. I cannot let her go!

She was here, where he'd longed to have her—in his chamber, in his grasp.

She stood watching him, still bearing the traces of their morning together—or was it the betraying signs of another man's fervent touch? Her hair was down, coiling over her pearly shoulders like golden silk and her lips were swollen by another man's impassioned kisses.

He wanted to toss her from the house. He ached to wrap his arms about her knees and beg her to stay with him. He longed to turn back the clocks an hour and be laughing in her bedchamber with her, blissfully unaware of her wayward nature!

Worst of all, he craved her still.

Though she was still somewhat dressed, Deirdre felt naked before him, her stomach shuddering slightly from the cold and the twining unease and need within her. She did not move or speak now, her saucy words useless against the black lust in his dark eyes. She was about to meet the Beast.

He reached out, but instead of wrapping his hand about her breast, he took the thick rope of her hair and wound it slowly about his fist. She let her head drop back a bit from the weight of it, but he did not pull.

He moved in, close enough for her to feel his erection press to her belly through her wrapper. His dark gaze burned into hers. "What have you done to me, Deirdre?" The question was real, the loss and doubt harsh in his deep voice.

Only love you. Only that. She must be the first, the only one to do so in his entire life, for he had no recognition of it. Melinda had wanted the title, Phoebe had longed for security and safety.

How could she be the only woman in the world to truly see the worth in this man, this noble, lonely wounded creature who had captured her heart across a crowded chamber of inquest so many years ago?

Then again, for all her acclaimed beauty, had any man ever gazed at her the way this man did now, his soul naked and aching in his eyes, asking without words for something he could not name?

He thought he wanted her submission, her body, her dark, soft, wet places to conquer. Any woman could give him that. What she had to offer was her heart.

Calder gazed down at the proud, outrageous beauty who now offered herself so compliantly to him. So beautiful, so soft, and soon so very naked. His cock pulsed so powerfully he felt the dizzying loss of blood to his brain.

She's only trying to distract you. She doesn't want you. She loves another.

God help him, he wasn't sure he cared.

Don't give in.

Give in.

Winning, losing, control and submission—all such thoughts faded from his consciousness. All that he felt roaring through his veins was dark, bottomless *need*.

Right now, more than air or life itself, he needed this woman.

So he took her.

Chapter Thirty~eight

Deirdre gasped as her back hit the wall, then forgot it as Calder's big hard body pressed against her from shoulder to shin. He took her face in both his large hands and kissed her hard and deep, a parched man at the first well he'd ever seen.

She kissed him back desperately, willing him to feel the love in her lips, in the hands that clutched at him, in the body she offered freely. His hands slid down her jaw to wrap themselves gently about her throat, holding her still but not tightly. She arched her neck and opened her lips to him, her trust complete. Master indeed!

The thought excited her deeply, making her tremble, threatening to steal the starch from her spine as his hands roamed further down, over her shoulders to cover her full breasts. The sensation of his hot riding-roughened palms on her already tender flesh sent a new rush of heat to her lower belly. She felt herself throbbing, dampening until her thighs were slick with it.

She slid her fingers into his thick hair and pulled him close to kiss him deeper still, the action grinding her lower body harder into his, but that only made the ache spread. His hands left her breasts and slid back to cup her buttocks and pull her hard into the rigid swelling of his groin.

Then shock chased away the lingering alarm when he bent to hike her wrapper high to her waist, and slipped his fingertips between her buttocks, softly stroking the tender place between. Then he lifted her, his hands supporting her bottom, and hefted her thighs high. She wrapped her legs about his waist and held on tight as he ground his trouser-trapped hardness into her soft, parted groin.

It was rough and harsh and she shook with the pleasure of it, curling her arms about his neck and letting her head drop back in surrender. He could free himself now and take her upright like an alley whore if he wanted—she was fairly sure she wouldn't lift a finger to resist him, unless of course he required help to free himself. She was certain she could manage to lift a finger then.

Yet as thrilling as this clothed play was, she was dying to see the man beneath the woolens once more. As he bent his head to kiss the tops of her breasts, she began to tug at his cravat. The knot was another complicated invention of Argyle's and quite beyond her. She gave up with a growl of frustration.

Argyle must pay.

Later.

Still, she accomplished drawing Calder's attention to his state, for he swung her in a circle to deposit her easily upon the mattress. She fell back on the softness, spreading her arms, urging him on with her eyes as he yanked brutally on the offending cravat. In moments he was down to his shirt, which he pulled from his trousers and yanked over his head.

Deirdre purred with pleasure. Her big handsome husband was a sight to behold, all broad shoulders and rippling pectorals, the ridges in his hard belly contracting as he gazed hotly down at her. She let her eyes rove over him, making no effort to hide her desire. When his hands went to the buttons of his trousers, she rose on one elbow to watch. She would never tire of this part.

Her boldness excited and confused Calder. How could she be so open and free after being caught with her lover? Yet he needed her sapphire eyes gleaming hungrily as she gazed at him. He even slowed his motions in order to prolong her suspense a bit longer.

If she was a wanton, then she was *his* wanton and he was determined to benefit from every moment of her bad behavior—even if it meant he had to lock her away in Brookhaven afterward!

Then he stripped away the last of his clothing and stood before her naked. Her eyes widened when she saw his rigid, jutting cock, fully enlarged this time. He waited for her to protest, to demure, to give any sign that she was the virtuous woman he'd once thought her.

With her gaze still locked on his groin, she licked her lips.

Well, hell. He shut away the disappointment and rode the answering surge in his lust, giving up on the dream woman in favor of the lesser, harlot version. Let her work to please him, then. Let her service him once more before he sent her away.

He strode arrogantly forward to lift her chin with his hand until she blinked, her eyes focusing upon his at last. "Perhaps you'd like to use that lovely mouth for something other than arguing with me?"

She swallowed. "All right," she said faintly, but then

made no move to wrap her soft lips about him. He slid his hand into her golden hair and urged her downward. She bent toward him hesitantly, then stopped. He moved closer, until the thick tip of his cock was nearly at her lips.

Slowly, she leaned forward and kissed it softly. At his murmured encouragement, she opened her lips slightly to tentatively touch her tongue to him, her hot, wet tongue like a lance of fire on his flesh. He flexed without intention, but the motion succeeded in pressing him between her parted lips.

At Calder's groan of pleasure, Deirdre endeavored to open wider to take the swollen head of his member into her mouth, as he seemed to wish. Unsure but curious, she slid her tongue around it, exploring the taste and texture. He seemed to enlarge further and the hand in her hair began to tremble. Relishing such a new-found power, she dared to let his length slide further into her mouth, until she could take no more.

Instinctively, she reached a hand to touch the rest of him, sliding her fingers over him in hesitant exploration. She began to move backward then, forcing a harsh sound from him, making his hand fist in her hair. She froze, then when he did not pull away, she repeated the motion, taking him as deeply as she could, then pulling back, letting her tongue play around him as he slid in and out of her.

He was panting now, his hand heavy on her head as she moved closer, then away, helpless with pleasure in her hands. This must be a very naughty thing indeed, for she'd never heard of it at all. Then again, anything worth doing was worth doing well, wasn't it?

An accidental bit of suction caused a strangled cry to

rip from his throat. She played with this knowledge, letting his reactions tell her what felt good to him, until she could feel his great body trembling.

Finally, he pulled away from her. "My God!" Then he lifted her in his arms to stand on her knees on the mattress, pulled her hard to him and drove his tongue into her mouth, mimicking the motions she'd just created for him.

Her jaw ached and she'd lost a bit of her fervor in that time of experimentation, but his powerful need soon overwhelmed her once more. When he fell with her back down to the mattress, she welcomed his warm, muscled weight over her. When his knee pressed between hers, she parted them willingly, ready to be his at last.

Until his mighty erection pressed hard into her and pain ripped a shrill, surprised cry from her throat.

Chapter Thirty-nine

It was too soon. Calder knew the moment he began to enter her. She was still too sore from this morning.

He withdrew at once, kissing her lips softly in silent apology. Then he worked his way down her curves and slopes, kissing and tasting her creamy skin, her sweet nipples, the salt of her slitted, hidden self. When she gasped and tried to pull away in shock, he held her wrists in a gentle lock and spread her thighs with his body. So innocent she'd never heard of such a thing? After what she'd just willingly done to him?

He pushed such whirling doubts to the back of his mind and slid his tongue between the plump hot lips of her, soothing, stimulating, determined to make her entirely ready for him.

Deirdre lay captive in his grip, flayed by startled embarrassment and aware of a crazed pleasure rising through her from his busy mouth. This was mad—and marvelous—and more than she could bear, oh heavens, the *pleasure!* Lost in the ecstasy of his darting, twisting, restless tongue she gave in, submitting completely, spreading her thighs, rolling her hips, madly panting as each stroke drove her higher to a wild, aching place she'd never been before!

The darkness exploded behind her closed eyes. She dimly heard someone keening high animal noises, but she ignored it as the rippling waves of pleasure swept her thoughts away.

When the world righted itself and her breath returned to her in rasping gasps, he was smoothing his large hot hands back up her body, rising from between her thighs to kiss her breasts and her neck, whispering soothing words as the last shudders still racked her body.

She limply allowed him to wrap her in his arms once more as he pressed his erection slowly into her. This time, he slid more easily in the wetness and relaxed heat of her. Touched, she slid her hands up his arms, relished the corded muscles there for a moment, then moved them down over his wide back, daring at last to cup his rigid buttocks in her palms.

When she relaxed at last, he stroked the hair back from her face to gaze down at her in the dimness. "Is all well with you?"

She melted further as she nodded, suddenly shy again. This man, this powerful, dark, brooding creature—who people called Beast—had not a cruel bone in his body. She curled her arms about him, tucking her face into his neck to hide the sudden dampness in her eyes, for he'd think them tears of pain, not of empathy and aching, bone-deep understanding.

Slowly, he began to withdraw from her, then press deep again. She forced her body to relax into the movement, feeling the tightness easing a bit with every stroke, although she didn't think she'd ever not feel stretched to the limit by his largeness!

Then the tight ache began to be replaced by a sliding, growing ecstasy. She knew this pleasure! Eager now, for it would be a lifetime before she tired of that place of exploding stars, she lifted her hips to take him in, unable to resist sliding her hands back down to those delicious hard buttocks to feel them flexing and thrusting beneath her palms.

She slipped her fingertips between them, just a bit, the way he'd done to her. He hissed a startled breath, but she felt his member swell further and a new tension in the controlled rhythm of his thrusts. She appreciated his taking such care with her, but she was bloody well tired of his everlasting control! On impulse, she squeezed his buttocks hard and bit the rigid muscle wrapping his chest.

The animal roar that erupted from her husband vibrated deep within her, sending up an answering tremor of wildness that emerged as a wordless cry as he lost his grip on that famous control and drove deeply into her!

Lost in her now, he bucked and thrust powerfully, driving into her, forcing guttural cries of maddened pleasure from her throat as she reveled in his wild strength.

Then she fell, or rose—she knew not, nor did she care. All she knew was that this raging vortex of pleasure sent the memory of the exploding stars right out of her mind. She wanted more now, she wanted something darker and harder and so true that the resulting ache would only prove its certainty. No barriers of thought, no walls of prudence or planning lay between her and her man now.

With a final roar, he thrust hard, swelling into her, erupting within her, stretching her to her last fraction of room, driving her pleasure to a new height until she wailed freely at the rapture flooding her.

Then . . . silence but for their mingled gasps and thudding hearts. The dimness enveloped them, protecting the moment, keeping them still and wordless long after their breathing eased and their pulses slowed.

Then she felt him stir and stiffen and knew the walls were rising once more, though he still lay half-hard within her, though her arms still clung to him, though he still held her naked next to his heart. When he lifted his head to look at her, she could see in his eyes that her beloved Beast was caged once more.

"I hurt you."

She sighed. "You did not. I am fine. A little . . . saddle-weary . . . perhaps, but otherwise perfectly well."

He withdrew from her slowly, but her quickly stifled gasp gave the lie to her claim. She was *sore!* He climbed from the bed and strode naked to the washbasin to wring out a fresh cloth. Deirdre didn't let the very attractive view pass unnoticed. She might be sore, but she was not dead!

"I should not have allowed you to shake my control," he said stiffly when he returned. "That was more difficult than necessary."

She could not resist a disbelieving laugh at that. "That was difficult? Were you *there?*" She blushed. "I think I might have disturbed the Tower ravens with my caterwauling!" Then realization made her bite her lip. "Do you think the servants heard?"

He grunted at that. "No. They're paid extremely well to hear no such thing." He reached to cleanse her, but suddenly shy, she took the cloth from him. He did not turn away, however, but lay back next to her.

Then again, it was his bed.

Deirdre swiftly cleaned her thighs, though there was

little she could do about the stain on the coverlet. She looked up to see if Calder had noticed, only to find that he was sound asleep, naked and unwary, the strain of the last weeks clear on his handsome face.

She'd driven him mad, she knew. Mostly it had been intentional. Some of it was definitely mutual. That didn't keep her from being sorry at what she'd put him through.

Tossing the soiled cloth beneath the bed—a childish move, but she couldn't bear to leave it out—she curled up on the bed next to her husband, watching him sleep.

His lovemaking had held a trace of bitterness—or was it hopelessness? She had held him so tightly, but now she wondered if he had felt her arms about him at all.

She would protect him from his own darkness if she could—rip out the years of loneliness and regret and replace them with contentment and joy.

Yet how to make him know that? This man had heard every lie a woman could tell and he'd believed them— once. How was she to make him believe in her now, when she'd done nothing but push him away since she'd walked back into this house as his lady?

He'd damaged her pride. He'd knocked down her expectations as if they'd been nothing but a house of cards. He'd barked orders and given ultimatums without a single care for her opinion. She'd known right then that he hadn't the slightest idea what sort of woman lived behind the perfect face, beneath the stylish gown. She'd loved him from the age of sixteen. He didn't even know who she was.

She stroked the dark hair back from his proud forehead as he slept. "You stupid man," she whispered. "Honestly, I don't know why I love you so."

He didn't love her. How could one love a stranger?

Her first mistake, it seemed, was to propose to him in the first place. She'd done it all wrong, thinking she was so clever—seizing the most vulnerable moment, offering the arguments most likely to win him.

She'd behaved just like Tessa—only worse, because Tessa's motives were always clear, always true. Tessa wanted what was best for Tessa, in the most material sense.

She, Deirdre, had been after bigger game. She'd proposed a heartless union—a lie, for every word had been uttered in the hope of capturing his heart. Now she had no hope of making him see the truth.

So now what to do? She could not turn back the clock. She could hardly go back to that house on Primrose Square, don her virginal gowns and win him through the usual means, the age-old ritual of courtship. A man need not court his own wife!

Unless . . .

She rolled onto her back and gazed intently up at the tester above the bed. Shadows from the dying coals turned the vast room into some primeval cavern, without corners or straight lines.

Coming at her husband sideways had failed her.

Perhaps it was time to try something a bit more direct.

Chapter Forty

A few hours later, Deirdre arrived back at Tessa's rented house, Lementeur's bounty packed and piled upon the carriage roof. She'd not expected to receive such help from the staff, but Fortescue had spotted the bruises Baskin had left on both her arms and gone completely ashen.

She'd begun to protest, but Fortescue held up one hand. "I was here the day Lady Brookhaven died, my lady," he said cryptically. "I know it is possible for even a man such as his lordship to go too far."

When she alighted from the carriage in front of Tessa's house, Sophie had already come out to greet her. "What is this?" The first pile of trunks grew to two. She stared at Deirdre. "Are you mad? Are you in danger? Can I move to Brook House and take your place?"

Deirdre snorted. "Don't you even want to find out if I'm in danger first?"

Sophie shrugged. "Not particularly. Anything is likely better than here, although Tessa is out at the moment."

Deirdre let out a breath of relief. Her stepmother was difficult at the best of times—and this was definitely not one of those! When Tessa learned that Deirdre had left her not-quite-duke husband, she would fly into such a rage that they'd probably lose another entire servant staff!

"Well, that's a mercy, at least." She tucked her arm into Sophie's. "Why don't you show me to my old room?"

Sophie raised a brow. "You've forgotten already? You've been married less than a week." Still, she guided Deirdre to her room and sat beside her on the bed.

"Calder doesn't love me."

Sophie blinked. "Does it matter? I thought it didn't matter."

Deirdre sighed, letting her eyes close for single exhausted moment. "It matters."

"But you thought Phoebe was mad for turning down a marquis!"

Deirdre shook her head, a rueful twist to her lips. "No, I thought Phoebe was mad for turning down that particular marquis. I wanted him so badly . . . loved him so very much . . ."

She shrugged. "I've never had the slightest problem in prompting men to proclaim their undying love. I suppose I thought it was a given that he'd be as mad for me as I am for him." She gazed up at Sophie, trying to blink away the tears that welled forth. "I've been quite thoroughly hoisted on my own petard, haven't I?"

Sophie tilted her head and gazed back without flinching. "Yes, you have." Then she sat next to Deirdre and put a comforting arm about her shoulders. "Yet it is truly sad nonetheless."

Such kindness was the last thing Deirdre expected. She'd never been terribly good to her gawky cousin, although they'd forged a sort of truce when Phoebe had needed their help. Now, that compassion quite laid waste to the last shred of her self-control. She leaned her head on Sophie's neck and cried for Calder and Meggie and her own unhappy ending.

It didn't change a thing, this moment of consolation and support. Calder still despised her, she was still going to be alone for the rest of her life and Tessa was still going to be the most hideous bitch about the entire matter—but it helped all the same. Knowing that she had Sophie and Phoebe to turn to in the world—well, it was more than she'd had since she'd lost Papa and quite possibly more than she deserved.

At last, empty of tears and her pain reduced, for the moment anyway, to a throbbing in her head and a sick turmoil in her belly, Deirdre lifted her head and sniffled away the last of her sobs. "Th—thank you."

Sophie handed her a plain white square to dry her eyes with. "I thought I was going to have to build us an ark there for a moment."

It wasn't that funny, but Deirdre laughed helplessly into the handkerchief. Somehow lighter, though still devastated, she managed to give Sophie a watery grin. "Horrible. You'll have to settle for marks for effort on that one."

Sophie smiled, lending her thin features a flash of splendor seldom seen. "You're welcome." Then she stood and smoothed her skirts briskly. "Now time to get off that lovely arse of yours. You have plans that need making."

"Plans?"

Sophie folded her arms. "Are you telling me that you're going to give up just like that? Haven't you learned anything from those tales I've translated for you? There can be no great reward at the end without first passing some great test. This is yours. You must prove yourself to Brookhaven and win him back."

"Prove myself?"

Sophie reached out to flick Deirdre on the ear like a recalcitrant student. "Don't be a parrot. Now, we must figure out where you went so terribly wrong—"

Deirdre rubbed her ear and grimaced. "Well, I certainly didn't flick his ear!"

Sophie grunted. "Perhaps you should have. Men can be so very thick."

Deirdre narrowed her eyes. "Since when did you become so conversant with the opposite sex?"

"I—unlike some I could mention—am a very quick study. So, did you make yourself available to him?"

Deirdre blushed and looked away. "Sophie!"

"Oh, please." Sophie waved the air. "I was brought up in the country, Dee. I know how mating works. It is only the *social* intercourse that I haven't a clue how to pursue."

Deirdre cleared her throat. "Ah, well . . . yes, I made myself available."

"Did he want you?"

Want was far too pale a word to describe the dark hunger that had possessed him. Lust was too simple and love—well, had love, other than hers, even been present? "It was . . . complicated. Yes, he wanted me." At least for a moment in time.

Sophie's eyes brightened. "Ah! That is excellent. Ambivalence we can work with!"

Deirdre laughed even as she frowned. "What are you talking about, you mad thing?"

Although they discussed it for what seemed like hours, Sophie could come up with no better plan than

Deirdre's, which was to lure Calder into courting her properly—starting over, so to speak.

The conversation began to drift, and then there was the sudden and intense need for sweets . . .

Sophie shook her head and popped another piece of toffee in her mouth. "I used to think how unfair it was," she said around the sweet crunching. "After all, I have the same number of eyes and ears and limbs that you do. I have blue eyes—well, gray-blue, at any rate—and fair hair. Yet the overall effect is so different. . . ." She shrugged. "I always thought things were so much easier for you." She rolled her eyes. "Except for Tessa, of course."

Deirdre snickered. "Oh, yes please, let's except Tessa. Where is my dear stepmother, anyway?"

Sophie took a deep satisfied breath. "Gone." At Deirdre's startled look, she laughed. "Oh, I didn't do away with her or anything, though it crossed my mind once or twice or a thousand times." She leaned close with a conspiratorial grin. "Lady Tessa has taken a *lover.*"

Deirdre simply shrugged. "I can't imagine what took her so long. She rarely goes without."

Sophie's eyes widened. "She was like this when you were young?"

"She was like this within a month after my father's death." Old fury stirred, then subsided. "It doesn't signify. Tessa is an amoral cat. One can only hope that her looks go before her stamina does."

Sophie rolled over onto her back to gaze at the ceiling. "Tessa is so beautiful . . . almost as beautiful as you are."

Deirdre raised a brow. "Thank you. Most people say it the other way around."

"Until she opens her mouth, I'll wager."

Deirdre laughed. "Too right."

"Beautiful, yet so awful. And here you are—beautiful, yet so sad. And here I am, unbeautiful, yet I'm having the most marvelous time . . ."

Her voice faded softly—a little too softly. Deirdre looked up sharply. "Why, Sophie Blake, you've met a man!"

Sophie grimaced. "Hardly. You and Phoebe nabbed the only two bearable gentlemen in Society and I'm not allowed to move in other, more interesting circles."

Still, there rose a faint blush that brought something altogether new to the mix of features that made up Sophie's "unbeautiful" face. She looked . . . pretty? *My, my.*

Whoever he was, he must be quite the fellow to see past the ungainly shyness to find the fine wit beneath. Who might he be? As far as Deirdre knew, the only man Sophie wasn't a complete goose around was—

Oh no. Oh, dear heaven. "Sophie . . . Sophie, it isn't . . . you haven't lost your head over *Graham*, have you?"

"Of course not!" Yet the brief, panicked glance Sophie cast her said it all.

"Oh . . . but *Sophie.* Graham is—" Graham was too handsome, too highborn, too light-minded. The list was long and it led to one certain outcome—heartbreak for Sophie.

The blush deepened. "You needn't worry, Dee. I don't have any illusions about Graham. It would be like he said, a tiger and a giraffe." She shrugged away the impossibility of being loved as if it were no more than an irritating thought.

She was an idiot for thinking she deserved anything less. Damn Graham for teasing his way into Sophie's heart when he wished nothing but a clever playmate to ease his boredom. Now every man who followed, every bookish banker or scholar who might appreciate Sophie's finer qualities, would be seen through the misty glass of first love. Who among them could survive being compared to handsome, charming, dashing in his own useless way Lord Graham Cavendish?

"I'm going to disembowel him," Deirdre bit out clearly. "With a very dull spoon."

Sophie laughed, covering her face in embarrassment. "You'll do nothing of the kind. What's the harm, anyway? He likes me and I make him laugh. I've a new friend and I've a lovely fancy to take away after the season, which is so much more than I came with."

Deirdre wilted in the face of Sophie's wry elation. She was happy now, but she had no idea of the pain in store for her when Graham grew bored and moved on to other, more interesting playmates—which he always did, sooner or later.

"Sophie, it—" *It hurts to be unloved. It leaves one hollow and aching and, oh, so very cold inside.*

She couldn't say it aloud, not with Sophie's eyes softening simply at the thought of Graham, any more than she could say it aloud to herself.

Instead, she smiled and made a long arm to crack two more chunks of toffee from the batch. Handing one to Sophie, she raised her own chunk high. "Then here's to lovely fancies," she declared.

Sophie smiled crookedly and raised hers as well. "And here's to new friends as well."

Deirdre blinked back the mist that rose at the

knowledge that she wasn't completely alone anymore. "New friends, then."

They solemnly clinked the toffee, which promptly crumbled to the coverlet at the impact. They both looked down at the mess in horror, then sapphire-blue gaze met blue-gray gaze.

Their laughter could be heard throughout the halls of the house . . . if there had been anyone there to hear.

Chapter Forty~one

Left undisturbed by his uneasy staff, exhausted by the weeks past, and having found physical release for the first time in a long while, Calder slept through the evening and night, waking early the next morning alone in his enormous bed.

Of course, she would have returned to her own chamber. It was best that way. He would see her again in a civilized manner, a cool morning greeting over breakfast, perhaps a desultory conversation about the weather or Meggie's progress—and then he would inform her of his decision.

The only problem was . . . he hadn't actually made it yet.

To most men of his station, the matter would be cut and dried. Unfaithful wives were banished to the country where they couldn't get up to mischief until they'd borne an heir. Then, if they didn't invite too much ridicule with their "activities," they were allowed to come to town and conduct their affairs with decorum and discretion. That was the way things were done in the aristocracy.

Calder disliked the casual immorality that surrounded him. His own father had sprouted a bastard along with himself, careless of the differences in their futures which had caused the brothers endless pain over the years. Calder had never lain with a married woman, preferring to take his rare pleasure with the occasional widow, and he had always taken precautions against bastards. He would never wish such a future on any child of his.

So what of Deirdre? She'd claimed herself innocent of Baskin's plans, yet he knew she'd entertained the fellow on a regular basis for quite a while.

She had not slept with the blighter at least. So was that scene he'd stumbled on yesterday one of illicit passion or something else? If she'd not been willing, then why not cry rape? She'd even stopped his vengeful beating of the whelp—which, looking back now, he was—mostly—glad he'd not killed the idiot.

Yet there was her daring in the bedroom, her willingness to do things that even now the memory of brought heat to his groin. She'd done them well, but perhaps not actually with skill.

So who was Deirdre: bold, flirtatious but virtuous wife, or calculating creature playing both sides of a dangerous game?

Argyle tapped his way into the chamber with a pot of coffee and a breakfast tray. Calder scowled. "I did not say I wouldn't come down to breakfast."

Argyle busied himself with the tray. "I'm sorry, my lord, but your usual breakfast hour was over long ago. I thought you might be hungry by now."

Calder blinked. "I overslept?" He never overslept! Ever! Since childhood he'd been an early riser with no prompting whatsoever.

He rubbed a hand over his face. He'd been more worn by recent events than he'd realized, he supposed.

He felt a flash of guilt. Had Deirdre awaited him at the table for hours? She would think him angry or disappointed, when he was—well, he didn't quite know what he was yet, did he?

"What time did her ladyship rise this morning, Argyle?"

Argyle made a great deal of noise with the tray. "I'm sure I wouldn't know, my lord," he mumbled.

Calder frowned. His staff knew he disliked evasions. "Argyle, when did her ladyship rise?"

The valet's narrow shoulders slumped. "I would have to inquire of Lady Tessa's staff, my lord, for Lady Brookhaven left the house last evening."

Calder's eyes narrowed. "Left? For a family dinner?"

Argyle looked absolutely miserable. "She packed, my lord. Everything."

She'd left him. *Deirdre!*

This was his fault. He'd lost control with her, so soon after her first time, yet. He'd frightened and hurt her and she'd fled him! Flinging aside the covers, he sprang from the bed, ready to race to her side, to beg forgiveness. Then he halted.

Baskin claimed she wanted to run away and now she has.

Guilt and loss and insidious doubt mingled in a tangle within him. He would not chase another runaway bride, not after Melinda, not after Phoebe.

They wanted pretty words of love, he suspected, words he'd never used. It would be easy to simply say them, truth or not—that is, it would be easy if one weren't Calder. He was never less than completely truthful. His strict code of honor permitted nothing less. So if he was to get his wife back—and he did want her back, for she'd left an emptiness behind her that he didn't want to look at too closely—he must find a way to appeal to her wiser, more practical self.

He'd seen what excess and emotion could do to people, causing loss and destruction. He'd seen where lies and betrayal could go. He would not forgo his own honor, not for anyone, nor could he have faith in people who were less rigidly honorable than himself. He only wished he knew which category his wife fell into. He suspected that the answer was not the one he'd like.

Yet responsibility tore at him. "Was she well, when she left?" Was she in good spirits, happy to escape her dull marital duty? Was she cowering and frightened, fleeing the Beast?

Argyle took too long to answer as he took out Calder's clothing for the day. Then, with a furtive glance at the master's set expression, he caved. "She was in fair shape, my lord . . . but for the . . . the bruises."

Bruises. Oh God, he was a brute, just as the world claimed! He could scarcely recall what he'd done during those lost incandescent, orgasmic moments when he'd taken her hard and fast and—

He covered his eyes with one hand. "Leave me!"

Argyle left speedily and then there was no one left in the room but Guilt, Remorse and Self-Loathing. Those guests, he feared, were here to stay.

MATTERS AT THE house on Primrose Street had gone from relaxed to raging when Tessa reappeared at last.

A crystal dish flew through the air to shatter on the opposite wall. "You stupid cow!" Tessa was ever careful with her beauty, but apparently she'd never looked in the mirror when in a temper. Deirdre had always marveled how someone so beautiful could look so like a gargoyle when angry.

Another valuable dented the wallpaper. "If you wanted a bit of pudding on the sly you ought to have been more careful! And then to leave—what are you thinking? You must go back to him at once!" Tessa demanded between shrieks of rage. "Seduce him from his anger, blind him with lust, make him forget the whole matter! It shouldn't take much to make him forget his jealousy. After all," she sneered, "it isn't as if he actually loves you!"

Deirdre felt the shot of that truth but would never give Tessa the satisfaction of seeing the arrow penetrate. Instead, she gazed at her stepmother with cool disdain.

"That is your maternal advice? To distract him with bedroom acrobatics while I have my 'pudding on the sly'?" Deirdre exhaled slowly. "Really, what was Papa thinking when he chose you to be my mother?"

Tessa's head snapped back and bitterness flared in her eyes. "I should never have agreed to his proposal! First he makes an idiot of himself with those shipping investments, then when the ships go down in a storm, he has the nerve to die and leave me with nothing but his brat to look after!"

Tessa's face twisted with resentment. "I told him not to risk everything, but he insisted that you have a worthy dowry. He didn't want you to have to try for a duke, he said. He wanted you to marry for love!" She spat like a cat. "*Love!* What a ridiculous fool!"

Deirdre didn't retort, too stunned to care if Tessa scored a point.

He wanted you to marry for love!

Papa had not been party to the conspiracy of modeling her into the perfect bait for a duke. Papa had not wanted her to endure the endless hours of "figure-training" and semi-starvation and punishments at Tessa's vicious hand.

That had all been Tessa's idea, in order to win wealth and connections for herself.

Of course it was. Oh, Papa. I'm so sorry I doubted you.

The irony of it was, she had blamed Tessa for the loss of her father's wealth, when it had been herself at the source of it all the time.

Nothing is ever quite what it seems, is it?

Truth was the only constant in this world. If nothing else, all her manipulation and calculation had taught her that. If Calder had spoken the truth about having a daughter, or if Deirdre had spoken the truth to herself about her reasons for keeping Baskin close by, or if Tessa had spoken the truth about Papa's wishes . . .

No, that thread didn't wind, for Deirdre had loved Lord Calder Marbrook, Marquis of Brookhaven, from the very first moment she saw him. From then on, she had trained as diligently as Tessa could ever ask for, for she had one goal in mind . . . to have him for her very own.

And how did that wind up?

She'd ruined everything, of course. Yet, she could not regret aiming her own arrow toward Calder's heart. Should she never feel his touch again, she'd known more happiness with him in her short time as his wife than she ever had. How could she regret that?

Tessa was pacing, her tirade escalating. "What if he decides to dissolve the marriage? Have you thought of that? He has the money to pay the bribes, and he has no honorable reputation to uphold. The man's a scandal three times over! Do you think he'd stop at something like divorce?"

Doubt wormed through Deirdre. Calder was a good man, but he might think himself in the right to divorce her. After all, he needed an heir. What if he didn't believe her faithful enough to produce a true Marbrook?

It was an ugly thought and she didn't think him capable of it—yet the doubt wouldn't dissipate. Tessa was right about one thing. Calder didn't love her. What if Tessa was right about this as well?

"We'll be ruined!" Tessa, when highly wound up, required no actual response. "No one will want you now, and we've nothing left, not a farthing!" She whirled on Deirdre, her lovely face twisted with hatred. "This is all your fault!"

Deirdre nodded calmly. "Of course it is, but really, how could you expect matters to end any differently when I haven't the faintest idea of how to live happily ever after, like in one of Sophie's stories!"

She shook her head, suddenly unbearably wearied by Tessa's self-absorption. "Tessa, since this house was rented with mine and Sophie's money, I think you had better take yourself off to that lover of yours."

Tessa blinked in surprise, then snarled, advancing on Deirdre with her hand raised. "I'll do no such thing! How dare you? I am your guardian, you little—"

Crack! Tessa's head whipped to one side at the force of Deirdre's open hand on her cheek.

"Oh, my," Sophie breathed. "That was lovely."

Tessa scurried backward, her eyes wide over the hands she pressed to her reddening cheek. "You dare!"

Deirdre ran her hand down her skirts, for her palm stung fiercely. "Get out, you nauseating harpy, or I'll drive you out with my own hands." Her voice sounded oddly calm, but her stomach trembled with rage and disgust.

"I'll help," Sophie murmured, but Tessa only had eyes for Deirdre.

"I'm done with you, Tessa," Deirdre continued. "I am a married woman now, so you no longer have a reason to speak to me, or call on me, or wave to me when I pass you in Hyde Park." She stepped forward, but took no real satisfaction when Tessa stepped quickly back. Bullying Tessa made her feel soiled. "*Done,* do you understand?"

Tessa slid a look in Sophie's direction, but perhaps some scrap of common sense remained in her vain and vicious mind, for she did not play the chaperone card at that moment. Instead, she straightened and tilted her head arrogantly at Deirdre, who decided not to notice that her stepmother's hands were trembling at her sides.

"I have things to do, in superior company, mind you, so I shall take my leave for a time." She turned with twitchy dignity and nearly ran from the room.

Sophie came alongside Deirdre and placed a gentle hand on her arm. "She can't leave forever," Sophie said. "It would not be acceptable for me to stay here on my own." Then she gave Deirdre's arm a little squeeze. "But I'd definitely enjoy a brief respite from her 'superior company'!"

Deirdre was too bruised, inside and out, by recent events to give an answering laugh, but she put her hand over Sophie's, wordlessly thanking her for making the effort.

She sighed. "Tessa is the least of my worries at the moment. What am I going to do about Calder? He thinks I'm in love with *Baskin!*"

Sophie shook her head. "Sometimes I think I was better off not knowing any men. I truly had no idea they could be so very stupid." She sighed. "It's quite disappointing, really."

This time Deirdre did laugh, a small damp sound that might have been a sob.

Damn Baskin anyway!

Chapter Forty-two

Baskin strolled jauntily, if a bit stiffly, up to the familiar door of the house on Primrose Square. For the first time in what seemed like forever, the gray skies that followed him had been parted by a ray of golden light. His beloved had left her husband behind!

His new friend—the fellow had told him his name, he was sure, but he could never seem to remember it—had come to his rooms last night where he'd been nursing his wounds and weeping for worry for his Deirdre and informed him that she had moved out of Brook House, trunks and all!

That knowledge had soothed the aches and healed the pains, making it possible for Baskin to eventually rise this morning and make his way here, to where she had taken refuge from the monster she'd married.

Now he tapped the knocker, desperate to see her, eager to plan their future, dying to touch her hand with all the right in the world!

He nodded archly at the disgruntled butler who answered the door. "Good morning. I am here to see Miss—er, Lady Brookhaven."

Instead of opening the door wider and giving

welcome, the fellow only soured further. "Her ladyship is Not At Home."

Baskin scowled. "Oh, for heaven's sake, you haven't told her it's me!"

The doorway narrowed visibly. "Her ladyship is Not At Home."

Something snapped in Baskin, something too long held down, too long kept in check, too often failed and too readily ridiculed. With a snarl, he shoved at the door with both hands, knocking the sour-faced servant backward. Striding past the stumbling man, Baskin entered the house. "Deirdre! *Deirdre!*"

At his shout, she appeared at the top of the stair. "Mr. Baskin! You—you should go."

She was looking around nervously. Why? No one could stop their love now. He started up the stair, but he'd not made one step before she pulled back, her eyes wide and . . . frightened?

"Deirdre? What is it, my darling?"

The other girl, Sophie, came up behind Deirdre and put a hand on her arm, then she glared down at him. "Get out, Baskin."

He'd never liked the scrawny Sophie. Her plainness was an affront to Deirdre's golden beauty. In addition, she was terribly arrogant for someone so lowly and unattractive. He hated the way she looked at him, the same way his father looked at him, as if he were too stupid to draw breath on his own.

He ignored the red-haired girl in favor of his golden goddess. He smiled up at her. "Deirdre, what is wrong? You need not be afraid of the Beast any longer. We can be together now!"

Deirdre stared at him as if she didn't know him. "Mr. Baskin, don't you remember yesterday?"

Sheepishly he fingered the bruises on his face. "He got the drop on me, darling. I'll make better show of myself next time, I swear it."

Sophie snarled, "She means when you brutally assaulted her, you cretin."

Baskin blinked. "No, no, it was magical, our first kiss—"

"Magical?" Sophie held out Deirdre's arm and pushed up the loose lace sleeve. "Do you find this magical, you rotter?"

Baskin recoiled from the black bruises he saw there—right where he'd taken her into his arms—where his hands had touched her—defiled her—

"No!" The word was a gasp, a shout, a plea. He ascended two steps, desperate to make her see. "I would never—I could never *hurt* you! I love you, Deirdre! You're my angel, my savior, you're the light in the dark—"

"You're a rapist," snarled Sophie. "Do not return here or I'll send for the law myself!"

Baskin had eyes only for his love. "Dee—"

She flinched from him. "Do not call me so," she said, her voice low and hard. "Baskin, you have misunderstood every—" She halted and swallowed. "*Everything.* I'm not your love. I'm not your light. I am Lady Brookhaven and I will be for as long as my husband walks the earth. I do not want you to return, do you understand me?" She gazed at him, her stunning eyes without light or laughter. "*Ever.*"

His heart shrank within his chest, leaving only a great emptiness that threatened his very breathing. He gazed at her pleadingly, but there was no relenting in her stare. Defeated, broken and empty, he numbly stumbled back down the stairs to where the butler stood, the front door still open. When he passed the man, the servant snickered vengefully as he rubbed at the mark on his forehead from the door.

Out in the day again, though it seemed the blackest, soulless night, Baskin staggered to the walk as the door slammed firmly shut behind him.

Bruises. Loathing. What had he done? How could he have done such a thing? His eyes burned and he wiped at them, then winced as his fist encountered his sore cheekbone.

Bruises. He blinked. His bruises, caused by that brute Brookhaven. Her bruises . . .

He clung to the thought, the hope, until it became truth in his desperate mind. For some reason, out of fear for his safety, probably—oh, my lovely brave darling!—she'd decided to drive him away. She didn't want Brookhaven to kill him, of course!

He tossed his head back and laughed aloud at the relief flooding him. Then he remembered his mission, his true and rightful purpose on this earth. He was Deirdre's chosen champion. He must free her from Brookhaven's cruel domination forever!

The night receded, the bleakness faded. Life was once again worth living.

THAT EVENING AT dinner, Calder sat across from his daughter at the silent table and tried very hard not to take it personally that she appeared grubby and tattered, her hair a tangled mass, a purposeful streak of soot across her nose.

And she relentlessly kicked at her chair legs the entire meal.

He made no comment, for he had no idea what to say to the child now that he'd driven off yet another mother.

Eventually, she flung her fork down on her untasted plate with a clatter and glared at him. "You buggered it, didn't you?"

Calder put down his own fork, for everything tasted like sawdust anyway, and leaned back in his chair. "I'm not sure. I might have."

Meggie folded her arms. "I heard you, you know. I know you made her bawl."

"Mm." He really must reinforce the walls of this house. Then again, what was the point?

"You made her run away, just like Mama. Maybe I'll run away from you, too. She didn't even say good-bye to you. She hates you."

Another noncommittal grunt.

Meggie lifted her chin. "She said good-bye to me. She said I could visit her and Sophie, at least when the wicked witch isn't home." Then her gaze narrowed. "I saw the bruises, too."

God, had Deirdre stripped naked and posed for the entire household? He wasn't sure where he'd bruised her, but he was fairly certain it was somewhere rather private.

Meggie continued. "Her arms looked like you beat her with a stick!"

Her arms? He'd not grabbed Deirdre's arms, had he? No, he'd taken her hand, he'd filled his palms with her full breasts and he'd definitely squeezed her buttocks—but he could honestly say he had no memory of touching her arms!

Meggie gazed at him with a new hesitance in her eyes. "Did you beat her with a stick, Papa?"

He pushed back his chair. "Excuse me for a moment, Lady Margaret."

He found Fortescue on his way back into the dining room. "Fortescue, where was her ladyship bruised?"

Fortescue gazed somewhere over Calder's shoulder, cold disapproval faint but definite in his lack of expression. "I saw only her arms, my lord, as I helped her into her spencer."

Had it been Baskin, after all? Had the fellow nearly raped his wife in his own bloody house?

Had Deirdre fought him off, but been helpless against him when no one came to her aid? And then he, Calder, had accused her, had misused her—

Passing a hand over his face, Calder blindly made his way back into the dining room and into his chair. Meggie still sat, her little face crumpled with anger. She'd asked him a question, hadn't she? He couldn't remember.

Automatically he took a bite of his food, only to discover that somehow it had become covered in a crust of salt. Meggie glared at him, waiting for him to shout, to punish. A test? Fortescue appeared at his elbow. "Shall I take that, my lord?"

Calder waved him off, never taking his eyes off his daughter's. "No, thank you. It's just how I like it." He forced himself to chew and swallow, then take another bite, watching as Meggie's confusion grew. He didn't know what to say to her—how could a man fix losing the woman she'd come to love as a mother?—but he wanted someone, anyone by God, to trust him!

Besides, he deserved worse.

Chapter Forty~three

Meggie roamed in the gardens, refusing to enjoy them. There were blooms everywhere, but she had no interest in them. All sorts of creatures rustled and slithered aside at this rare passage of anyone but the gardener, but she ignored them as well.

There was Something Going On. It was one of the times that the adults had decided it was better that she not know anything. Even Deirdre had been close-mouthed as she'd packed her things.

"I must go, at least for a while, Meggie. I can't say why right now. It isn't because of you, truly it isn't. I'm glad I came here and met you, sweeting." She came to sit in a chair and gazed into Meggie's eyes. "I think I'm doing the right thing, for us all. I hope—" She'd shaken off the thought with the first false smile she'd ever given Meggie. "Well, you and Mr. Livery will keep each other company for a time, won't you?"

The kitten's name changed every time Deirdre said it. Sometimes it was Little Fortescue—when Large Fortescue wasn't in the room, of course—and some-times it was Foppish McMaster or once the Violent Valet when Dee had discovered teeth marks on her shoes. Meggie tried to think of something clever to call the little cat chasing at her feet, but it was Dee who always came up with the best names.

She went to the place by the garden wall where she could sometimes hear the neighbor's servants gossiping. There was a little bench there next to a statue of a man with goat legs that she liked to climb on to listen better.

There was a piece of paper fluttering from the goat-man's wrist. Meggie pulled at it, only to discover her name on the outside. "Lady M."

"Dee!" Meggie plunked down on the bench to read it, sounding out the florid script with difficulty. Oh. It was from that man, the one Dee liked to visit with, the one who had told her about the chipped mantel.

"Lady Margaret, if you'll come to feed the swans with me in Hyde Park today, I'll tell you all about your dear mother and why your father is to blame for what happened to her—and to our dearest D. Your friend in secret, Baskin."

D. Dee. Meggie thought about the black and blue marks on Dee's arms and how her father had never answered her question at dinner and how the mantel in her mother's—Dee's—room was chipped, just like the man had said.

Hyde Park was nice. Patricia had taken her there just the other day and they'd had ices and fed bread to the swans in the long skinny lake. It wasn't far at all.

She folded the note into a tiny square and shoved it deep into her pocket. No one was watching her, for Patricia had gone with Deirdre.

She looked up at the cloudy sky, but she couldn't tell if it was early or late. One could never see a proper sky in London. She'd already had dinner, so it must not be very early. If she didn't hurry, Mr. Baskin might not wait for her.

She looked down at where Silly Cat—it was the best she could do—rolled belly up in something damp. Moments later, the kitten wandered into the kitchen alone, mewing for the milk he knew the cook would give him.

In the meantime, Meggie was nothing but a fluttering coat and short legs moving fast in the distance.

"MEGGIE! MEGGIE, COME out this instant!" Calder knelt to peer beneath Deirdre's bed. No skinny legs, no fierce scowl. Worry began to clutch at his gut. The servants were tossing the house upside down, attic to cellar, front gate to privy, but so far there was no sign of his child.

Meggie was angry with him—furious, to be exact. She missed Deirdre and she was simply too young to understand. Not that he understood all that well himself.

She would go to Deirdre. Yet it was a long, treacherous way to that neighborhood, with plenty of opportunity for danger both accidental and more sinister. The cart traffic alone was deadly to the uninitiated! He wasn't even sure if Meggie knew the way, for she'd never been to Primrose Square in her life.

Knowing his stubborn child, that might not be enough to stop her from trying. He strode from the room. "Fortescue!"

Fortescue popped up, breathing heavily and dust-smudged, but prompt as always. "Yes, my lord?"

"Have my carriage readied." Would it be faster to simply send a groom? No, for he'd want to keep an eye out on the way. "I'm going to check at Lady Tessa's."

Fortescue's eyebrow rose. "Indeed. Good thinking, my lord."

"In the meantime, have the staff search the garden."

"They already have, my lord. Twice."

"Then make it thrice, Fortescue. She must be somewhere!"

It was only moments before his carriage came around, but still he chafed at the delay. The night was gathering quickly and the thought of his child alone in the lawless city at night brought his fear to a place he never knew existed.

Damn him, if he had been less worried about his own heart and more worried about his daughter's, less bound by his own stupid standards of honor, he would have done anything to bring back the stepmother she loved so much.

If he lost Meggie now as well . . .

Though he searched the streets carefully on the way, he saw nothing of her. Once at Primrose Square, he bounded down from the driver's seat of the phaeton and was pounding on the door in an instant.

Lady Tessa's incompetent butler answered at last. "You're fired," growled Calder as he pushed past the man. "Meggie! *Meggie!*"

"You can't fire me, I don't work for you!" The man faded before the glare Calder turned on him and stepped back, muttering, "Blighters pushin' in the door, bellowin' for ladies . . . Oy, we don't have no Meggie here!"

Calder ignored him. "Meggie!"

Deirdre came running, her skirts in her hands, Sophie close behind. "Calder? What is it? What's happened to Meggie?"

He could see on her face that his daughter had never

made it to this house. Icy terror stole his breath. "Oh God, Deirdre . . . she's gone!"

As her arms opened, he fell into them, their difficulties forgotten as she held his trembling body close to hers.

It was Sophie, ever practical, who disturbed the moment. "Lord Brookhaven, you must widen your search perimeter. If we gather everyone at Brook House, we can begin a systematic search."

Sophie spoke his language. The solid, practical words pulled him from the pit of terror and gave him something real to do. He straightened, though he did not give up his grip on Deirdre. "Right. Sophie, gather the staff here and get them over to Brook House. Deirdre, get a warm cape. We'll take another route back and look for her as we go."

"Oy, milord . . . am I still fired?"

Calder didn't spare the humbled man a glance as he passed him. "Not if you find my daughter."

Chapter Forty~four

Once Calder and Deirdre had arrived back at Brook House, they immediately sent the servants out on Sophie's "widened perimeter search." Calder had scarcely shut the door on the last footman when the knocker sounded.

They answered the door together, in a rush, for Fortescue had already taken charge of the search. There was a grubby fellow at the door, holding out a folded piece of paper. Out of habit, Calder tossed the fellow a coin from his weskit pocket as he unfolded the sheet. The man disappeared before Calder had even begun to read.

"If you wish your child back unharmed, you will bring Lady Brookhaven to the crossing in Hampstead Heath by midnight. We will exchange them, along with your promise to dissolve your unconsummated union immediately. Bring no one else. Baskin."

Calder stared at the paper. Kidnapped. He'd not even thought of it. Meggie was rebellious, angry. His only thought was that she'd run from him, just like her mother.

Just like Deirdre.

Deirdre. He turned on her. "Your lover still wants

you." He thrust the note at her, his fury and fear overwhelming.

The confusion on her face was plain, then she read the note. "Oh, my God. Oh, Meggie!" She turned to him urgently. "Calder, Baskin is a madman. He's dangerous!"

Calder gazed at her, his eyes narrowed. "Is this a ploy to frighten me into conceding? It isn't necessary, you know. I could easily have this marriage dissolved. It would be costly, and neither of our reputations would ever recover from the scandal, but you'd have your lover and I'd have my daughter back."

Deirdre snapped her fingers before his face. "Calder, listen to me! There's no time for your jealousy! I'm telling you, Baskin assaulted me in my bedchamber yesterday. He climbed the bloody *tree,* for pity's sake! His mind is going, I tell you! He thinks we're in love, that I can save him from the darkness or some such babble—" She shoved up the sleeves of her gown. "Look what he did to me!"

Calder looked. The bruises of legend were indeed something to behold. Very clearly, the shape of a man's hand was outlined in purple and black on each of her upper arms. Calder slowly reached out his own hand and covered them gently, matching finger to finger.

His hands were too large to have made them. Somewhere inside him, beneath the gibbering fear for his child, relief welled up that he'd not harmed Deirdre thus.

Then the cruelty of those bruises struck him. "So much force—you were fighting him, weren't you?"

"Of course I was fighting him, you stupid man! It was as if I swatted at an elephant with a handkerchief. He's out of control, I tell you!"

So, just like that, his wife was returned to him—but his daughter was still gone, somewhere in the dark, in the hands of a madman. If he'd had faith in Deirdre, he would never have lost her. Pity something that simple wouldn't bring Meggie back.

Deirdre realized it as well. "You're thinking of doing it."

He took the note and folded it carefully. "I have no choice but to go to meet him, but you'll not come with me." He turned away. "Fortescue, prepare the phaeton. I'll drive myself."

She stepped before him, protesting, "I must come! He's expecting me—and I can talk to him. He'll listen to me, he loves me."

Calder reached to stroke his fingertips over the bruise on one arm. "Did he listen to you yesterday?" He moved past her. "Fortescue, her ladyship will wait here. Is that clear?"

"Yes, my lord."

"Calder, what are you going to do?" She tried to press past Fortescue, who simply took hold of her skirts with one hand. Deirdre pushed at him, trying to twist away, but the butler's grip was steadfast. "Calder! *Calder!*"

Chapter Forty~five

In his small but respectable house in London, Mr. Stickley woke to a pounding upon his door.

He sat up abruptly, alarm chasing through him. "Is it fire?"

Then he recognized the sodden howling from outside. "Stiiiiii—" *Hiccup.* "Kleeeey."

Eyes narrowed in disapproval, Stickley left his comfortable bed and went to his door to let his drunken partner in before the neighbors sent for the watch.

Wolfe hadn't been to his home in many years, perhaps not since their boyhood. "What do you mean by this?"

Wolfe grinned at him. "Gotta game waiting, ol' Stick. All out, I'm 'fraid." He leaned forward. "Can't stop now—I'm in the middle of a lucky streak."

Stickley sniffed. "Then why are your pockets empty?"

Wolfe shrugged. "Need a bit to tide me over until the next turn of the cards."

Wolfe stank of spirits and women and other unwashed amusements. Stickley drew back. "I don't have anything here!" This wasn't precisely true. What might have been more precisely truthful would have been, "I don't have anything here for you!"

It wasn't surprising that a practiced sinner like Wolfe

saw through that feeble lie. He advanced on Stickley, his gaze flashing from amiable drunk to dangerous in an instant.

"I need that coin, Stick. I'm owed, after what I've done for us this past week."

"What have you done?"

Abruptly Wolfe's mood swung again. "Saved the Pickering caboodle!" he crowed. "Lady Brookhaven won't be the Duchess of Brookmoor. Can't be a duchess if you don't have a duke!"

Stickley, who had been contemplating simply handing over a small portion of his emergency nest egg, just so he could get back to sleep—without having Wolfe's malodorous self passed out on his fine carpet, thank you—drew back warily now.

"You didn't kill him?"

Wolfe blinked and put one hand upon his chest in mock offense. "Me? Why, I could never do such a thing!" Then he snorted. "But Lady Brookhaven ought to have been more careful who she flirted with. Lovestruck young men do tend to take drastic measures!"

Stickley went cold. "Brookhaven is *dead?*"

Wolfe shrugged. "Don't know. I suppose we'll find out tomorrow, won't we?" He belched then, his face taking on a greenish tinge.

"What precisely do you have to do with this matter?"

Wolfe's gaze went glassy and distracted. "Not a thing, not a thing. It's all that young Baskin's doing. All he needed was a bit of guidance from someone with more . . . life experience."

Stickley backed away. "Where is Baskin now?"

Wolfe giggled. "There's a party on Hampstead Heath tonight," he sang. "A spot of murder and then a pretty little wedding, all at the point of a pistol! 'A sacred place,' " he mocked in a reedy voice, posing his hands in an effete manner, " 'Where we can announce our vows before the gods themselves,' etcetera, etcetera. I tell you, Stickley, that boy might be a lousy poet, but he's got a real imagination for crime!"

No longer quite so worried about his carpet, Stickley hurried to the desk in his tidy little study and pulled a small sack of gold from one of many such hiding places. "Here." He tossed the bag at Wolfe, who caught it easily, not even drunkeness likely to make him drop his coin. "Now go on to your game."

Stickley shut the door on a suddenly gleeful Wolfe, then turned to his wardrobe instead of his bed. He only prayed he wouldn't be too late to stop matters from turning dangerous!

CALDER DROVE THE phaeton as quickly as he dared, for the midnight hour was fast approaching. The city was far from empty—the carriages of the rich were transporting from ball and musicale to late supper. Out of Mayfair, there was less traffic and he allowed the horse its head, the phaeton tilting dangerously on the corners.

Once on the deserted plain of Hampstead Heath, he slowed, letting the horse pick its way with care. "The crossing" was where Baskin had said to meet him. Two roads intersected in the Heath, if one cared to call them roads. They were more like earthen tracks, created by picnicking commoners and drunken rowdies coming and going.

Then, ahead in the limitless blackness, he saw a man

standing by the road with a lantern and a small bundle on the ground at his side. Baskin.

The man waved the lantern at him, stupidly, Calder thought, for there was no mistaking him at this point. He didn't see Meggie anywhere—

As he drew nearer in the phaeton, the bundle lifted its tangled head, revealing a white face. Baskin, the bastard, had tied his tiny daughter in a sack!

"I'm going to kill you," murmured Calder beneath the creak of the wheels. "For Deirdre's bruises and for treating my child like a kitten you want to drown. I'm going to kill you with my bare hands and then I'm going to resurrect you just to kill you again."

In the rear of the phaeton, behind and somewhat under the seat, in the spot where one might stow a picnic lunch if one were on a drive with one's lover, Deirdre braced herself in the unpadded space.

Fortescue had watched her climb the stairs to her room, but he'd not set a guard on her window. The climb down the blasted tree had been harrowing, and she was quite sure she'd scandalized several squirrels with her gown rucked up to her waist, but she'd managed to reach the waiting phaeton before Calder.

Now her body ached beyond imagining. She'd been knocked about rather thoroughly when Calder had been driving fast, and more than once she'd nearly given in and called out to him to stop.

Now, as the phaeton, normally a rich man's plaything, slowed to a stop, she took advantage of the creaking to fling herself bodily from her prison.

Once on the ground beneath the phaeton with her sleeping limbs tingling to wakefulness, she crept forward carefully, listening.

"Free my child at once!"

"Not a chance. She's a biter," Baskin said disapprovingly. "Really, Brookhaven, you ought to see to your unruly brat."

Calder made to swing down from the seat. Baskin raised his hand from where it had been hidden by his coattails. A dueling pistol glinted dully in the lamplight. "I'll thank you not to presume, Brookhaven."

Then Deirdre saw Meggie in the sack and wondered at Baskin's fearlessness. Didn't he realize that he was already dead? And when she was done with him, she promised herself she'd give Calder a moment with him as well.

Meggie, however, seemed to be taking matters quite well. She looked grubby and tattered, but then she usually did. She also seemed monumentally bored. "Hi, Papa," she said calmly. "Bastard's a liar."

Baskin turned on the child in a fury. "Show some respect, brat!"

She shrugged inside her sack. "Sorry, *Mister* Bastard."

Baskin aimed a kick at the bundle and Meggie cringed.

Calder couldn't bear it. He leaped down and started forward. "You wanted Deirdre, Baskin!"

Baskin looked up, his kick unfinished. "Yes! Where is she?" He peered at the carriage. "She isn't with you!" In his fury he aimed the pistol at Meggie.

Calder's blood turned to ice. He held up both his hands. "She's just down the road," he lied. "I left her there because I didn't trust that you'd bring my daughter."

Baskin lifted his chin. "Well, I am a gentleman, Brookhaven. I keep my word."

The idiot's oblivious smugness underlined his madness as nothing else could. This fellow had no idea what he was doing. He was obsessed with Deirdre. Nothing and no one would convince him that Deirdre didn't want him just as much in return.

Calder doubted that telling Baskin that the marriage had been consummated would accomplish anything but to madden him further.

This was not going to end well, he saw now. Reason was useless, as was bribery. The best he could hope for was to save Meggie. There wasn't much hope of saving this stupid boy as well.

So be it. Calder wasted no time dithering. He took a step forward, his hands still held up.

Baskin jolted at his movement. "Stay where you are!"

Calder moved slowly but he continued to move. "You have the pistol, not I. You can hold it on both of us more easily than one."

Baskin blinked but could find nothing wrong with that logic. He sneered then. "Deirdre said you were all that is efficient and mechanical. That's why she doesn't love you, you know. You're as cold and cruel as ice."

Calder knew the young man was deluded and let the sting of the truth pass unremarked. Meggie was all that mattered. If he could get between her and the pistol, he could take the single bullet that lay within. He might even survive it, though that mattered very little at the moment.

Thank God he'd left Deirdre safely at home.

Deirdre began to move backward, away from the phaeton, into the deepest shadow. If she could get around Baskin, she could distract him while Calder overcame him. She was very fond of this plan.

Her second plan, formed in the last few seconds, was to give herself into Baskin's possession voluntarily. He felt himself to be a gentleman. She might be able to persuade him to allow Calder and Meggie to go free.

She was not fond of this plan at all.

Now if Calder would just stop moving . . .

"Halt, damn you!" Baskin's cry was shrill but all the more frightening for it. Deirdre froze and the tableau before her, framed in lantern light, froze as well. It was Calder who faced the pistol now, but Baskin had moved to stand just behind the bagged Meggie, so the child was still in just as much danger as before.

For the first time, Meggie seemed to be showing fear. She was hunched small, her sack-covered hands covering her face. Only her wild curls showed above the crude sacking. Poor little one. Poor wee frightened—

Then Deirdre got a glimpse of what Meggie had in her mouth. The child was chewing the cord with all her might as her gaze flickered this way and that, keeping an eye on proceedings.

Deirdre longed to signal her, but she would only endanger them all by doing so. Better that she stay concealed and work her way around . . .

She stumbled on a stone, sending it rattling into some others in the darkness.

"What was that?" Baskin cried out in alarm. "Who goes there?"

On instinct Deirdre dropped flat, hiding her pale face and hair beneath her darker-clad arms. She waited, her lungs too frightened to expand, willing herself to sink into the soil and disappear entirely.

Calder took advantage of Baskin's distraction to

move forward several quick steps. When the young man whirled back around after searching the darkness behind him, Calder was as he had been—only slightly closer. Too bad the idiot hadn't fired a wild shot into the darkness. Once that bullet was fired, Calder could mow the slighter fellow down with one blow.

And this time he wouldn't stop.

The breeze picked up, the cool air coming at Calder's face and Baskin's back, but Calder ignored it—until he saw something pale and wispy flutter into the circle of lamplight.

A narrow bit of ribbon, pale blue and shimmering, now fluttered from a twig just behind Baskin—a ribbon that he himself had purchased for Deirdre's hair not two days ago!

Dear God, she was here! The valiant little maniac must have secreted herself in the phaeton and now planned to do something incredibly stupid!

He must keep Baskin from seeing the ribbon. The fellow had been obsessed with Deirdre for months. It wasn't possible that he wouldn't recognize it.

Then the ribbon let go its tentative hold on the twig and whirled along the ground, flying to Baskin as if he'd called it to him!

Meggie must have seen the growing horror on Calder's face, for she twisted her head about to see what was coming behind her. His darling conniving daughter took one look at the oncoming ribbon, made a tiny sound of surprise, then proceeded to fall over—

Directly onto the pale strip of silk that now lay just in front of Baskin's right foot.

Baskin looked down. Calder started talking fast.

"I know you want to trade for Deirdre, Baskin. Why don't you let me take Lady Margaret now? Then we'll all ride back down the road and I'll give her to you."

Baskin's eyes narrowed. "Is she really there?"

Calder shrugged. "Of course she is. I would give anything and anyone to get my child back. After all, I only met Deirdre several weeks ago. I'm not all that attached, to tell you the truth. She's lovely, but I really wanted someone more . . ." He couldn't think of a thing, damn it! God, if he'd ever needed to be glib and persuasive, it was now!

"More *efficient*." It was Meggie, a little sideways but definitely still in the match.

"Absolutely." Calder nodded vehemently. "Deirdre is perhaps the least efficient woman I've ever met. Illogical, impulsive—really, we don't suit at all. I'm sure she'd be happier with someone more . . . poetic."

For a moment, it looked as though for once in his life he'd said precisely the right thing. Baskin was looking more convinced, even calmer.

In fact, when he looked back up at Calder this time, there was a firm decisiveness in his bland face that Calder had never noted before. "In that case," Baskin said slowly, as he raised the pistol and took fresh aim at Calder's heart, "I suppose I'll just kill you now."

Calder's heart sank then, for he realized the truth. He'd underestimated the young man entirely. Baskin had never meant to drag Deirdre through a prolonged and public annulment scandal. How much more efficient to simply turn her into a widow.

He'd fallen right into the trap, allowing his concern for Meggie and Deirdre to cloud his perceptions. He'd moved closer and closer as well, making it very nearly a sure shot, no matter how ill-practiced the gunman!

He watched helplessly as Baskin cocked back the hammer and tightened his grip on the trigger. His only comfort was that Deirdre lay in the darkness where she could help Meggie, now that he'd been so stupid as to allow himself to be removed from the game.

The barrel of the pistol gleamed darkly sinister in the lamplight, the black hole seeming to grow as Calder watched Baskin's ink-stained fingers tighten slowly.

"*No!*"

A cry, a fluttering blue whirlwind, a sharp *crack!*—

And Deirdre lay on the ground between them, gasping and pressing her hands to the blossoming red patch on her side.

Chapter Forty~six

Deirdre!

Calder lunged toward her fallen figure, but Baskin reached into his shirt and pulled forth the dueling pistol that matched the first. "Get back from her, you beast!" Baskin waved the second pistol wildly. "This is all your fault! Look what you made me do!"

Calder would have ignored the wild pistol threats if they hadn't included Meggie. His daughter lay curled up on the ground, her eyes wide and horrified as she stared at the blood coming from Deirdre.

Baskin knelt at Deirdre's side and awkwardly patted her face. "My love, my heart—what have I done? Speak to me!"

Deirdre grasped his hand in one of her bloody ones. "Baskin, it's over," she gasped. "You must let us go. I need a physician. Just put the pistol down and let us go."

Baskin twitched. "No! I need you with me! I—" He stood, pulling Deirdre awkwardly to her feet. She cried out, but when Calder moved toward her, Baskin trained the pistol on Meggie once more.

"Even trade, Brookhaven," Baskin called out wildly, his voice breaking. "Take your sniveling brat then." He backed away, toward the phaeton, his arm holding

Deirdre tightly. She went with him, barely able to stand, but cast a look over her shoulder at Calder.

He stood there, unable to help her, unable to leave Meggie alone, torn into agonized bits as he watched Baskin drive away at high speed, reckless in the night, Deirdre nearly unconscious at his side.

Then he ran to Meggie. It took several moments to wrench loose the knots that held her tied, but then she was free and in his arms. He held his little girl tightly, his cheek on her hair, her skinny little knees poking sharply into his side. She clung to him for a long moment, sniffling as her scrappy bravado faded away.

Then she pulled her head back to gaze at him. "Papa, is Dee going to die?"

He didn't have an answer for her. Sickening worry had taken the place of a regular heartbeat. All he could do was to swing Meggie up to ride on his shoulders, grab up the lantern Baskin had left behind and take to the road. Baskin had headed farther into the Heath. Though it killed him to do it, Calder took the other direction.

There had been a few places of commerce and spirits edging the Heath down this road. He needed to get Meggie to safety and he needed help to search for Deirdre.

God, Deirdre! Hang on! Please hang on!

BACK AT BROOK House, Sophie paced the floors, her long legs scissoring endlessly over the same piece of carpet.

Fortescue had not returned. Neither had any of the rest of the devoted Brookhaven staff. Only Patricia remained, for she'd been meant to tend both Sophie and Deirdre in their time of need.

Except Deirdre wasn't here. She'd gone to her room, only to disappear. Sophie had paled, thinking about what the climb down the tree in the dark must have been like, but since there was no broken body next to the trunk, it seemed Deirdre had made it safely down.

To go where?

Sophie knew where she would be—following Lord Brookhaven to Hampstead Heath to find Meggie—which only made the worry worse within her.

Patricia brought her another pot of tea, but Sophie only waved it away. "Patricia, I think you ought to go out and find the staff. They should all go to Hampstead Heath to search."

Patricia, as she had several times in the last hour, stood firm. "His lordship told me to stay here with you, miss. I'll not leave you alone with madmen running about!"

"Madmen? What madmen?"

Both women whirled at the deep voice to see Graham standing at the door, his evening clothes showing the signs of a night well-spent.

He stepped into the room, concern on his face. "What the hell is going on? I was on my way past when I saw all the windows lit up. I walked right in. Where's that intimidating butler? Where's Brookhaven?"

Sophie was so glad to see him that if she hadn't been so preoccupied, she might have been appalled. She barely kept herself in check, for she'd have liked nothing better than to dampen his broad shoulder with her worries.

She clenched her twined hands together instead. "Little Lady Margaret's been kidnapped. Brookhaven and Deirdre have gone to Hampstead Heath to find her.

The rest of the staff is still out searching London, for the ransom note came after they'd set out."

Graham blinked. "Brookhaven and *Deirdre?*"

Sophie grimaced. "Brookhaven didn't know she was following him."

He rubbed his face. "I should hope not." He looked about the silent house for a moment. "What now then?"

"Now we find Lord Brookhaven," said a reedy voice at the door. Mr. Stickley, the solicitor, stood there clad in a wrinkled coat and untied shirt. "For the whole thing's a deadly trap."

After he'd briskly related what he knew, Sophie was only more confused. "A sacred place? In Hampstead Heath?" She turned to Graham. "What is he talking about?"

Graham worked his jaw, thinking. "There's nothing *on* Hampstead Heath. It's just a wild place, a picnic spot. There's no church there, not even a chapel."

Stickley nodded. "I concur. If I'd recognized a location I would have gone there instead, but the Heath is miles of nothing."

"Pardon me, sir . . ." Patricia stepped into the conversation. "Did he say a church exactly?"

Stickley's brows rose. "No, not exactly. But if he wants to marry her once he's made her a widow—"

Patricia held up a hand. "Excuse me, please. I'll be right back—" She was gone in a flutter of dark skirts and flapping apron, only to return in moments, breathing hard. She pushed some sheets of paper into Sophie's hands. "I took these—yesterday—from the grate—" She blushed. "I didn't think they were wanted—and I needed some readin'—don't want to dirty his lordship's books—"

Sophie flattened the wrinkled sheets. "It's Baskin's poem." She glanced up at Graham. "The one he gave her." He gazed back somberly. He felt as she did, she knew, that they ought to have seen Baskin's madness and desperation sooner. Comforted a little, she looked back down at the script in her hands.

"There's a bit right there," Patricia said, leaning in and pointing. " 'Sacred places,' he says."

" 'I shall steal you away to sacred places,' " Sophie read aloud. " 'And upon Bodicea's breast I will sing my love for the moon to hear me.' "

"Oh, my God," breathed Graham. "Bodicea's Barrow."

Stickley blinked. "Oh, yes. Of course. That makes perfect sense, doesn't it?"

Sophie twitched. "Translate!"

Graham shook his head. "No time! I'll tell you all in my carriage. Come along, now! You, too, Patricia. If Brookhaven's been attacked, we might need many warm bodies for the search."

Chapter Forty~seven

Each jolt of the racing phaeton ripped at Deirdre's side like a fiery knife. She was terrified of the speed in the dark, terrified of this crazed new Baskin and terrified at how much blood seeped from her with every passing moment.

She pressed her hand hard to the hole in her body, praying that Baskin would be thrown from the speeding carriage and land on his head.

"Don't worry, my goddess! I'll get you there in time!"

Get her where? "Baskin, I need a physician. I'm badly hurt."

"Our love will heal you, you'll see! I'm proof of that!"

She leaned away from him, her thoughts whirling and useless. She didn't even know where they were. She'd never been to Hampstead Heath in her life, for Tessa thought it common, preferring the elite crowds at Hyde Park.

The darkness was so complete that she didn't know how Baskin could see the road before them with only the jouncing carriage lanterns to guide them.

Then the wheel hit something that wasn't road and

Deirdre got her wish. Unfortunately, she was also flung from the carriage, landing hard on the grassy bank.

Her breath left her lungs and her head swam, but she struggled to rise and run away, into the dark, anywhere where the madman who'd shot her couldn't find her!

Then hands came out of the dark. "There you are, my dear. Come, it isn't much farther now."

He pulled at her. She sagged back, unwilling to leave the frail safety of the road in his company. "I'm injured, you idiot! I'm shot and now I'm quite sure I've broken my ankle!"

His hands traveled down her. She pushed at them, but he was only trying to feel her ankle. "Nonsense, my pet. It is only a bit twisted. Here, I'll help you."

He dragged her unwilling to her feet. Where did he get such unfailing strength? Did he burn within with madness, like one of Calder's relentless steam engines?

He looped her arm over his shoulders and more or less dragged her off, stopping to pick up one of the fallen carriage lanterns that still burned dimly.

She had to try, although she didn't think he'd listen. "Baskin, I need to tell you. I love my husband."

He only laughed. "There's no need to pretend now. You're well away from him. I didn't manage to kill him for you, but he'll never find us now." He smiled at her, a childish, blissful smile. "I know you're only trying to save me from him, my brave love."

She shoved at him. "I don't love you, Baskin! I never did!"

His smile disappeared. "Stop. Don't say it any-more."

His grip slipped and she took advantage of the moment to pull away, though she staggered weakly. A wave of dizziness struck her. When had it grown so cold? She pressed a hand to her head.

"I . . . I don't love you, Baskin. You're nothing to me. Less than nothing. For God's sake, man, if I'd wanted you I could have married you anytime before I became engaged to Brookhaven!"

He shook his head. "No. You were forced to wed him. I've seen your aunt bully you. She made you do it."

Deirdre laughed shortly. "You cretin, *I* proposed to *him!*" She wiped the back of her hand across her brow. "I've loved that stubborn idiot for years. It broke my heart when I thought he'd marry my cousin."

Something in her voice seemed to pierce his delusion at last. He gazed at her as if he'd never seen her before. "But . . . you saw how I loved you. You saw and you smiled to see it! What sort of monster are you, that you would toy with me so?"

It was insane that she should feel guilty at this moment, yet she did. "I thought . . . I didn't think. I'm so sorry that I caused you pain. I didn't mean to, but neither did I take care. Manipulating people—it's all I know, all I've been taught."

His breath caught, the pain audible in the sound. "You—you don't love me, do you? I can see it now. God, what have I done? I'm ruined! I ruined my life for you and you gaze at me with nothing but pity—damn you, I don't want pity! Love me, damn you—love me!"

He grabbed her and crushed her to him. The pain in her side made her gasp. The world went white, then gray, almost fading to black. *No. You must stay alert. You must not let him steal you away any farther . . .*

She came back to herself to find she was horizontal, her head cradled in Baskin's lap, his hand in her hair, stroking back the strands from her face. His touch was shaky, jerky. She opened her eyes to gaze into his whitened face.

"I've killed you. Oh God, I've ruined everything. I've killed you, and now Brookhaven will kill me, and rightly so. I deserve to die."

Dimly she saw him raise the pistol.

No. She meant to scream. She might have whispered. Either way, it did nothing to stop him.

The flash blinded her. Hot ash sprayed her face and the explosion made her ears ring.

Oh God. Her head swam. Weakness seeped through her bones. Willing herself to move, she could only roll away from Baskin's limp form until her face smeared into the cold damp leaves on the ground.

The clean smell of wet earth finally replaced the stink of gunpowder as she counted her breaths. At ten, she pushed herself up on her hands, disregarding the sting of the cold ground on her abraded palms.

She did not look at Baskin. She did not want to see what she had wrought with her manipulations. She was not the only one who had done wrong here. She was not so pure as to take that on—yet she could not ease the hard regret that filled her belly.

Baskin had been disturbed and lonely and not very bright. She had used his adoration as a sop to her tweaked vanity. He was not a good man, not an honorable one, but he had been worth more than that to someone.

Of course, the fact remained that he thought their simultaneous deaths would be some sort of poetic, romantic end.

He truly was an idiot. Or perhaps he was merely so immersed in fantasy that he expected to be saved magically at the last minute. Now the poor, deluded fellow was dead and no one would ever know.

You cannot take it back.

You can only take it onward.

Yes. She must find her way out of this wood, back to the road where someone could find her—eventually.

She pushed herself to her knees, then rose to her feet, steadying herself with one hand on a tree trunk. The dark was nearly complete. Baskin's lantern had gone out when the shot was fired.

Broken, too, she could smell the kerosene. Another night, she might have been able to allow her eyes to get used to the light of the moon or the stars, but there was nothing but the blackness and a drizzling rain now.

Her clothing was soaked. She shuddered, her knees going weak. God, she hoped it was only water.

Chapter Forty~eight

Calder strode along the road, Meggie on his shoulders. He'd tried to run, but she couldn't keep her grip. The best he could do was to walk fast, his racing thoughts spurring him like thorns.

He'd lost Deirdre because he'd judged her too harshly. So sure of himself, so sure everyone else in the world lacked his own moral fiber, so ready to be judge and juror and hangman. People were flawed. His father was flawed. His brother was flawed.

He himself outshone them both. He'd judged his brother unworthy of Miss Phoebe Millbury and had stepped in to claim her for himself, despite knowing his brother's feelings perfectly well. He'd isolated Meggie because she didn't live up to his exacting standards. He'd imprisoned his bride of only hours because she didn't meet his absolute approval.

And yet Deirdre was the one who'd never betrayed him, who would never betray him. He knew that now—now when it might be too late!

Dear God, don't let it be too late!

Desperation coursed through him. He ached to undo, to replay, to turn back the hands of the clock, to be a different man who would cause a different course of events—

Miraculously, he heard the rattling wheels of a carriage approaching them. He swung Meggie down and then stepped out into the road to wave it down.

It creaked to a halt just before him, so close he could feel the hot breath gusting from the horses.

The driver tipped his cap up. "You lost, guv'nor?"

Before Calder could answer, a shriek came from inside the vehicle. "Humbert, how dare you stop! He could be a highwayman! Drive over the rotter if you must!"

Calder held his hands wide and approached the side of the carriage. "No, please! You must help us! My wife's been kidnapped. If you let us on, we can catch them still!"

A round, angry face framed by a silk turban appeared at the window. "We'll do no such thing!" The woman shook her finger at him. "We want nothing to do with such matters, do we, Harold?"

Calder tried to put on a soothing mein. "Please, madam, sir! They are only moments ahead but if we delay—"

"Humbert, drive on!"

The driver raised his hands to snap the reins, then he halted, his eyes wide on Calder. Or rather, what sat in Calder's grip, black and shining and deadly. It was Baskin's spent pistol, which he scarcely remembered tucking into his shirt. Calder regarded it with some surprise himself. That had been entirely too easy to do.

"Oh, dear," he said mildly. "It seems I'll be taking the carriage after all."

There came a muffled squeak from the general direction of Meggie. Calder sighed. All those hours of etiquette lessons, gone in a flash. Oh, well. There was no help for it.

He waggled the pistol at the occupants of the carriage. "Madam, sir, out you come."

The small wiry man helped his large gasping wife from the vehicle. Calder looked at the driver. "I fear you'll be coming with us, my good man. I'll give you fifty pounds if you'll do so willingly."

The woman shrieked. "Humbert, you wretch, it'll be the end of you if you do!"

The driver looked at the couple with a slight smile, and then back at Calder, his grin widening, and nodded. "I'd have come for five."

The small man paled further. "You—you cannot mean to leave us here alone! Why, it might be days before someone else comes this way!"

Calder looked at the driver. "Is that true?"

Humbert shrugged. "Might be. The weather's turnin'. Not much call to come this way when there's mud for a road."

Meggie folded her arms. "Can't we leave them, Papa? The lady's voice makes my teeth hurt."

Calder glanced at the couple. They were ill-suited to last more than an hour on their own. "What if they don't survive?"

Meggie shrugged. "I'll bet no one likes them anyway."

Humbert grimaced in agreement.

When Calder still hesitated, the woman shrieked in rage. "You horrible man! You wouldn't dare! What sort of father are you, to commit such a crime!"

Calder rather doubted that the woman was truly concerned for the state of Meggie's moral character. "It cannot be helped," he replied shortly.

"You should be ashamed of yourself! You're a horrible influence on the child!"

He grinned at his daughter, feeling fierce and free and hopeful for the first time. She grinned back at him, a matching light in her eyes, so like his. "It's quite the other way about, you know."

He tipped his hat at the couple. "So be it. You'll stay here. I'll send help, once I've accomplished my mission." He swung Meggie into the carriage and clambered aboard. "Drive on, Humbert!"

It didn't take long, going at speed, to catch up to his phaeton, for it lay abandoned in a ditch. Calder and Meggie leapt from their carriage and examined the broken phaeton, but it was empty—

Except for a great deal of blood.

They have to be close by, for Baskin can't get far carrying Deirdre, but the Heath is so large and so dark, they could be anywhere!

They needed manpower.

Driving fast, Humbert had them at the outskirts of the Heath in moments, but it seemed like hours. He ordered the driver to stop at the only sign of life, a grimy public house that still seemed to be serving.

He had no choice but to leave Meggie to watch over the carriage. He didn't think the driver would disappear without his fifty pounds, but he could not afford for the man to escape and call the watch down upon him. The consequences for tonight's madness would come eventually and he would face them gladly—if he had Deirdre by his side.

The outrageousness of leaving a nine-year-old to hold a grown man at the point of a pistol faded next to the thought of bringing her with him into this scabby, stinking cesspit of humanity. A child shouldn't even know places like this public house existed.

The noise—composed of drunken male shouting, drunken female shrieking, and drunken puking from both sexes—forced him to give up on any civilized form of communication. Oh, well. In for a penny, in for a pound.

He leaped to stand on the most crowded trestle table, casually kicking mugs of stale ale into the laps of the unsavory clientele. It was likely the closest they had come to a bath in months, so he counted it as a favor to the world in general. He hefted one of the tipped mugs, then threw it across the room to shatter against the stone fireplace. It exploded loudly enough to catch the attention of all but the most cataleptic sots.

"Oy!" The innkeeper, identified by an apron that ought to have been burned for violations of basic human cleanliness, strode forward. He was a big fellow, nearly as big as Calder himself. He was backed by enough men that the sheer poundage would be enough to defeat Calder's desperation and fighting skills. Then again, he could be quite the bastard when he drank. He swept up another mug and drained the nasty ale in one swallow. Then gagged.

Bloody hell. "Bloody hell." It felt rather relieving to say it out loud. He tried it again. "Bloody fucking hell." He wiped his mouth. "This swill isn't fit for fucking pigs."

The innkeeper reddened. "Toff bastard. Let's teach 'im what for, lads!" The mob, well-lubricated by swill-ale and general hatred for the Quality, moved forward en masse, surrounding the table.

Bloody hell.

Calder jumped high and grabbed the beam overhead with both hands. He took out the innkeeper with two bootheels high in the chest and then swung himself up to stand on the beam, bracing himself with one hand on the ceiling. Dirty, sweating, upturned faces swirled beneath. He saw a pair of eyes just like his own . . .

Meggie.

"Bloody *hell.*"

Meggie frowned up at him. "What're you doing up there?" Her high voice piped clearly above the murderous mutterings of the crowd. "I thought you came in to get help for Dee."

The surly rabble turned as one to gaze in astonishment at the tiny, well-dressed girl-child in their midst. She glared back at them with equal or perhaps even superior surliness, but they were a hardened lot and scarcely seemed to notice. They had no idea who they were dealing with—a fortunate thing, for Lady Margaret Marbrook, daughter of a wealthy marquis, would make for a fetching bit of kidnapping—witness the reason he was here in the first place!

"Meggie, up!"

She didn't hesitate but clambered right onto the table he'd emptied with his ill manners. She stood and reached her hand high. He dropped to his knees on the wide beam and swept her up beside him before any of the scum realized what she was about.

Meggie balanced calmly next to him and surveyed their situation with no apparent fear of the height. "You've buggered it now, Papa."

"Yes, it would seem so."

She patted his arm. "Don't worry." She reached into the puffed bodice of her little dress and pulled out the pistol.

He reached for the firearm, but she pulled it out of his reach. "Wait . . ." She gazed up at him soberly for a moment. "Papa, do you trust me?"

God, she couldn't do any worse now than he had. And she was right. They *were* buggered. He nodded. "I trust you."

She grinned evilly. "Just pretend you're . . . well, not you. All right?"

"I think I can do it. I've been practicing," he said seriously.

She patted his arm again. "I'll help you." Then she turned to face down into the pub. "Oy!" she shouted. Again, her clear childish soprano cut through the noise like a fine knife through privy-muck. The mob gave her their surly attention.

She waved the pistol. The attention grew more sullen but the room quieted somewhat. "We need men to search the Heath. You've all just volunteered."

The innkeeper was still down, so the second largest man took it upon himself to be the leader of the mob. "Who're you t'be tellin' us what to do? You're a child."

Meggie laughed rudely. "I'm not a child. I'm the meanest pygmy you've ever met."

It was so ridiculous that it would have been laughable—if the dwarf hadn't been waving a gigantic pistol with complete ease. There was something rather convincing about cold steel and gunpowder.

The man, who also seemed to be the mental giant of

the crew, came up with what he thought was a vital point. "Yer wearin' a little girl's dress."

Meggie widened her eyes gleefully. "Stole it, I did," she growled. "Right off'n the little girl I killed with this very pistol!"

Calder closed his eyes briefly in apology to anyone who had ever tried to get Meggie to speak properly. It was going to be a long road back to propriety after this. Then he joined in—in his own voice. "She did. I saw her. She killed several people, actually. She killed the man I stole these clothes from. She kills often. I think she likes it." He glanced down at his little daughter in her stockings and tiny buttoned boots. "She wears the dress to make ladies think she's lost—and then she robs them."

Meggie shot him a glance of respectful appreciation. He nearly took pleasure in it, until he remembered it was for spouting atrocious untruths. She grinned down at the men. "So, who wants to try me aim first?"

The big fellow shifted restlessly as his gaze flicked about him. Now that he'd taken up the job of spokesman, he seemed to realize that this also made him something of a target. "Well . . . what you searchin' the Heath for anyway?"

"My—me sister," Meggie replied. "She was took by a man—a bastard toff—and he's hidin' in the Heath."

The man rubbed his unshaven chin for a moment. "I had me a sister once. I reckon I'd want to find the toff what took 'er."

The man next to him snickered. "Yeah, so ye could hit the blighter up for a quid!"

With a swing of his giant fist, the spokesman struck down the wit standing next to him without so much as glancing at him first. Then he gazed up at Meggie and Calder. Calder could almost hear the clockworks grinding away in his head.

"Say we find the toff and yer sister—you say you been out robbin' ladies. What you got to trade?"

Desperation welled up, choking Calder. God, they were wasting too much time here! He pulled his purse from his pocket and jingled it. "Gold. We stole gold from the ladies. You can share it all if you find my—her sister. I have more elsewhere I can give you after."

Meggie closed one eye and aimed the pistol directly at the big man. "Or you can die now."

Damned if she didn't sound completely serious. Calder hid a slight shudder.

The man held up both hands. "No need for that, missy—er, ma'am. Why, we'll be 'appy to 'elp, won't we, lads?"

The ridiculous story, the pistol, the gold—Calder didn't much care what had convinced the lot of them to try. He simply took the gun from Meggie, swung back down to land feet first on the table and reached to catch his daughter as she flung herself trustingly into his arms. Unwilling to put her down in the milling herd of heavy boots, he put her on his shoulder. She wrapped her hands under his chin to hold on.

"Come on, then! Quickly now!"

They left the inn and went into the night, an army of the unwashed exhorted to speed by the curses of a little girl who was very nearly a princess of the realm.

The unlucky innkeeper and the half-wit were left on the floor to sleep off their misfortune.

Chapter Forty~nine

When Graham, Sophie, Stickey and Patricia reached Hampstead Heath, they found it alive with men and torches. Before they could ask for Lord Brookhaven, Sophie and Graham were captured—a sister and a toff, right?—and dragged before Calder.

He turned from his torchlit search to blink at them both, then at Stickley and Patricia, who had warily followed behind. "What—"

"Bodicea's Barrow," Sophie blurted, smacking away the hands that held her. Surrounded by rough men, her worst nightmare come to life, she didn't know whether to scream or laugh hysterically. The only thing that mattered was to find Deirdre, but she could scarcely make her mouth form words!

She felt Graham take her hand in his, a warm link to someone safe. Her heartbeat steadied. "Baskin's taken her to Bodicea's Barrow—his sacred place! It's in all his poetry!"

Calder's eyes lit with hope. "Yes, of course! Everyone, to the Barrow!"

"Oy," the man holding her protested. "I'm not goin' there!"

Other protests came from all around them. "It's a

grave, ain't it? We orn't goin' to step on no grave at midnight!"

Calder had no time for such nonsense. With a quick look of gratitude toward Sophie—beautiful, brilliant Sophie!—he grabbed the spindly, swaybacked mount of the man nearest him and swung astride it. He kicked the protesting man aside with one boot.

"Stealing your horse. My apologies." This crime thing was becoming a habit.

The barrow was a mound in the southeast portion of the heath. Whether Queen Bodicea of old was truly buried there or not, legend had her bones lying there for hundreds of years. The mound was large, with a copse of full-grown trees on top. Calder knew that the superstitious believed that Bodicea walked the earth at night, bemoaning her betrayal and the betrayal of her daughters.

At that moment, he didn't bloody care.

The night was complete and moonless. Calder finally had to pull his mount to a fast walk, for the poor beast had no stamina and the path was not easy.

At last he found the barrow—and at the top, he saw the faintest gleam of a light, like a lantern nearly out of oil.

Calder flung himself from the horse, hitting the ground and scrambling on all fours to reach her. She lay a few feet away from a body—Baskin's—but Calder only had eyes for her still white form.

Just as he was about to pull her roughly into his arms, Graham ran up with a fresh lantern in hand. The sight of so much blood soaking through her gown froze Calder in mid-reach.

"Oh, Papa, she's bleeding so!"

That small horrified exclamation rang through the sudden silence of all those gathered around the still pale body on the ground.

Calder reached a trembling hand to brush the fallen golden hair away from that lovely, marble face. Her skin chilled his fingers.

Deirdre wasn't hurt. Deirdre was dead.

Calder's breath left him. *Lost.* All that fierce pride and vulnerability, all that shimmering beauty and defiant loyalty, gone forever—because of *him*.

Slowly, carefully, as if she would shatter in his hands, he drew her into his arms. "Oh, my beautiful darling . . . don't leave me, I beg of you. Don't leave me . . . alone."

"Papa . . . are you crying?"

Tucking Deirdre's cool face into his neck, he pulled her onto his lap, sprawling awkwardly in the dirt and dead leaves. In the circle of watchers who stood in the lantern light, no one moved a muscle as they watched the great proud man heave rasping sobs of heartbreak into his wife's flaxen hair.

Chapter Fifty

Deirdre opened her eyes to find herself in a creamy satin heaven. That is, if heaven contained slightly grubby, dark-haired urchins who glared at her from the foot of the bed.

"You're supposed to be dead."

Deirdre blinked and very carefully laid her palm to the wound in her belly. The pain radiated outward, pulsating through her until she wondered faintly why she wasn't screaming. "I think I wish I were," she rasped.

Meggie narrowed her dark eyes and folded her arms. She looked bloody annoyed. Knowing from whose loins the child sprang, Deirdre guessed that the little girl was actually desperately worried.

She tried to smile. "I'm all right." She didn't feel all right. She felt shaky and chilled and weak—and the hole in her body seemed to be larger than it once was. "They took the bullet out?"

Meggie scowled. "I wanted to keep it, but Papa made me leave the room."

"That's too bad," Deirdre said faintly. "How terrible for you."

Meggie dropped her pose and picked at the coverlet with her well-chewed nails. "The physician did it."

"Better he than Fortescue, I suppose."

Meggie didn't look up. "He said you might die anyway."

Suddenly Deirdre no longer wished an end to her pain anytime soon. "I showed him, then."

Meggie continued her fascination with the stitching on the coverlet. "I could be your little girl . . . if you wanted."

Deirdre tried to smile. "Meggie, I'm happy to hear that, but I'm really very tired—"

"Since you can't have any babies now."

Ah. It seemed she'd only thought she knew pain before. Now the real agony seared through her. She closed her eyes against it, but she was too weak to fight the small aching sound that escaped her lips. No children of her own.

She'd been so vain and stupid, thinking of saving her figure and her social ambitions, determined to put off the dreariness of childbearing until the last possible moment.

A vicious punishment indeed, but perhaps not entirely undeserved. After all, she'd been careless with Meggie, hadn't she? She'd let Baskin in this house, endangering Meggie and destroying her own never-born children simply so she could sop up his puppyish devotion.

The scar across her belly would be large and ugly, she could tell. Her body was marred forever now, the perfection upon which she'd based her entire existence now erased. She didn't care one whit. She'd willingly bear scars all over her body if she could only be whole within.

She was barely aware of Meggie quietly slipping down from the mattress. She ought to stop the girl, reassure her, be what mother she was capable of being— but the weakness made her too slow and Meggie was gone by the time she opened her eyes.

The bed was a lonely cold sea about her, the richness of the satin and silk chilly against her heated skin. She had a fever, she realized dully. It seemed she might die after all, as the doctor had said.

She gave it a try, just for a moment. She tried letting go, willing herself to fade away, willing her heart to stop pumping the blood that still seeped from her wound. The silence grew until she could hear that rebellious heart, still beating loud in her sensitized hearing. It was no good. She'd spent her life in the fight. She hadn't a clue how to give up.

So, then—if she couldn't give up, how was she to go on?

Calder . . . oh, God, Calder must know by now. The physician would surely have let the marquis know that his hopes for an heir were dashed. She'd failed him again, it seemed.

Poor Calder. It was really too bad that she'd not died. Now he was saddled with a scarred, damaged, barren woman whom he didn't actually like very much. If he had it to do all over again, she wouldn't be his sccond choice, she'd be his last one!

Tears leaked from the outside corners of her eyes, running down to trickle into her ears. She preferred to cry into a pillow, but she was too sore and weak to roll over! That pathetic thought tipped the scales until the tears swelled to a torrent, until she had to press hcr palms over her mouth to mask her raw sobs. They never seemed to end, racking her aching body and sapping her inadequate strength. She didn't even realize the moment when crying became sleeping once more.

CALDER ENTERED THE grand chamber of the marchioness and walked silently across the thick carpet to gaze down at the slender, frail treasure he'd placed so carefully in the center of the huge bed. She slept still, but when he stroked his fingertips down her cheek he wanted to believe that the fever was less.

A chair awaited him at the bedside. He sank into it without needing to look, for he'd spent many hours there already.

His fingers were damp from her face. Had the fever broken? Did she weep in her unconscious state?

She didn't know. She couldn't. He'd made sure that it hadn't been spoken of outside his study. The physician had whispered it to him as if imparting a shameful indiscretion.

"There's damage, my lord. More from removing the bullet, though it had to be done. Women are delicate beings. Even a bad blow to that area could make her barren . . . but a bullet? I fear there's little hope she'll ever be able to conceive."

Calder had listened and nodded in automatic response to the man's solemnity, but all he could think was "She's alive!"

He didn't give a damn if she didn't give him an heir. He was too bloody busy not howling with joy that he was sitting here beside her, not standing by her grave!

She mustn't know. Oh, he might have to tell her someday, if she fretted at their lack of children, but for now and the years to come, he intended to make sure she was too happy to care overmuch. They had Meggie and he'd be perfectly willing to raid the nearest orphanage to fill the house with children if she wished. He fancied he had a knack for crime.

Anything she wished. Anything at all, if she would only open her blue eyes and speak to him again.

She slept on, her hand small and limp in his.

Chapter Fifty-one

The next time Deirdre woke, feverish and fretful, it was to find Sophie sitting next to the bed, ready with a soothing word and a practical touch.

Her thoughts still fogged, Deirdre struggled to remember something very important. She'd been shot. She remembered the fiery brand of the impact. That was bad. Meggie was safe. That was better. Baskin was dead. That was best not thought about yet.

Then she remembered the worst. With a gasp, she reached for Sophie's hand. "The doctor said—oh, Sophie! No children!"

Sophie unwrapped her hysterical grip and then patted her hand soothingly. "I heard that Patricia heard that Meggie heard the physician tell Calder that." She took up a cloth from the nightstand and smoothed away the fever sweat from Deirdre's brow. "Physicians, you know, are just as fallible as anyone else." She snorted. "Or more so."

Deirdre blinked, not willing to hope so easily. "Wouldn't he know if I'm damaged or not? Do you think he could be mistaken?"

"Why not?" Sophie shrugged. "I've never put much stock in physicians. Cook's herbal concoctions seem every bit as helpful as anything the doctors ever give m . . . my mother. They've been dosing her for years and it hasn't done her a bit of good. Neither the leeches nor the dosing, come to think of it. Yet I've seen farm hands heal from the most terrible wounds, when all they've had are poultices and teas." She put the cloth back in the lavender-scented water. "I don't think anyone knows the future. Who is to say what is possible or not?"

Deirdre lay back on her pillows, her thoughts circling that single statement.

Why not?

Then she turned her face away. "Where is Calder?"

Sophie didn't reply. When Deirdre rolled to face her, the tall girl glanced away. "Lord Brookhaven has many duties."

Well, that was hardly a surprise . . . and yet, she was surprised. Did her sickbed not require his presence, at least for a short visit?

Apparently not.

Sophie stirred. "Deirdre, perhaps I should tell you. Calder is—"

Deirdre lifted a hand to stop her. "I don't want to talk about him."

Shaking her head, Sophie tried again. "Deirdre—"

"I'm quite serious. Do not speak of him."

Sighing, Sophic admitted defeat. "You're tired. Do you want me to leave?"

Deirdre closed her eyes, feeling the overpowering pull of dark, evasive sleep. "Stay," she murmured. Then she forced her eyes open to lock gazes with Sophie. "Don't tell him I asked for him." She gripped her hand. "Promise."

Sophie shook her head. "I promise."

Just as Deirdre gave in and darkness came to claim her, she could have sworn she heard one last word from Sophie.

"Idiot."

WHEN CALDER RETURNED from the ordeal and side-show that was poor Baskin's funeral, Fortescue awaited him in the entrance hall with a dry surcoat and a piece of toweling.

"I didn't suppose you'd want to take time to change before you checked on her ladyship, my lord."

Calder pressed his wet face into the towel and let out a harsh breath.

"Was it very bad, my lord?"

Bad? It had been dreadful. The world had come out to see the tragedy in three acts that was the life and death of one stupid, unbalanced boy in love. Baskin himself had fired the bullet that had caused his death, but Calder knew that the tale being told all over the city had at least three versions where he had pulled the trigger, several where Deirdre had done it, and a few circulating that held Meggie as the murderer. To stand beside the white-faced and rigidly mournful Baskin family and withstand the scrutiny and whispers while the poor lad was lowered into the ground . . .

"It was not a good day, Fortescue." He rubbed the towel over his dripping hair. "Why does it always rain at funerals?" It had rained when he'd buried each of his parents, and Melinda as well, come to think of it.

One wife buried, one fiancée fled, one bride nearly killed. The only constant in all that was him. He shook his head.

"I have no talent for marriage."

Fortescue raised a brow. "On the contrary, my lord. You very carefully and decisively chose your brides for all the wrong reasons. From the first it was clear that you and the previous Lady Brookhaven weren't going to get on well. I ought to have warned you, but it wasn't my place to do so."

Calder grunted. "Warned me that my sweet, demure fiancée was a whore? I don't suppose I would have listened."

Fortescue gazed at him pityingly. "Lady Melinda wasn't a whore, my lord. She was merely a young woman who loved a man and was thrust into marriage with another man."

Something inside Calder cleared, like silt running away to leave a stream sparkling and pure. He lifted his gaze to meet his butler's. "Like Phoebe."

Fortescue nodded. "Indeed, my lord. You do have a talent for choosing women whose hearts have already been stolen. Perhaps because you yourself have no desire to possess those hearts?"

Possess those hearts? No. Not Melinda's. Not even Phoebe's.

Deirdre's.

His hands slowly tightened to fists. Not in rage, but in longing. Deirdre's heart was what he desired, more than he'd ever desired anything—Deirdre's proud, stubborn, fiercely independent heart, which she'd offered to him like a gilded treasure and which he'd spurned like a soiled rag.

Oh, my darling. What have I done?

Sophie had the answer to that question, when he passed her on the stair.

"Essentially, my lord, you fulfilled her worst nightmare of a husband. I don't really think you meant ill by it. You must have worried that she was like Tessa—and one can certainly see why—but have you truly thought about what it must have been like to be raised by a woman like Tessa? A woman who cared nothing for her, a manipulative bully who only saw her as a means to an end?"

"Like me, you mean." He ran both hands over his face. "Oh, damn."

Sophie put one tentative hand on his arm. "I think— I think it must have been quite awful, really. She doesn't talk about it, but I've seen bruises—" She shrugged. "Deirdre seems very strong, I know. I once despised her for it, thinking her hard. It is an armor, really, against Tessa, against the world that left her in the hands of a woman like that. Underneath, I think she is very vulnerable and perhaps a bit lost as well."

Calder let out a breath and gazed at Sophie for a long moment. "I think all the Pickering granddaughters are a bit of a surprise beneath the surface."

Sophie blushed and glanced away. "I don't suppose I can bribe you to keep that quiet?"

Calder grunted. "Who would I tell?" The only person he longed to speak to was Deirdre, but what could he say to atone for his suspicions?

Sophie folded her arms, one eyebrow raised at his morose tone. "I don't feel terribly sorry for you, you know. You are entirely too intelligent not to realize that having brought this on yourself, you must be the one to make it right."

"But how?"

"I don't know how, but I have a suggestion as to

'when'." She tilted her head and quirked a smile. "Deirdre is finally properly awake, with no fever. It broke less than an hour ago."

Calder's fists tightened on a surge of overwhelming relief. *Thank God.* Beset by the desire to be near his wife, he turned his back on Sophie's knowing chuckle and took the stairs two at a time.

Chapter Fifty~two

Deirdre was sitting up in the bed, her face drawn but not flushed with fever or pale with blood loss. She was a tangled, unbathed mess and she had never looked more stunning.

Calder approached the bed with slow steps. "Good evening, my lady." Damn! Too stiff and formal! He tried again. "You look very nice."

She shot him a disbelieving glance. "Don't mock me. I feel awful." She tried to adjust her position, then winced. He rushed forward to help, but she held up a warning hand. "Stop. Don't touch me."

At a loss, he backed away a step. "Do you want me to fetch Sophie?"

Deirdre closed her eyes, shaking her head. "Heavens, no. I just got rid of her." She waved at the chair. "Please sit down, Calder. You're looming."

When he was seated, he leaned forward to plead his cause. He took a breath, but hesitated, unsure of what to say. *I love you. I need you. Love me always.* How could he, when he didn't deserve her? Blast, he hated being so unsure of himself! When things truly mattered to him, he had no words!

Then it was too late. In the moment of his strangled muteness, she spoke first.

"Calder, I think it's plain that we aren't going to get on well in this marriage."

Pain. Tearing, breathless agony. He was not to be forgiven. Dimly he realized that he hadn't made an actual sound. It was only his heart keening wordlessly and unheard.

"I've decided to reside at Brookhaven," she went on, her tone dull and lifeless, yet like steel beneath. "Phoebe will be there with Rafe, but I'm sure the house is big enough for the three of us. Meggie may come stay anytime she likes."

Meggie! That was the way through! Even as an inner voice warned him not to, he played that card. "I wed you to be mother to Meggie, not distant aunt."

"That shameful prod won't work," she said flatly. "Meggie needs you more than she needs me."

The gaze she turned Calder's way shocked him to his very core. The bold, outrageous woman he knew was gone. In her place was someone cool and hard and distant. Not to mention scornful.

And leaving him.

It is an armor, really . . . against the world that left her.

That was how she saw him, as a male version of Tessa. He was her worst nightmare come to life. How could he hope to overcome such rigid distaste?

Deirdre waited for his response. Not that it mattered, she reminded herself. She'd given up. She had wed a man who didn't love her and now she had to make the best of it.

She very likely owed him her life, but saved was one thing.

Loved was another thing altogether.

"I see," he said slowly. "I cannot ask you to reconsider?"

"Reconsider," like a man bargaining for a horse or a trinket. She uttered a hoarse bark of laughter. "Why should I?"

He nodded. "Of course." Then he stood. "I should let you rest. We'll . . . we'll resolve the details later." With a bow, he turned away.

Don't go! Don't nod and agree! Stay and fight, damn you! Fight for me!

Calder, it seemed, only fought for his machines.

At the door of her bedchamber, he paused, then turned to speak over his shoulder. He did not meet her eyes. In fact, he'd hardly met her eyes for the entire conversation.

How was she to know what he was truly thinking if he didn't meet her eyes?

"I spoke to Baskin's family," he said gruffly. "You should know that his lack of stability was not your doing. He was always prone to bouts of melancholy. This was not even his first attempt at self-murder. It was simply his most successful."

Deirdre thought about that for a long moment. Then she let out a slow breath. "Thank you, Calder. That . . . helps."

With that, he was gone. She leaned back on her pillows and closed her eyes. There. That was done. She'd made the most practical, intelligent decision. She'd chosen self-preservation over certain heartbreak. What could possibly be wrong with that?

It was a persuasive argument, yet somehow that didn't stop the tears from leaking out beneath her lashes and streaming down her face.

AGAINST THE PHYSICIAN'S orders, Patricia's worried pleas and Sophie's glum predictions, Deirdre was on her feet the next day. Unable to bear the noise of their protests, she finally threw them all out of her bedchamber, with the exception of Meggie, who seemed to share the outrageous notion that Deirdre should get up whenever she felt like it.

Now, slowly and painfully, her shaking legs carrying her on sheer will alone, Deirdre was packing for Brookhaven. Without any real chance of completing the job by herself, the act was more symbolic than anything, but she had to try.

The fine gowns from Lementeur she would leave to Patricia's capable hands. There wouldn't be much cause to wear them on the estate, but Deirdre couldn't bear to waste such exquisite work.

The ruined blue one, however, she packed herself with great care and a few secret sniffles.

"I've never seen Papa cry . . ."

Deirdre turned to gaze at her empty bed in astonishment. "Well, why would you, for pity's sake!" A man like Calder, weep? She shuddered to think what catastrophe might cause such a shattering of that stone-walled keep.

". . . until he found you dead on the ground."

The sheer will that was keeping Deirdre's knees locked and her spine straight left her on a single sharp exhalation.

"He wept . . . for me?" She sank into the chair that had materialized next to her sickbed sometime in the last week.

Meggie crawled partially out from under the bed and propped her chin thoughtfully on her knuckles. "We didn't think he would ever stop." Her eyes were wide and filled with awe at the memory. "But then you went like this—" Meggie demonstrated a harsh inhalation. "And then things happened awfully fast."

Deirdre stared down at her hands where they lay folded limply in her lap, unsure what to think of this stunning bit of information. "He felt guilt, I suppose."

Meggie rubbed at her nose. "For what? He didn't shoot you."

Deirdre twined her fingers together. "He takes a great deal too much responsibility for things. He is a man of honor and integrity."

Meggie grinned, a flash of pure evil in her pretty, childish face. "I don't think Lady Turbantop thought so when he played highwayman and stole her carriage so he could chase down Baskin."

Stole? Calder? *Highwayman?*

Deirdre gazed at Meggie in amazement. Meggie's grin faltered.

"Oh, blast," she muttered. "I wasn't supposed to talk about that." She started to inch back under the bed, but Deirdre sank to her knees on the floor and gently captured one long black braid in her fist.

"Meggie, tell me everything or your belly will never wrap itself about another piece of my toffee for the rest of your sticky little life."

Chapter Fifty~three

"By God, I have had *enough!* Enough, do you hear me?"

Shocked, Calder jerked his head up from his miserable contemplation of some facts and figures he couldn't have cared less about. In an instant he was out of his chair and across the study. "You little fool!"

Deirdre was braced in the study doorway, white-faced and shaking. He swept her off her unsteady feet and carried her to the parlor where there was a fire and a sofa. "Fortescue!"

The butler appeared instantly, already armed with a blanket and the news that Miss Blake was on her way to fetch the physician.

Deirdre lay limply in his arms but her eyes blazed. "Your physician can jolly well keep his hands to himself until I've finished what I have to say!"

Calder made a noise of objection, but Fortescue merely bowed. "As you wish, my lady." Then he left, shutting the door on his way out.

Calder knelt by the sofa to deposit Deirdre very carefully on the cushions, but she refused to loosen her grasp on his lapels.

"You have to rest," he protested. "What in the hell were you thinking, taking those stairs? You could have fainted and broken your neck and then I'd have to live the rest of my life knowing I'd killed you!"

Deirdre tried to shake him, but her arms were too weak and he was too solid. "Shut up, darling. I have something to say before I faint in your arms."

Darling?

Calder shut up. Easing himself down to sit with her in his lap, he kept her supported in his arms while he clumsily draped the blanket over her. Stupid, mad, stubborn, beautiful creature!

She weakly slapped the blanket away. "Calder, stop fidgeting and listen. I have had enough—no, more than enough—of your inability to speak your mind. We have been at odds with each other from the beginning because we are both too bloody tight-lipped!"

She curled her body carefully so that she faced him, then released his coat in order to cup his jaw in her soft hands. He was relieved to find them normal, not chilled and not fevered. Then he released his watchfulness, for to be touched by her sent his pulse racing!

She gazed into his eyes. "You started hiding before we were even wed. Let me tell you, my love, my stupid, stubborn darling—hiding will do you no good now. I am going to tell you the complete and entire truth, every minute of every day. You'll hear so much truth you'll run the other way when you see me coming."

Never. Having her in his arms again—feeling the curve of her backside against his lap, the weight of her breast against his bicep—

"Calder! Pay attention."

He blinked. "So sorry. You were saying?"

She frowned at him. "I'm saying I love you. I want to live with you. I want to be your wife, your lover, the mother of your child." She hesitated, a shimmer of doubt in her eyes for the first time. "But only if you love me as well."

His heart rose mute in his inarticulate throat. He choked on the poetic and beautiful words of love he wished he could cast into her lap like a thousand gold coins. He swallowed, but where to start? His feelings were too intense, too overpowering—he didn't know the words for such a longing!

She seemed to see some of his struggle in his face, for her eyes warmed with humor. "Say, 'I love you, Deirdre'," she prompted.

He cleared his passion-clogged throat. "I love you, Deirdre."

That was easier than he'd thought it would be. He tried again. "I love you very much." Still, the words were too simple, too tiny to encompass the depth of what he wanted to tell her.

He tried. "I—you were so ill—I thought—I found you on the heath—and then you wanted to leave—"

"Shh." She pressed tender fingers over his lips. "Don't rush yourself. There will be time to practice." She twinkled at him, her spirit undiminished in her shadowed eyes. "Years, possibly."

Years. At that stunning realization, something eased in Calder. They had the rest of their lives together. There was plenty of time to get it right.

Then, suddenly, he knew precisely what he most needed to tell her. "I did kill Melinda. I ignored and neglected her, yet when she left me I pursued her. The carriage turned over because I was gaining on it, drunkenly whipping my horse to a reckless speed. That regret was the most devastating thing I'd ever known . . . until

I met you." He slid her from his lap, then knelt on the floor before her. "I am wreckage before you. You have broken me, my love. All the walls of my life have come tumbling down and I stand in the rubble."

She smiled proudly. "You stand freed in the rubble." She wrapped his hands in hers. "You were already broken, my darling. Broken and badly mended. I had to take apart the pieces so you could become whole again."

He bowed his head over their clasped hands. "So what will hold me together now? I don't have the strength to rebuild myself, I fear."

She slipped his arms about her waist, then lay her head on his shoulder. "We both are in pieces, I think. Love will have to be the glue."

He gusted a sigh as his arms tightened carefully about her. "Well, we've plenty of that lying about, at least."

She choked out a damp laugh. "That we do, my darling. That we do."

Then she glanced down. "Calder, I hate to break this to you, but it might be some time before I can take care of that properly."

He laughed out loud, a deep rumble that brought her a whole new pleasure. She made an instant decision to make him laugh often.

"I'm sorry, my love," he said, his smile half-eager, half-embarrassed at his obvious erection. "But you do bring out the Beast in me."

Epilogue

The dream was of a place she'd never seen, although she knew it to be Brookmoor in her mind. Deirdre walked through a lonely wild space, with the wind pulling at her hair and the heather higher than her knees.

"Mama!" The small voice was hardly louder than a distant seabird's cry, yet she turned immediately toward it.

"Meggie?"

"Over here, Mother."

Over the softly rolling heather a girl came closer. She was tall and lovely, nearly a woman. Meggie's dark eyes flashed laughter as her hair was whipped about her face by the wind.

"Mama, look what I found!"

Deirdre looked down at the child who clutched at Meggie's skirts with one hand and cradled something in the other. "What is it, my darling?"

The boy looked up at her with great pride. "It's a bug!"

Deirdre peered at the slimy tail whipping indignantly from the boy's grubby fist. "It's a salamander."

He held it out proudly. "It's for you!"

"Oh, my," she replied faintly. "Thank you so much."

He waited, fist extended. She took a breath and held out her cupped hands. The wiry black creature dropped into them and went still as it assessed the new threat.

She was very proud that she didn't drop it.

Meggie chortled. Deirdre shot her a "just you wait" glare, then smiled at her tiny son. "It's marvelous. Wonderful. I love it."

Then she leaned forward conspiratorially and whispered in his ear, "I think Meggie's envious. Why don't you catch another for her?"

The child gazed up at her with Calder's dark eyes. "And one for Papa, too?"

She caressed his dark hair while surreptitiously letting the little creature slither to freedom at her side. "Oh, yes. For Papa, too. He's been simply longing for one."

Meggie's tinkling laugh rang out over the moor to dance with the wind. . . .

"Shh, Lady Margaret. His lordship and milady are still asleep," Patricia scolded with a smile in her voice.

Deirdre opened her eyes to the dimness of the private space behind the closed bed curtains. She was curled against Calder's large warm back, skin to skin with him. Drifting in and out of sleep still, she listened while Patricia shuffled Meggie out of the marquis's bedchamber and shut the door quietly.

There was no need to wake yet. She could sleep the morning away if she liked. Fuzzily, she wondered what Brookmoor looked like. She wondered if it was windy . . . and covered in heather. . . .

Reaching for his arm, she tugged Calder about to cradle her and snuggled deep into his sleepily welcoming arms. Hours yet to sleep . . .

Suddenly her eyes flew open in surprise. Scrambling

naked from the bed, she raced across the grand chamber to the tiny room that held the commode.

Calder joined her seconds later, still naked, his brow furrowed over sleepy, worried eyes. "You're ill. I'll send for the physician!"

Deirdre wiped her mouth and sat back on her heels. "No . . . I think I'm all right now." She shook her head. "That was so odd. You'd almost think I was . . ." Her heart stuttered. Her breasts were sore and she'd been quite inclined to sleep—

She lifted her head swiftly to gaze at him, hope dawning within her.

Something flashed bright in those dear, dark eyes. "That would be . . . quite delightful."

Deirdre pressed her palms to her belly, paying no mind at all to the long jagged scar there, healed for months. Calder's arms came about her as he knelt behind her, covering her hands with both of his.

"Is it possible, do you think?" His voice was careful, but she heard the joy behind it.

"Why not?" She leaned her head back against his bare shoulder, feeling his strength surround and support her. "Sophie never did put much stock in doctors." She closed her eyes. In her memory came the faintest call, hardly louder than a distant seabird's cry.

Why not indecd?

Turn the page for a sneak peek at
CELESTE BRADLEY'S

Duke Most Wanted

Coming in May 2008
from St. Martin's Paperbacks

"You've turned into such a lady," Graham teased softly. He made a grab for her hand and caught it. He tugged her around. "Sophie, don't let's be angry. I didn't mean to upset you."

She kept her face turned away. "I'm not upset. I'm just dead sick of you, that's all. No time for this, I fear. Too many more important people waiting for me outside."

He drew her chin about with tender fingers. "Here now. You've mussed your fancy doings." He pulled out his handkerchief and dabbed at her powdered cheeks, smoothing the lines of her tears away. "There now, all pretty again." He dropped a quick, meaningless little kiss on her lips, so close to his own.

Except . . . it wasn't meaningless at all.

SOPHIE FROZE AT the brief touch of Graham's lips on hers. So did he.

Time hung there, sweet and long, each unwilling to move away, unable to think or protest or do anything but *stay.*

The little room was a haven, the gathering outside

growing more distant with every heartbeat, the sounds faded and misted beneath the pounding of two hearts.

When she inhaled, taking in the heat and scent of him, it was as though he breathed some of his own life and vitality into her spirit. Suddenly nothing was to be feared, nothing was to be hidden. There was no one in the world but the two of them, and she reveled in that isolation.

He was here and he could be hers. All she need do was reach out—

His solid pectoral muscle flexed beneath her palm and she realized she already had.

It was all he'd needed, it seemed, for in the next instant she found herself pulled roughly into his arms, against that rock-hard chest, into the circle of his scalding sexuality.

She made no sound of protest, not even a gasp of surprise, for there was no surprise here. He was precisely as he ought to be and so was she, quivering for him, on fire for him—

Willing.

Nay, eager.

It was so easy to let go it made her doubt she'd ever held on. She slid both hands up to lace them around his neck, moving slowly as if in a dream. He exhaled harshly at her voluntary embrace and she was ashamed of how much she'd held back from him. She vowed she would show him herself, in such a way he might never forget it.

She twined her fingers through his hair gently, then tightened them. His eyes widened and he opened his mouth to speak.

"Shh." It was stunning how sure she was, how she knew just what to do. She'd never kissed him, but she knew just how to tilt her head to make their lips fit just so. She went up on tiptoe, sliding her body slowly up his hard stomach and chest, making no attempt to hide her enjoyment of the sensation.

He swallowed, hard. She felt the power surge through her, raw feminine power older than time itself. She claimed her seductress self, allowing her to well forth and play out the moment with slow, sure enticement.

He waited, his jaw tense, his eyelids heavy with un-expressed desire. He hardened against her. She smiled slightly and rotated her hips to press the softness of her lower belly into his rigidity. A rocky shudder went through him and the cords of his throat throbbed, but he kept his silence, still pinned in place by her entangled fingers in his hair.

He could have broken free, but Graham was finally in the place he'd dreamed of since . . . how long? Just this week . . . or for months?

He dared not so much as breathe too hard, although he could be panting by now if he allowed himself. She was so innocently, wickedly sensual—this was not his careful, restrained Sophie. This was the woman who had fought for him, the woman who had stood fiercely between him and Lilah's vicious insults.

Then there was no more time for memory, there was only now, for she kissed him at last.

Her lips were soft, her nipples were hard, her fingers in his hair causing him pain he would not have forgone for a thousand nights of heartless pleasure. She was the one. She had ever been the one. He'd known, in some place he'd never investigated inside himself, he'd known since the first time he'd rescued her from run-ning into a wall.

He stood there, taking her closemouthed kiss for as long as he was able to bear it, for he savored the innocence he tasted in it. She would never kiss so again.

Then he violated that sweet virginity with the tip of his tongue, a slow careful penetration that made her stiffen in surprise.

She wasn't one to quail. No, not his Sophie. At once she was back in the joust, her own dainty tongue slipping into his lips, the soft sounds of her pleasure vibrating through his mouth.

God, so sweet, so strong, so powerful—

He couldn't get close enough to her. In two steps he had her down on the fainting couch, her willing body at last pressed completely to his. Beneath his . . .

Soft and pale, her breasts emerged from her bodice when he pulled the neckline. The gift of her flesh in his hands as he impaled her mouth again and again with his tongue. There were other things he would do with that tongue, things she would enjoy, things he would get to in just a moment, just as soon as he'd had enough of fitting his hands around her small, high, perfect breasts.

Oh, the things he would do to his magnificent Sophie . . .

Outside the alcove room, the audience broke into applause. Jarred, Graham broke the kiss.

"Oh God." Not Sophie! He was a monster. He was a rotter, through and through. "Oh, bloody *hell!*"

He backed off her, turning away—*tearing* himself away, in fact, an act that cost him more than he could ever articulate. He rubbed both hands over his face, straining for sanity through the aching, heart-pounding lust . . . and need. Need like nothing he'd ever felt before. Need that nearly had him turning back and flinging himself upon her once again, just for one more minute of that sweet, pure hearthfire light . . .

He forced himself away, as far as the tiny room would allow. Leaning his forehead against the wall, he clenched his eyes tightly shut and beat back the aching loss until coherent thought returned.

Mostly.

Losing himself in Sophie . . . when had she become a pool of cool clean water? When had she become the unpolluted air in his lungs? Why hadn't he seen it sooner—why had she kept it from him, like a secret, like a treasure hoarded away for someone more worthy, someone less blind?

Too late.

No. Never. He needed this—needed her—needed—

You need Lilah's pile of gold.

No. He could not trade this . . . this pure, clean creature for a tainted harpy like Lilah!

Then trade her for the folk of Edencourt.

The pale, sunken faces . . . the blank, enduring eyes that held no faith in his promises . . . the rot and the waste and the damned, squandered years he'd walked right by . . .

Trade Sophie for his people? That . . . that he could do. Must do. To live without kissing Sophie would be torture. To live with destroying Edencourt . . . that would be hell on earth.

Resolute, he turned his heart to stone. Only then did he dare to turn back to her.

She was upright and dressed again, although her

hair was down from its elaborate coil, falling untamed and coppery over her delicate ivory shoulders as she sat tensely on the fainting couch, her hands knotted in her lap.

He was an idiot. Looking at the girl before him, the most lucid, non-babbling thought he could form was just that.

I am an idiot.

She gazed at the floor, her cheeks bright with a flush. "This was not a mistake. Don't you dare say it was a mistake—I couldn't bear it."

"Sophie . . ." He wanted her but he couldn't. "That was a mistake."

He would not be his father. He would not please himself at the cost of Edencourt's people. He was only glad he'd managed to stop before he'd gone too far.

No, you aren't. Too far is precisely where you want to be.

"So that is all, then?" She raised her chin and gazed at him evenly. He steeled himself against the stain of disappointment and hopelessness in her expression.

He gazed back at her solemnly. "Did you expect more?"

"Of course not. Who am I to expect anything in this world?" She lifted her chin proudly and stood. Shaking out her somewhat the worse for wear skirts, she moved to the door. "My congratulations on your imminent engagement, my lord."

With a dip and a careless tilt of her head, she was gone, striding back into the noise and crowd of the musicale as if she had more important business kept waiting.

Worry slithered through Graham's relief. Her gray

gaze might seem calm and disinterested to others, had, in fact, seemed so to him once upon a time, but he now knew what raged beneath that still surface. His Sophie was a hard-headed, fiery, unpredictable creature.

Who now seemed to think she had nothing to lose.